DATE DUE

At the Full and Change of the Moon

AT THE FULL
AND CHANGE
OF THE MOON

a novel

DIONNE
BRAND

GROVE PRESS
New York

First published by Alfred A. Knopf Canada in 1999
Printed in the United States of America

FIRST AMERICAN EDITION

Library of Congress Cataloging-in-Publication Data

Brand, Dionne, 1953–
At the full and change of the moon : a novel / Dionne Brand.
p.   cm.
ISBN 0-8021-1649-3
1. Trinidad—History—Fiction. I. Title.
PR9199.3.B683A92 1999   813'.54—dc21   99-18152

Grove Press
841 Broadway
New York, NY 10003

99 00 01 02   10 9 8 7 6 5 4 3 2 1

For Leleti,
love, the way one covets the flight
of swifts and terns and nightjars.

CONTENTS

Marie Ursule d. 1824

Kamena
Marooned to his last direction, 1824

Bola b. 1821 - d. 1921
Who was Marie Ursule's vanity and whose eyes wept an ocean and who loved whales

The one unrecalled
b. 1841

The ones left in the sea b. 1846, 1849, 1850

The one she made in the dry season b. 1856

Eugenia, the one who went to Bonaire
in a basket b. 1858
(Grandmother)

Rafael Simon, the one who loved gold things
and who was taken to the Main (Venezuela) b. 1860
(Grandfather)

Emmanuel Greaves b. 1905 ——————— m. ——————— Cordelia Rojas b. 1903

Hannah, Gabriel, Alicia

The one who was taken in a hurricane b. 1869 taken 1875

The one who loved dolls b. 1863

The one she washed out with lime b. 1865

The one who ran to the Rupununi b. 1872

The one who pointed to the sea saying "Boto bayena" and who
loved to iron clothes and who was taken to Curaçao b. 1865

Dovett b. 1890 - d. 1925

Dovett b. 1920 - d. 1978

Maya b. 1952

Adrian b. 1959

The girl who was flooded in everything b. 1987

The one who stole her footsteps b. 1869, who left
and found Terre Bouillante without looking, 1881

Augusta, the one for the blind man
whose head she loved b. 1881

Private Sones b. 1898

Dear Mama b. 1919

The sisters who went to England b. 1936 & 37

Priest b. 1940

Eula b. 1957

Sese b. 1939

Job b. 1945

Bola b. 1982

At the Full and Change of the Moon

...BUT A DRINK OF WATER

I

Marie Ursule woke up this morning knowing what morning it was and that it might be her last.

She had gathered the poisons the way anyone else might gather flowers, the way one gathers scents or small wishes and fondnesses. Gathering a bit here, wondering at a fiercely beautiful flower there. Tasting the waxiness of some leaves, putting her tongue on the prickliness or roughness of others. And she had been diligent and faithful the way any collector would be, any fervent lover. Scientific. Passionate. Every new knowledge, wonderful. She had even felt the knowing sadness, the melancholy that lovers feel, the haunting not-enough feeling, the way one covets the flight of swifts and terns and nightjars. She had sorted out the most benign vines from the most potent, collecting them all, and anything else she could find, recognizing the leaves through resemblance or smell or bitterness.

She had heard talk. She had listened to whispers from the Caribs and had made dealings with those of them left alive on the island after their own great and long devastation by the Europeans; their six-thousand-year-old trek over the Andes was close to ending here in Trinidad after four hundred years of war with the invaders. Meeting under curtains of heavy rains or unrelenting night, they had told Marie Ursule of a most secret way to ruin. *Woorara* they called it, their secret to rigour and breathlessness.

Wandering when she could wander, Marie Ursule husbanded the green twigs, the brown veins, the sticky bitterness, the most sanguine of plants. She loved their stems, their surprise of leaves as veined as her palms, their desperate bundles of berries, their hang of small flowers, and most of all the vine itself, its sinewed grace. She ground the roots to their arresting sweetness, scraped the bark for its abrupt knowledge. She had thought of other ways, bitter cassava, manchineel apples, but their agonies could last for days. *Woorara*, the Caribs had told her, was simple and quick, though it had taken her years to collect. And wait.

Marie Ursule waited for evenings like a lover waits, wanting soft light to embrace her. She looked over the ranges of cocoa trees, their green and red leaves young and old with longing. She imagined love waiting for her beyond the hectares of ripening fruit. Evenings—when clouds descended between the thick growth—kept secret her walks in search of smells and exchanges, her meetings with a straggle of Caribs, two men, three women, one boy, one baby. The Caribs were becoming ancient and extinct even as she looked into their faces, the last of their language vanishing. Marie Ursule offered them her company, her limp, her wish to die. Risking lashings she would to go to their small encampment where she and they sat in each other's contradictions, the straggle of Caribs moving reluctantly toward memory, Marie Ursule, willingly.

The last time, she had gone in a brief rain at the beginning of December but they had broken camp and disappeared, like the rain itself, the kind of quick rain that raises the smell of the earth, steams the roots of things, then vanishes leaving no trace of its passage. Their fire, smouldering from the rain, was almost imperceptible. Perhaps she should have left with them. Perhaps.

Hiding supplies in dugouts here and there, Marie Ursule collected woorara as patiently as she had worn the iron ring around her ankle. She collected it like a lover collecting sorrows and believed hurts. Faithfully.

Marie Ursule woke up this morning knowing what morning it was. Her flesh felt heavy. She could not get it off the board. It was as if her body was tied taut across the wood house like a hammock. She lay there for a while, gathering her legs and her arms and commanding them to wake up. She turned on her side to look at the door, giving herself a direction, but no resolve came. It was to be her last morning and she had prepared everything long before, and now her flesh would not move.

She heard the early birds' noise outside cross with the late birds' noise. She heard all the night insects go quiet, all the dawn insects shake light-shouldered light. She heard the morning coming, its uptake of breath. She had to move before the dark air turned vermilion and then white. She had to empty the gourd of woorara into the small copper pot hidden in the fire below the big pan full of cornmeal pap. Hammock-like her back winged on its hinge as she shifted again, tasting the early-morning taste of her mouth. It was full of spit unswallowed in the night. If nothing else, to stir her she must empty her mouth of bile. She felt her fingers in the dark, swollen and stiff as the rest of her, and started at the numbness in her feet. A numbness she had awakened to each day since January eighth, 1819—a deadness which always startled her at first—when one foot had been ringed with ten pounds of iron and the other had taken all the weight of walking. Now both were numb, the one in sympathy with the other.

This was her second morning to boil the cornmeal. She had taken this task to be near the fire, to be seen cooking the cornmeal, so that she might also warm the tar of woorara she had collected.

Marie Ursule turned again. The reluctance of her body recalled the sentence she'd been given on January eighth, 1819: two years with her leg in an iron ring and thirty-nine lashes. That was her sentence. And Marcelle Dauphine next to her sentenced to work in chains for life. Two years now, two years and more. But the memory of that ring of iron hung on, even after it was removed. A ghost of pain around her ankle. An impression. It choreographed her walk and her first thoughts each day.

She rose now with only the force of her middle and the urge to empty her mouth of bile. Going to the door, swifter than she'd felt only moments ago lying on the wood, she heard the breath of others taking their last before rising. Their last, praying not to rise. Praying that the dark would not turn vermilion, would not turn to white day.

She would often stay awake to hear them breathe, hours. She would listen, wondering if she slept like that, so deeply, so restfully. Breathing in sleep was the only time you owned the movement of your chest. When breath was all that was left to you, how light and heavy and in your middle it was. How limbs went limp but moved by some instinct to turn and turn only to help breathing. She wanted to lie there and inhale the breaths of those sleeping, inhale the smell like inhaling the smell of milk on a baby's mouth. She wanted to inhale the living. She didn't want to get up and bring an end to it. She stopped for a moment, listening and swallowed up by the breathing. Changing her mind then changing again, she slipped the wood latch and was outside.

The air resembled blood gone bad. She hoped it wasn't another morning to end up in ten-pound irons. That thought made her foot heavy. She limped to the shed but somehow swift swift. But if it was such a morning, bring it. She spat the bile out and wiped her hand over her mouth, pulling the film of sleep away. Her eyes did not need adjusting to the dark, she knew this way by heart. Marie Ursule, queen of the Convoi Sans Peur; queen of rebels, queen of evenings, queen of malingerings and sabotages; queen of ruin; who had lost an ear and been shackled to a ten-pound iron for two years after the rebellion of 1819 had been betrayed, after the plan to kill de Lambert, and all his own, discovered. While some had been put to death, their heads hung on sticks near the bell and their bodies tied to the walls in chains, she had been given a ten-pound ring to wear. She had been given thirty-nine lashes. She had been given her own ear in her mouth. She had been given a heart full of curses and patience.

The stink of that day was on her breath this morning, turning to white, not just yet, now vermilion, the colour of old blood. She spat. Soon the day would almost break, *petit jour*. On an ordinary day she would take her skipping walk into the fields of cocoa with the others. On an ordinary day the others would awake and stumble to the shed; stumbling out of their sleep and into the field, into this season and another season and another season to follow, an endless season.

Soon seasons would not matter and the iron imprint at her ankle would be light.

Only her little girl, Bola . . . she would send her to Arauc or Terre Bouillante. She would try and send her to the secret hills, to the secret places even beyond those secret hills, to those places where she, Marie Ursule, could not go herself because of her limp. And even more because of her heart, so skilled now, so full of wrath. She could not think of escape for herself. She could not imagine the mountains, or Arauc or Terre Bouillante where they said life was free. She could not imagine or believe any place like that. She was ruined already. She was tied to this morning. But sending Bola far into the hills and the impenetrable bush beyond, beyond the reach of de Lambert and his like, that was her one conceit now, her one little ambition. Hopping swift and lighter than her legs, she worried only if it was too much, and too boldfaced, to try and send the child to Terre Bouillante with Kamena.

The names of secret places had dropped from Kamena's lips in whispers. Terre Bouillante, Arauc, Casse Terre, Morne Diable, Morne Macaque, Morne Maron. He had said them so softly, so gently, she was tempted to believe they existed. He had heard that some who ran away made it to those places. It took days of walking, he had heard, perhaps weeks, perhaps luck, and perhaps waiting, to arrive there. And he had escaped, promising to return for the child. She had told him, just in case, if he didn't find the place, he should go to

Culebra Bay where there was nothing but the ghosts of two Ursuline nuns who had once owned her. Just in case he couldn't find his way, she said, in case, then he should go to Culebra Bay; because his voice soughing on the names of Maroon places could not persuade her that such havens of runaways existed, let alone that the militia would not find them. But Culebra was rumoured to have leprosy and so no militia would chance there, though she knew it was only the nuns' old craft, she was convinced that, dead and all, it was their own mystery still hovering. He had escaped, promising to return for the child, not listening to Marie Ursule. Because Bola was his child too and his mind did not linger on hurt like Marie Ursule's. He wanted lightness, he wanted peace.

Marie Ursule wanted peace too but nothing that could be settled in escape. She had lain too many nights listening for rain. It was with rain that the vines sprang and ran. The thought of rain was the only thought that filled her with crying or longing. The sound of rain was comforting, reaching the balata trees windguarding the cocoa—the sound of rain on broad leaves gave her the sense that each drop contained a life, an elliptical limning life like hers. She tried to grasp it before it broke against a leaf.

Did she read the morning right? And who was she to try to save anything? Well, it was already decided and beyond her and now it was too late to discover if she was wrong. Now she couldn't change her mind. If Terre Bouillante existed and if Kamena had survived to find it, he would return today for the child. And if not, then it would be too late: she would have to mark the child then. This morning was the end of the world.

The one vanity she'd had was that child. Like Marcelle

Dauphine and Marie Bastien and Marie Rose, she had washed out many from between her legs. Like them, she had vowed never to bring a child into the world, and so to impoverish de Lambert with barrenness as well as disobedience. Not one child born in that place for years, except what de Lambert could make himself with his own wife. Until one day, Marie Ursule made one with all itself intact. Her one curiosity and her vanity. The eyes of the child emerging between her thighs, round and robust, were startlingly open as if to say, "I'm coming, Marie Ursule. Don't lay a harmful hand on me." Its mouth was full of milk, grey drooling milk. It came as if already feeding itself, and if Marie Ursule would not help it, it was ready to survive on its own. She laughed as the child tumbled out of her and the gush of afterbirth followed like an ocean and a torrent between her legs. It sailed Bola away from the hands of Marie Ursule and landed her on the dirt floor, balled into a moon.

The child was not a disappointment. From the moment she was born Bola's eyes saw too much. She was born with teeth, which was a sign of gifts or curses, and from the time she first spoke she sang Marie Ursule's name. Marie Ursule had to contend with people calling the child "jumbie" because she had a mind of her own and would say something to anyone who maliced Marie Ursule. She was a child born out of curiosity and prodigiousness. Though not a good four years old, she was a one-word child, *jealous, thief, spirit, goat, hiding, naked*. Certain people drew the length of her tongue and shut up right away. This morning Marie Ursule left Bola sleeping, for Kamena to come and take her to Arauc or Terre Bouillante, whichever he had found safely, as they had planned. And, if not, to Culebra Bay.

This child who was her vanity was now her leavings.

She had to fix the small copper pot of woorara, make it boil to its most potent, get ready to put the knife in it. She stepped, lithe now, over the mud drain, feeling a shadow cross the yard and enter the barrack behind her. It was Kamena. She didn't look, she didn't want to change her mind. Let the child go. She herself had to avoid every moment now when her body wanted to do something else, walk back to the barrack, go back to sleep, perhaps walk away herself to the distant place where Kamena rolled under the sky. Her body wanted living. And she had to twist it round to another task. She did not look round to see Kamena carrying the child through the cocoa fields, the fruit reddening and yellowing under the leaves, the morning soaked in mist. She knew Kamena would run through the field to her left, which fell away into dense high bush. Then they would disappear into days of walking.

Well, Marie Ursule, thank God for the beginning of the morning and the end of it too.

In this early early morning when morning wasn't morning and nothing was anything yet; this morning when trees and grass and rock had not yet gathered themselves into their shapes, when life was not even life itself, when anyone could change into what they might be, this morning like any morning in the world for Marie Ursule was not a sign of anything certain. Hadn't life ceased to be certain long ago, hadn't every turning stood still, hadn't every stillness turned to motion long long ago? And what was memory when she felt it loop and repeat, when what she was about to do she had imagined done already, like a memory.

She was owned by M. de Lambert, and before that by the Ursuline nuns who had moved from place to place, from Guadeloupe to Martinique and then here, Trinidad, this last island before Venezuela. They and she had run out of islands. Her ears' tips had been cut for rebellion there in Guadeloupe and many charges laid against her for insolence.

She had come to the Ursulines under false pretence. M. Rochard, her owner before the nuns, saying he was in debt, offered Marie Ursule as his most valuable to the Ursulines, who were always needing for the amount of runaways they had. Rochard wanted to be rid of her and make his money back but the Ursulines didn't miss her ears or the set of her face and bargained him down to take her off his hands.

Mère Marguerite frightened Rochard anyway, streaking toward him when he got off his horse, streaking toward him like a spectre of a century past. Marie Ursule on the rope, walking behind him, smelled communion powder and smoke and spat the taste from her mouth. Soeur de Clémy, following Mère Marguerite de St. Joseph, summed up Marie Ursule in one look, taking in the ears but also her strong legs, her stare that said you'd only get half the work out of her but also the strong large hands, the broad back but the eyes with their own business. She summed her up and offered half of what Rochard wanted.

Rochard handed the rope over and left without arguing, not even bowing before getting back up on his horse, not bothering after all to recite his story about leaving the colony, about stock to get rid of in a hurry, better opportunity in the Guianas; these were only half-truths and anyone could tell they were lies after seeing Marie Ursule. Most of all the Ursulines, who had seen everything. He had heard about but did not believe that he would ever see this vision of the Ursulines, eroding like dead coral and dusty like an eternity. What he saw was more seductive and fatal than his own greed. Why they looked so old he put down to leprosy, but he fled, leaving them in what he knew was another century.

Soeur de Clémy untied the rope from Marie Ursule's hands. When she came close Marie Ursule warned her, "*Pain c'est viande beque, vin c'est sang beque, nous va mange pain beque nous va boir sang beque.*" Bread is the flesh of the white man, wine is the blood of the white man, we will eat the white man's flesh, we will drink the white man's blood.

Running out of islands themselves, the Ursulines had fled the claims of the Jesuits for their estates in Martinique and Guadeloupe. They came to Trinidad with nineteen slaves and their belongings. Having bought a small plantation on Culebra Bay, they arrived at its remote rock face and its bush face. They arrived at a place that was barren and unimaginable. Having no more funds, they settled into its waste and decrepitude. Only the water, the sea at Culebra, showed any bounty. Whales and sharks perused the bay, trumpet fish and bonito, and sometimes wild water and sandy winds. The nuns had been duped, sold a useless piece of rock, which the sea salt took inch by inch.

They were a hard lot, the Ursulines. So much kneeling down for disobedience and so much for lateness and so much more for indolence. The industry of slavery was how they kept God and flesh together. And like all who came to the colonies, they had to make their money out of punishment in some shape. Mère Marguerite de St. Joseph and Soeur de Clémy baptized all their slaves, hoping for obedience, but they could not depend on baptism strictly. The lash was handy. It was as dutiful as praying. And their baptisms were often in blood.

"Go, before you send us to hell," they finally told Marie Ursule after her rebellions and plots. Mère Marguerite's face was already paper-thin, blistering to powder. Soeur de Clémy bit her fingernails to their dry quick. "You in hell already if is up to me, Marie Ursule," Marie Ursule whistled at their powdery skins.

So Marie Ursule was sold to de Lambert when all the beatings did not turn her and when she became so unmanageable that their punishments could not sit well with prayers to their own Virgin Mary. And when their estate at Culebra seemed to be sinking into the coral reef that it really was, they sold Marie Ursule on their suspicions that it was she who had blighted them. Merchants would not come out to Culebra, and whatever goods they made took so long to arrive at Port-of-Spain that the ships were gone and they had to sell cheap. Suspecting the nuns of leprosy because of Mère Marguerite's blistered skin, good commerce abandoned Culebra.

De Lambert had bought an estate on this last island, retreating down the archipelago himself, bringing twenty slaves with him as well as buying Marie Ursule when he arrived. Buying her from a bedraggled nun circling the wharf like a man-o'-war bird, when the boat docked at Port-of-Spain. A nun who looked more weary than her slave but who haggled for a good price nevertheless and who looked out of the corner of her eye and smiled at Marie Ursule, and turned cold when Marie Ursule said, "You going to live long. Take the money from him. You owe me an eternity."

De Lambert had married a free coloured woman who you could hardly see was coloured and who never faced the sun directly. She took care that no one saw the darkening knuckles on her fingers or the tips of her ears. Moving like a ghost herself in dark rooms of the estate house, only her shadows crossing windows. One good sitting in the sun and the African in her would come out. De Lambert was her cousin twice removed and mercifully removed from any black blood. Ten of his slaves belonged to the free coloured wife, bought for her as a dowry by her father, Toussaint Voisin, whom she hated—another free coloured, much closer to Africa.

Toussaint Voisin smiled too much for his oldest daughter's tastes, he smiled and touched his light-skinned daughters as if he were drooling. He touched everything like that, cloth, horses, francs, Madame Voisin *née* Lavigne, his Creole wife, slaves. His daughter was happy to leave him on Martinique and lighten into her husband's prestige on this last island in this chain of islands floating into the Orinoco River.

Mon Chagrin estate. Why de Lambert called it that was in his own past, some blight he felt he'd suffered, some little hurt he'd kept or some romance he held about himself and his industry. Or perhaps some cognition. Mon Chagrin.

And this is where Marie Ursule had her ear cut off, and got her iron ring for two years, and her thirty-nine lashes, after the first uprising of the Sans Peur Regiment was betrayed by the dog-traitor Vargas, who thought he would be freed for his trouble. And, well, she knew then she would wait, would have to wait. She would learn how to finish something. And she would wait until after they took off the ring and after she looked like her mind was repentant and even after that.

Sans Peur, without fear they called themselves, Sans Peur. They gathered each night thinking and plotting and praying in the old ways that they could remember. They had planned that first insurrection, which was to see the planters rounded up and killed, with the Macaque Regiment and the Mon

Repos Regiment, from the two estates to the west of Mon Chagrin. They were also betrayed, and so most of their night army of slaves had ended up in irons, a few dead.

She herself had listened to her own sentence in disappointment, wishing death. "Marie Ursule in Sans Peur Regiment to receive thirty-nine lashes, to have an ear cut off, and to have an iron ring of ten pounds weight affixed to one of her legs, to remain thereon for the space of two years." She, Marie Ursule, would wait and plot another way. It would take that long to plan again and when they did she took the place of Marcelle Dauphine as queen, because Marcelle Dauphine had succumbed to the madness of the weight around her leg for life.

Marie Ursule had waited until this morning. This morning waking up and smelling the sweet breaths of last sleep and tasting the bile in her mouth which caused her to move, this was the morning then. She lit the fire, put the small copper at the bottom and over it the pan of cornmeal to hide the darkening mixture of curare. Somewhere she sensed Kamena and the child, heard the child singing "Marie Ursule, Marie Ursule," calling her. She held the pan full of water and molasses now boiling. Her fingers did not feel pain from the heat. It was long since burning could harm her so she didn't use a rag. She would add vine of the soul and god's breath leaves to the cornmeal, just to make their going easier. These plants would give them visions, dreams and sightings, pleasure at the coming life. They would see where they were going more clearly when they took the knife of woorara to their veins.

The small copper, hidden in the flames under the cornmeal pan, reddened. It would not take long. By the time the morning came and they were all of them gathered, the curare would still the muscles and stop their breath and their hearts.

Kamena moved away without a sign to her. He knew that she saw him, he knew that she heard the child's singing. He could not be sure that he would not be recaptured. But no one would be looking for him once they discovered what the Sans Peur had done. He hoped that the child would not sing all the way to wherever they were going. He hefted the child on his back, felt for a brief moment her weight as heavy as the ocean, felt for a moment a sudden difficulty standing, then stepped away from that place where he was leaving Marie Ursule, her eyes never meeting his or his eyes hers but knowing what they knew. He hoped that the child would not sing all the way to where they were going anyhow.

And it was Marie Ursule's last morning. And the last morning that anything like will would make her rise and live. Those mornings were hard to summon. She could only count a few—the mornings of doing something that was not directed or ordered from outside. What woke her also this morning was dreaming the thing she had to dream. Dreaming her generations. Dreaming a safe place for Bola. And she only remembered to dream when she heard the child singing in the damp ochre shade of the morning. Her hands were already stirring the poison, already hefting the cornmeal, her hands were already burnt on the fire. She had done this thing already, it was a memory when they found her sitting near the dead ones, it was finished. She had lived it already night after night when the Sans Peur Regiment met to dream it and to make it true.

She was already condemned; her eyes were already closed when they opened suddenly to the child's tune of her name, when they opened to Kamena's hesitation and his sinking knowledge of where he should go, when they opened to a vision of red birds and skittering eyes. And for a moment she too hesitated, she too thought of continuing when she foresaw the little girl stooping in the crablands, smothering in her own breath, and Kamena lost. Then she remembered the last thing she had to dream. The two miserable nuns in Culebra Bay whom she had set in stone. Dead now perhaps, dead to the world but not to her vision. Their evanescence thickening into sight, she called their mystery into shape. If Kamena could not find Terre Bouillante, then she would lead him to Culebra Bay. Their way out and their long destination.

Marie Ursule faced the world turning white from vermilion. She faced the bodies of the Sans Peur Regiment moving toward her, shaking and humming. Her hand ladling cornmeal trembled and was still at the same time. They walked close to each other for warmth and assurance. The morning was cold. She saw the others' indecision and their fright but perhaps it was her own. It made her own heart more determined. They sat in their accustomed way, emptying their gourds of cornmeal, then waiting for Marie Ursule to bring the small copper and the knife wrapped in cloth at the hilt.

They saw visions of where they were going, blues and whorling reds and spirits beckoning. Their faces were stricken, whether in pain or relief she could not tell. They each took the knife and drew a mark in their own hands. For the one or two breaths they lived after, the woorara tar was a river flowing through their hands. A river they were going to, to wash themselves of this life and Mon Chagrin and all the other places they had been. Who didn't die, Marie Ursule knew, would be no good after and de Lambert would die too in his own way. "One thing," she thought, "dead is where we all is going." On a morning turning from ochre to white with the smell of frozen blood, dead is where everybody was going.

Her whole body was rigid except for her hands passing the small copper pot to each one. And as the Sans Peur had planned, so no one would see the other dying and lose courage, they marked their palms one after the other without hesitation, cutting the tar-like poison deep into their flesh, humming their accustomed tune. They knew that the body was a terrible thing that wanted to live no matter what. It never gave up, it lived for the sake of itself. It was selfish and full of greed. The body could pitiably recover from lashes, from weight and stroke. Only in the head could you kill yourself, never in the body. It would thrash and heave its way back. So their minds were made up, knowing this. And each night, in the months before, they had plotted together, they had given the mind this mystery to work out, how to ignore the body, how to reach the other shore.

Marie Ursule used to sit at their head, humming a tune. A tune so tuneless it lay between individual breaths and a common sound. It began the way anyone begins walking along alone and needing a sound. Sometimes it began like a moan from a headache or it began from the sound of someone stumbling on a careless stone. Any one of them began. Petit Dominique or Pompey. Sounds catching in their chests like gasping in an airless room. Marcelle Dauphine knocking the iron on her foot with a stone, hoping, the way only madness can hope, that little by little the way she had it calculated the iron would break in thirty years or she'd be dead. Her breath would thicken to a tune with exertion. Then they would all join the tune, which became an enchantment, a going to somewhere dark and empty of things that had happened and dark and empty of failure and dark and empty of history and dark and empty of their bodies burning to live.

Valère, Dominique-Rivière, Pedro, Petit Dominique, Marie Rose, Pancras, Florentine, Adelaide, Gabriel, Eustace, Jean Noel, Pompey, Sayman, Louis, Nero, Marcelle Dauphine, Marie Bastien, Avril. All now breathed the dark emptiness where they were going. Each swallowed darkness. They breathed time. They breathed wholeness. Marie Ursule continued the tune, tuneless and stilling, taking the falling pot from the last hand. She herself would not take the knife to her veins. She wanted to see the faces of de Lambert and the rest when they discovered her. She wanted to vow to them that it was she, Marie Ursule, who had devastated them.

Steady, steady she watched until it was done, waiting, watching the sky break and the world end, watching the Sans Peur swoon to death, their hearts stopped, watching the day end before it truly began.

In another century without knowing of her, because centuries are forgetful places, Marie Ursule's great-great-grandchildren would face the world too. But even that forgetfulness Marie Ursule had accounted for. Forgetfulness is true speech if anyone listens. This is the plain arrangement of the world, they would think, even if they knew different, even if they could have remembered Marie Ursule. They would say: This is the plain arrangement of the world, this I have suffered, this I have eaten, this I have loved. When she woke up that vermilion morning, stepped out of her sack on the floor with her limp and her plans and her poisons, looked through the holes in the wood planks lashed together for the barrack, smelled the air of ripening and mouldering cacao, and limped out to the morning, she had taken account of forgetfulness and remembrances.

De Lambert turned in his sleep now, drinking in the same air as Marie Ursule but not tasting the breaths that she tasted and hesitated at. His blood would run the same through him to his generations. Generations needing a new language, because de Lambert turned in his bed to get the rest of his sleep before waking up to kill Marie Ursule. His generations would melt into his secrets. They would take other names. They would even forget de Lambert, the man in their faces and in the faces of the photographs that would speak of a great family. De Lambert. De Lambert spread across their mantelpieces in the faces of great-grandmother, grandfather, uncle and great-grand-aunt, little boy, young man in regimental wear in medals from the Boer expedition and the First World War.

They would forget that this morning de Lambert rose to unusual quiet, called for his boots and his cocoa tea, which did not come, and rose in his shirt to open a window and wonder where those black bastards were. De Lambert prostrate in more faces now added to the ones in photographs on the mantelpiece—the mantelpiece in the old house built after the old house was ruined by fire—capped and gowned from universities abroad or soaked in rum as fishermen, debauched in the slack eyes of uncles who had fingered young girls' dresses, wrapped in the smooth hands of merchants, their spendthrift sons, the daughter who became a poet, the cousin who was a recluse, the owner of a discothèque, the one in the jersey who liked cocaine. They had forgotten, or forgiven like family, what they had no way of forgiving or worse even knowing. They had forgotten, not needing to remember.

No need. What Marie Ursule is leaving she knows she cannot put into a face. Perhaps she can leave it in bones or gestures muscular with dispossession—though she cannot think of anything but what she will do this morning. The lives of her great-great-grandchildren, their lives would spill all over floors and glass cases and the verandas and the streets in the new world coming. Their hearts would burst. When asked they will say they had no reason for knifing someone or blowing a kiss. They had no reason at all for sitting numb, with cocaine or gin or music coursing through their fingers. Singers will pierce them dipping into their ribs. They would come to be whatever impulse gathered the greater in them, like threatened forests flowering.

Sending Bola away light as her singing, heavy as her weight on Kamena's back. Deciding to send this child through a breathless dawn when the morning wasn't morning and the light was still dark was like sending messages, but not knowing their destination. She was long past caring. Everything had happened already. She had seen it, and sent Bola to that life.

When they found her she was sitting in the dirt near the bodies. Her burnt hands were outstretched soothing a face. She was cooing the song they used to hum at night in their meetings. She sat with the dead, cooing to them like babies, strumming the heaving and clatter of air passages and limbs until someone came. The overseer, the driver, de Lambert himself. The morning had turned to day. It was the bluest driest sky. The grass dew-wet only an hour ago was now dry and stiff, a few cicadas whining, a donkey braying from thirst. Day here always stunned by sunlight, Marie Ursule sat there humming like any night.

"This is but a drink of water," she told them when they killed her. "This is but a drink of water," they heard her say after they broke her arms dragging her. After they put the rope around her neck, after she confessed gladly to her own name alone, "This is but a drink of water to what I have already suffered."

But she'd sent eyes full like an ocean. She'd sent singing. Even she dense with her poison did not understand the exact reason why. What she understood was plain as a rope and a whip, so she sent Bola, and her singing and her eyes full like the moon when the ocean rises. She had counted more than all the counting-house clerks and merchants and ship's captains and nuns. She had calculated in no more than a vanity and an iron-ringed foot.

Marie Ursule would not have changed her mind if she'd known that what she had saved was girls eighteen years if a day with liquor on their breath and razors in their panty hose and men casually holding their genitals, standing on streetcorners and hovering around community-centre halls. Yes, it was true these might be her sums. Clothes on their bodies undone and their own feet breaking, breaking like dried earth, and their throats yelling out on roadsides or in madhouses, hair standing wide, and open and desperate looks in their eyes. She'd summed up all these outpourings of the body and cracked mind.

She'd sent her vanity and her joy, and that morning, when she woke up in the vermilion light and dreamed her child singing from far off on the shoulder of Kamena, she'd sent whatever wasn't spoiled, with no hope of gratitude or remembrance. If her descendants might emerge, sore and disturbed, in another century—well, it reflected only a moment in her mind, a little passion which she indulged herself in, and Bola would add the rest, all beginnings, all catastrophes, like lust.

And yes, she heard Bola calling but she, Marie Ursule, was from another life, done already, and no charm could make her leave off and run with them to Terre Bouillante or where they might go. Though charm could make her feel the broken chest of Kamena deciding and not deciding to leave the child, charm could make her see Bola's crushing flight of red ibises and battle of crabs; charm could make her own conjuring of nuns' dust assemble a spectral estate for her child's safekeeping. To run, to step from where she stood in front of the pan bubbling with curare, to have followed or answered Bola's singing—"Marie Ursule, Marie Ursule"—would have blighted it all, pushed her out of her time and blighted it all. All was beyond her now—something that belonged in the water in Bola's eyes.

She, Marie Ursule, was not someone who could live another century. And she could not afford longing or pity for herself. She would wait only that moment, her feet tied now, and her hands lifeless already. Waiting in the stocks, showing them how she, Marie Ursule, had devastated them. Her face was swollen and bleeding and her eyes almost shut from their beating. Her grey dress was clotted with blood. The threads were stiff and rewoven in the bleeding of her body. She would wait only long enough to dream the man-o'-war nuns spreading black wings to hide her child. She would wait only long enough to resurrect the damned— the one with her muttering and counting, the other with her hovering shame. Long enough to dream them back to what they owed when they were finished with her and passed her on to de Lambert. The one holding the rope, the one looking at her.

Marie Ursule waited only that moment, for her memory to thicken their shapes so Kamena could see them and the child hear the ocean beside which they lived, and that was enough. Kamena with his heart bursting from fatigue and the child sleeping on his shoulder. She would make him see their shapes knowing that they could not hurt him anyhow. Then she would succumb to torture, peel off her skin in the flamed bonfire they had prepared for her as if hanging her were not enough. Then she would leave, leave the dream dreaming itself, then and only then. "This is but a drink of water. . . ."

She did not spare de Lambert her last look, she had seen all she needed to—their faces, de Lambert's, mashed and broken in incredulity and terror and loss and sadness—she was too busy going her way now. To tell the truth he didn't look at her any more either. She was a catastrophe but one he would recover from. He had to go about his business proving that the rebellion was instigated from another estate, proving liability and weaning sympathy from the Governor and calling for harsher penalties and punishments of slaves. He had to get compensation for the dead slaves and for his temporary ruin.

It was the day before New Year's day, one week since his bad fortune. He had a christening to go to, his youngest child's, and the week-long sentencing of Marie Ursule was all but over. Her hair matted in blood, her face so battered she was unrecognizable. The missing child Bola he surmised was buried already. There was no sign of her. A small grave would turn up some day in the field. Marie Ursule was about to hang, saying calmly and bluntly, "This is but a drink of water to what I have already suffered."

II

"Stay here," Kamena had said. In the grand swamp miles and miles away now. Stay here. Someone will soon come. One day a village had sunk and the swamp rose up with swamp grass and enamel fish and frogs, and the village had subsided under. A whole village, bell and garrison, big houses and barracoons. Crabs and mud had taken over, hard fish and walking birds, sucking water and pools of dry ground that came and went. Someone would come. Bola saw Kamena's shoulders moving away, shoulders she had been sitting on, had fallen asleep on, bitten and sucked. The sun had burned her head until she fell asleep and then he had let her down and said, "Stay here, someone will come." Half a day or longer she could not tell. Days were not how she measured time as yet. She measured time with the face of Marie Ursule. So she stooped in the swamp, waiting. She listened to trees squeak and bush breeze, and stooped with her dress knotted around her small knees.

Crabland. No one but runaways came here. The sunken village did not frighten them as much as what they'd run from. All around her were holes busy with crabs skittering in and out. Brown and white thick-shelled land crabs crawled out of their holes, waving their big gundies at her. Their eyes would rise perpendicular, wave and tremble, curious at her presence. Bola opened her mouth and sang tuneless *ahs* and looked up at the sky between the bush's *ahs* and the trees' *ahs*. Then she opened her mouth to drain spit onto the soft tenuous floor of the swamp. Kamena had left her on a round stump of land damp and grassy, a tree growing out of it. The swamp was misty and quiet and she listened to it, afraid and not afraid. "Stay quiet, someone will come. Don't answer until you hear your name," he'd said. "Stay quiet."

The swamp was quiet, the birds were quiet, the village, bell and garrison, big houses and barracoons, all dying quiet. So she let out *ahs*, *ah*ing with the bush and trees and heard her sounds hush the mist and the heat. Sometimes flies buzzed around her and she clapped them hard, giggling. She heard her clapping returning to her and she heard her giggling returning and snatched them back remembering Kamena's "Stay quiet."

Hearing her clap, a crowd of red ibises sprang to flight and she was so startled she coughed to catch her breath. A catastrophe of red choked her, its swoop upward sucked the air out of the earth, lighting the swamp with fire, only to sweep back again to where she had not seen them till now red from their toes all the way to their beaks, blood feather red. She lost her breath as they took over the earth, the small sky that was over her, and she coughed and coughed to catch her breath. She breathed the colour red and it was dusty and full of feathers and she raised her small arms over her head to stop it.

Someone will come. Was this someone then, this red fire deluge of birds that made her cough? Marie Ursule, her mother, said, "Everything is a sign. What don't meet you don't pass you. Not every message come by hand or by mouth. Sometimes the beasts and birds is telling you something." Did Kamena say wait for someone or wait for a sign?

Fire birds must be a big sign, crabs' perpendicular eyes and fire birds burning the air. A sign.

It is close to night and crimson birds swoop in again to roost, sucking the air from her small sense of earth and she is covered in them, still coughing to catch her breath. She cries for Marie Ursule as evening is coming. She only knows time in the memory of Marie Ursule now. She has not seen her since the early dark of another morning and all these signs do not look like the face of Marie Ursule.

～～～

Kamena has left her here. He will come for her two days later after he finds his way to Terre Bouillante, and if he cannot find his way to Terre Bouillante he will have to take her to the nuns. He cannot travel with the child any more. He has to move faster to find the Maroon camp and so he decides to leave her in the crablands, no one will look there, no one will go near a drowned village with a dying quiet bell and garrison, big houses sunk in silence and barracoons crushed in stillness. And Kamena will tell her how to pray and set her mind to one thing until he returns. So, "Stay here, I go come back soon, soon," he says.

Kamena had made his way to Terre Bouillante before and he had not made his way so much as dreamed it, and been so lost he'd found it. Terre Bouillante, the Maroon camp everyone had run to after the militia had surprised them in the Arauc hills. And Kamena, not knowing then that the militia had overcome the Maroon camp in the Arauc hills, had first headed to Arauc, setting off in a shower of rain. Three dead and fifteen recaptured, but many had escaped, away, twenty-eight, farther away to Terre Bouillante. Terre Bouillante was

undetectable because of the rain that fell around it and grew
the forest so thick. And the fugitives had left it undisturbed,
so that the militia could not pass through.

One season ago, in a heavy heavy rain, as rains are here,
Kamena had made his way from Mon Chagrin to Arauc only
to find everyone gone and the dead bodies of three, their
heads on sticks as warning. He arrived fortunately days
after, by the look and smell. He had felt an uneasy birdless
silence as he'd made his way there. Some sense had told him
to cover himself with bush, making day for night. Sleeping,
if he could call it sleep, in the day, and skirting the hills at
night, pushing closer and closer to the camp or where he
thought the camp might be. Then he had come upon the
abandoned place with its rotting smell and warning. He
didn't know what to do next but he was sure that some
had got away. Sure. They couldn't kill everyone and they
couldn't take everyone. So he roamed the bushes and bam-
boo, giving each direction two days. That is how long he
determined that the dead ones had been dead. How far they
could get to in two days is how far he imagined they'd go,
leaving some sign in their hurry. And how far he went, until
his legs turned to wooden spikes and then to lead; until
lying down one night to sleep, after doubling and tripling
his way to this certain night, he heard a sucrier, the sugar
bird, whistling.

Sucriers didn't whistle at night, nor had he seen any
during the day. This was either Terre Bouillante or else the
militia had found him. Maybe he was so tired he had made
his way back to where he'd started out, Mon Chagrin, and
it was morning and his eyes had deceived him and light
was dark or dark was light. Hunger had confused him many
times already and he had been compelled to sit down and

sleep even in the broad daylight with his eyes wide open. And so the sucrier singing in the night was a sign, if it was night, and if it was a sucrier, and if not it was the militia or Terre Bouillante, because he imagined Terre Bouillante as somewhere where sucriers sang at any hour just to make him feel good in his heart. But if it was the militia, then he felt sick, sick and unable to move out of their reach. He was asleep covered in whole sheets of rain so steady, so blistering, he felt himself drown far from any ocean, far from any river up here in thick forests, which mangled his breath and did not leave light, but made way for infinities of rain.

The land was steep, hundreds of feet high, and the Maroon camp he determined must be at the highest point for safety. It was rainy season when Kamena tried to find the camp. Sheets of rain fell. Slate sheets that were sharp and stinging. Rain, which now confused him, beating him, unceasing, blocking his way to Terre Bouillante. But rain had been his thinking when it fell so many days and so relentlessly that he was sure of the season. Rain, which had made his mind up for him to find Arauc. Rain, when no one would follow him or notice for some time that he was gone from Mon Chagrin, and although it would slow him it would also slow whoever was behind him. They wouldn't spare a company on one man in the rainy season, and he was only one man and not a dangerous man just a tired man, not even a man who knew where he was going, only that he had heard and knew somehow the general direction.

So when he got to Arauc and found the heads on sticks only two days new, he sat there under them, trembling for a while, and then he prayed to them and asked their direction and thanked them for leading him here without the militia seeing him. And then he buried them after saying more prayers and thanked them again, touching them gently as they had not been touched, showing them that he did not scorn them and talking to them as they had not heard, not to curse him or leave their jumbie on him but to bless him and move his feet again. When he was finished giving them their rest and whatever little ceremony he could afford, he headed wherever five days took him, when he thought that it was two in several directions. The days had spun him around, and the slaking rain beat him so hard he lay down in surrender and opened his mouth. If he was not to drown in the sea he would drown in the rain. And then he had heard the sound of a sucrier. The fatal knowledge of his life sang the sucrier into capture.

Terre Bouillante was more than two days away from the last Maroon camp, more than five. And Kamena had wandered more than five. He'd wandered so far as to be right in Terre Bouillante, but his body was his only register, where hunger takes over sight and worry turns to gloaming. All he saw was the rain and the thick forest of teak and bullet trees and primeval tangle. Red macaques screamed through his ears. Bearded birds and jacamars lived there too, parrots, red and blue macaws high in the silk cottons. Feather and fine bones landed on his tongue. His blood singing in his ears sounded as sweet as sugar birds. They were flying close to his face, brushing his head, and he heard the beat and flutter of wings as incessant as the rain until he thought that it was his own heart, and his skin was covered with feathers and the silk of birds.

The sky closed to his feet, closed in rain and cloud until he bent and seemed to share one sliver of a horizon with flying birds and monkeys and insects. He crawled along the horizon now with the closing sky, room enough as under a bed, and the flutter around him beat more furiously and he felt the hearts of birds and rain and monkeys next to his own. He felt their hearts and his as if he were holding them in his hands, and he felt his body weep as if it were melting.

When somebody had tied a rope around his belly in the rain and half dragged him to Terre Bouillante through the mud and forest, he was not alive in any plain way. He had only stumbled through the screaming forest, hoping that he was not being dragged back to Mon Chagrin. Whoever was pulling him would not stop and he fell many times, hooked into the big roots of silk cotton, his face slashed by palmiste hanging low down. Whatever was around him was dense, and he still felt the soft veins of birds and heard the red 'monkeys' cackle, raucous and grating; he saw their eyes' black light and heard the whip of their limbs in the trees. Entering Terre Bouillante was like entering his own blood. Tangled in the rope and in the trees, he gave up any control, his body becoming porous and falling apart like rotted meat. He was sure that when he arrived it was just his torso left with the rope tied around. He was sure that he was what the forest leaves, like what a shark leaves, or a hoe leaves in a root or time leaves in a crevice.

When he arrived at Terre Bouillante he woke up to the smell of coconut smoke. Bony legs filled his swollen eyesight when he turned his head. His head was numb and felt dense as if he were a small thing inside his great flesh. He lay on a mud pallet unable to move except for the pained movement of his neck. For some time his eyelids could not rise beyond the ashen legs of those he wanted to thank if only his lips would help. He saw only a grey-black face when it descended beside him to check his breathing or put water in his mouth. He heard an argument about what to do with him, and silence after it was decided to give him a little of what they had until he could do for himself.

In the days that followed, fingers fed him a pap of crushed roots and seepings of warm brown metallic water. The parameters of his gaze extending with the unswelling of his healing body, he made out the ragged group, their faces gaunt from hunger, their limbs emaciated to sticks. Yet the mist of Terre Bouillante shrouded them in glowing, their movement soft and blissful as delirium. He could not tell how many of them there were even after he had fully recovered. Fugitives came and left, looking for food or looking for other places to hide. In Kamena's time there no one who left returned.

Terre Bouillante was desolate. A clearing cleared by streams and fissures of hot water bursting as if in fright. A constant mist and hiss, which nevertheless Kamena learned to read quiet in, utter quiet. The hiss of fissures became the quiet itself for the Maroons, melding into its definitions, so that they could detect a change in the day, a coming attack by the militia if it ever arrived, or the dreamed-out swollen body of another fugitive.

On the edges of the clearing, the Maroons tried to plant a few roots, wild tania and yams which came up poor and stunted. They hunted agouti and iguana and managed a half-starved living. In the flat heat of days they languored on the edge of the clearing, on the edge of life itself. Terre Bouillante was desolate and better, better than Mon Chagrin or Mon Repos or Calendria or Petit Valley or Belmont or any other estate they had fled. Terre Bouillante was peace.

Kamena acquired its ghostliness. He had arrived with his own quiet. He had no memory of his own mother, and what he knew of his life was not worth remembering. Only the whispering of names of places to escape from slavery. Only Marie Ursule, whom he loved and envied, with her one ear and her skipping walk. He would have died with her if she'd willed him to, he knew. He loved her fatal resolve but he himself could only think of escaping. He realized with a blessed relief that she did not mean him to follow her. Following was not what was needed for that journey, no one could take you or compel you. To embrace the thought of death the way the Sans Peur needed to was to embrace it with willingness. He was not willing. He had not come to the end of himself yet. He loved Marie Ursule going her way and expecting him to go his. He wanted peace. Terre Bouillante with all its boiling hiss and hunger made him peaceful.

Their only pact had been that when he had found his way he would return for the child that morning: the day before Christmas, 1823. He had been turning into a ghost in Terre Bouillante since the rainy season began. Now it had ended and he had returned to Mon Chagrin for the child.

Now having left Marie Ursule in a vermilion morning with her hands burning, now having taken her child on a promise, he was not sure if he could find his way back to Terre Bouillante again, to find the place where he would roll under the sky with the child, to find the sliver of horizon with the crowd of macaques and parrots and hearts. What had happened to him before had become sacred to him and unimaginable and perhaps something he could do only once. If he had to follow every step he made the last time, then he was likely lost. It was another season and a different place.

Now there was no rain to drown him, only Marie Ursule's vermilion morning going about its own business.

III

It was as if Terre Bouillante had never existed or as if he needed days of walking and thirst to find it, days of hunger and confusion; it was as if he needed bewilderment and sheets of rain, as if he needed the end of himself somehow and his last moment of hope and when he was beyond it. But now, with certainty in his steps, with a bag of water and a child singing, he could not arrive at the boiling mud or the impenetrable forest around it. He could not find the closing sky with the birds and macaques.

This time, with the child on his back and the season dry, he was alive, and could not summon up his way to Terre Bouillante. He had left her there in the mud swamp and he had gone circling himself, imploring the ground to open and let him in. When it didn't he walked back to the crab-lands to collect the child, thinking all the way to abandon her and vexed with himself, thinking all the way that she had spoiled his eyesight with her singing. Marie Ursule was probably in the stocks already and she would not know that he had not done what he promised or that he had left Bola there for crabs and birds to devour her in their own hunger. But whether it was what he owed Marie Ursule or fear of her, or the child singing in his blood now instead of the sucrier, he turned back to her.

His chest was breaking. All the fine passage to Terre Bouillante he had laid in it was lost. The child on his shoulder turning him into wood, his own memory deserting him. That wonderful day when he was dragged to Terre Bouillante and emerged in the clearing of lush peace—when he couldn't find it again he was homesick, homesick and homeless, and he wanted to lie on the ground and have it take him. He didn't want to go back for the child, he wanted to find Terre Bouillante as he had found it when he was dead, as if finding a childhood. But he could not remember for the life of him, so he returned for the child where he had left her and said, when he saw her calling for her mother, that Marie Ursule's dreaming was his next destination.

He was not Marie Ursule's man, not her brother and not her child's father, but they had lain in the same shack and breathed the same air of broken fields and broken hearts. And if something had been done between them, if their bodies had opened to each other like earth where too much has been planted and the soil gets weary and crumbles, he was still more her brother than the child's father. Marie Ursule had told him when to run and how to go and that was why he had to return to take the child, and when his passion for Terre Bouillante could not lead him back to it with or without Bola he had to return to her in the crabland to hear her sing, "Marie Ursule, Marie Ursule," so that he could gain his direction again.

He was a quiet man and made like wood, and her song told his green centre where to go, and when he saw Bola sitting crying and humming to the crabs and the red rain of ibises he knew that after he took her to where Marie Ursule led him he would find his country again. He would find Terre Bouillante and the place where he rolled under the sky and felt the hearts of birds. He was nobody in this world and he wanted to go to his own, he wanted the sky to close after him. He wanted his life and his quiet world. So he came back, and he lifted Bola to his shoulders and she drenched him in a shower of tears like a rain forest and he put one foot in front of the other and she led him out with her singing.

IV

The two old nuns are standing in the doorway. They are waiting in the place where Bola will end up, where she will discover the sea and the rock out in the sea. They have been here since her mother's time and before. Bola sees that they are from eternity. They are from God, and they are nothing that truly exists. It is a story that Marie Ursule has told her. She sees them in the doorway before she discovers the sea. And she sees that they are crumbling. She sees their figures in habits dampened by their strangled pores, pressed by countless suns, black and white turned black, their several hundred years particled in fine little grains. She sees their faces gone over by wood ants' and weevils' gnawing, moss drying for no moisture, the man-o'-war gowns held up like old cupboards for old keepsakes, and she screams. "Hush child," Kamena says, "what do you? *Ça qua fait na?*" "Dust," she screams, "Dust," and he cautions her, "Quiet, you and me alone see, keep your tongue in your head." His voice is rough with his own grief. They draw closer and Bola grips Kamena's shoulder, tightens her small legs around his neck and mutters, "Dust."

Nearer, Kamena walks across the marl stone yard, the child Bola growing from his neck. Nearer, toward the nuns, several hundred years coming into full sight. Her gifts bring them into a kind of being. "What live here?" she asks Kamena. "Nothing," he says, "Not one living thing but we." Moths and winged ants fly out of them, cincindela, aphids, parasol ants, chasseurs, boring beetles stirred, jack spaniards and razor grinders, disturbed, hum in confusion. Their several hundred years, long folded, shake out and hover together; two shapes held together by dust and insects and this time by Marie Ursule's dreaming.

There is time that is always happening. The time that is lost or forgotten or deliberately misplaced; the time well left unremembered or the time that is wasted on human stupidity; and the time that is unresolved and therefore unmoving, held there by frail wills, the acts of a day and all disappointments. Mère Marguerite de St. Joseph and Soeur de Clémy are buried in this time. There is time in this archipelago that returns and returns because no one truly belongs here except the Arawak close to extinction and the Carib retreating into denser interiors down the South American Main. The rest are cargoes of human beings without a recognizable landscape, whether they are slaves or masters. Marie Ursule counts on time's requital to summon the Ursulines. Kamena's walk, an unsteady dactyl, draws closer still to the nuns' regeneration.

"More dust, all dust, Kamena, all dust." This is the beginning of Bola's psalmody. Her art to living begins now, her art to time and determining what is more alive and therefore more of what she wants.

Long before Bola discovers the sea these two old Ursulines have been hovering and multiplying. Long after, they are still. They are dead by any empirical sign, their novices have died, their overseer, their cattle, have died, skins withered to paper with work; their goats dried to drum skins;

their convent crumbled to another civilization of rocks and chiton and cytheria, paludina vivipara and triton; crumbled to lancet bats and scorpions, crushed in the liquid silk of snails and the powdered gold of wood ants. All, died. Except, nothing dies. Nothing disappears with finality along this archipelago. Time is a collection of forfeits and damages.

Colonies of life's acts inhabit time here.

The Ursulines had long perfected their circumspect hovering, having to make their way without too much offence. To minister without ministering, to be there without being there, but to be called by God and to live and to minister to the vast amount of heathens—the endless work of God. Called. First to minister to the *Indians*, the Caribs, conceited heathens forgot the prayers the moment they were out of your sight and were baptized as many times as they could have new goods but went back to their own ways the minute your back was turned. Called. And invulnerable to resistance. Like man-o'-war birds, the great frigates that follow ships and whales, the Ursulines were even invulnerable to air, that is, time. Called to transform it into the breath of God.

So, like the man-o'-war, there and not there, the Ursulines had entreated to be sent, to make passage to the New World, since 1691. Begging the sols for board and lodging, on October twenty-eighth, 1691, they had embarked from La Rochelle, with two novices, on the ship *Tranquille* in choppy and treacherous seas and under the captain's compliments and his table they reached Martinique on the twenty-ninth of January, 1692. The dangers had only strengthened their faith and improved their quietness. And something else besides. The Caribbean taught the nuns how to multiply, as it taught all who came here mathematics.

How to multiply ground and tonloads of sugar and cocoa
and whale oil and anything they turned their hand and someone else's labour to.

And the Ursulines learned how to multiply their own
years also. They had moved, skittering down the archipelago
(as they had skittered down the centuries also), Guadeloupe,
Deasade, St. Vincent, since their jurisdiction was contested
by the Jesuits who had laid claim to their holdings as the
superior order on the island of Martinique. The Jesuits, being wonderful mathematicians themselves, claimed that the
Ursulines were under their rule according to the orders of
the king, and therefore owed them the profits of their slave
holding. And here the Ursulines came and remained, multiplying on the last Caribbean island—La Trinidad—before
islands exhaust themselves in coral and rock and cactus.

And Bola, hanging onto the back of Kamena, perceives
Mère Marguerite de St. Joseph and Soeur de Clémy more
than one century later. The gift her mother had given her,
allowing Bola to fall out of her belly like a moon, this gift
makes Bola see beyond the conclusions that flesh can come
to. There they are in the doorway, Mère Marguerite de
St. Joseph and Soeur de Clémy; a stilling whirl of their journeys, vanities, patience and penance, and what they could
not keep out. *Coronula diadema* adheres to their skins, and the
air they exhale is of castor seed and iron and lime, scorched
Guinea grass and rain.

Mère Marguerite de St. Joseph is the tall one; when her
arms stretch out powder falls, yellow clay with sand and
marl, particles of asphaltum, shells. Soeur de Clémy is the
one who resembles everything and nothing, her arms are
folded but her lips mutter multiplications of sugar canes
ratooning. Their skin is like smoke and rotted parchment.

Mère Marguerite opens her mouth in a kind of welcome and Bola sees gushing dust fall out instead of sound. She raises her arm to touch Bola who is afraid of falling into her mouth and ducks beneath her arm, whining, "Dust, Kamena."

"Hush up, I tell you already, child, you want me to take you back to the crabs?"

The big gundied land crabs wave in her memory. "These two is worse."

Kamena says nothing and stops, then continues thinking and discovers a metaphor, saying then, "Well, dust can't hurt you." For a few more steps, he says, "It could be fire." A slow man himself but certain, his neck is like a tree that she grows out of and to the incorporeal Ursulines it must look like salvation and resurrection coming toward them. A cross and something living growing out of it. Kamena's black chest like living wood and the child growing from him.

The first time she saw the sea she did not see it. It was night and she heard it break and wash before she saw it. She had heard its noise big as her breath when she'd opened her mouth in the swamp quiet and the red birds had fired into the swamp sky. Kamena had said to her, that is the sea, when she'd asked what noise was that that sounded like her breath. That is the sea, don't play with it.

Kamena had come back for her and fetched her from the swamp when it was so late she had thought that all her sighing would stop and the crabs collect her and drag her to their holes piece by piece. They had gathered around her, a whole riot of crabs, threatening gundies waving, and busily skittering sideways. The mud was puckered and dried stiff where the holes opened and crabs sidled in and out as if she were intruding and they had to be on their guard. She had stayed as still as possible, hoping that Kamena would return and thinking about what sign this was, and when she thought, they quietened, and when she noticed them again, they scrambled sideways toward her, clattering arms raised. Between the devastation of red birds and the running riot of blue crabs she had thought of signs.

Man-o'-war, in black and white, Bola saw the Ursulines waiting, floating like frigate birds at the end of the marl entrance. Marie Ursule had summoned them with all of her poisoned will, all her life boiling at the fire that morning. She had summoned them the way one summons a bad memory believing it to be as useable as a good one. They are a story Marie Ursule once told Bola, a juju to save her from pain by summoning pain itself.

The little girl remembers it now as she and Kamena move toward the entrance of Culebra Bay. The entrance is dead coral-white and empty, the nuns appear, called by several imaginations. And they, so seduced by penances, had come, though they had come with the industry they knew—slavery, and their regular regimen of prayer and punishment, passion and hesitation. But they had heard her nevertheless and collected themselves, dust and crushed debris, Mère Marguerite trying to hold the visitors to her bosom, Soeur de Clémy taking a rope in her hand.

These nuns who disappeared each morning and evening to mutter to themselves in a place with flowers and a man long dead whom they have placed in the stocks hanging above a table. Man-o'-war birds floating in and out, when only by looking up you would see them, not hearing them come in or leave. Not one sound sometimes. But they were good with money, purchasing this estate with their wit, with Soeur de Clémy's francs and letters patent and grants from their king, and trading and doing what quiet people

do, watching for their chance. They had bought the estate
on Culebra Bay and nineteen slaves from the filibusters, not
telling their king, not showing it on the accounts, and living longer than they were supposed to live, not letting their
king know either, not showing their longevity in their books;
a century of taxes unpaid. Quiet as ever, like man-o'-war
birds no one knows where they alight, but look up in the
mornings and they're ringing a bell and in the evening disappearing where, no one is sure.

They hover. Mère Marguerite and Soeur de Clémy. They
hover over the boiling house with its piercing odour of cara-
melizing sugar, the drying trays of rancid cracked coconut,
and the small stunted field and the sea. The nineteen slaves
exist now only in several imaginations. Even there, every day,
washing, digging, weeding, their movements are infected
with the nuns' hovering. The boiler keeper's hand lingers in
the air and the plantain grove keeper's cutlass hovers over
the grap before descending. The weeders notice weeds grow
again in the middle of pulling. The donkey stops in the middle of walking around the mill, or in the middle of eating it
grows thin. So everything is slow and hesitates on the estate,
tripling and doubling its time. The air is humid with fer-
mentation. Yet a step toward the sea and rusting spray and
wind begin abruptly, undoing the spell of the Ursulines.

Mère Marguerite de St. Joseph is the tall one, the one
who hovers the most, she moves in wisps like smoke. Soeur
de Clémy is the one who looks like no one and everyone and
cannot be seen. The one who is good with figures, calculates
in leather ledgers the lard, the hogs, the gallons of oil, the
digging tools, the steps to the boiling house, how long it will
take, how many ratios of cornmeal, how many bananas, the
plantains, the cassava, the spoonfuls of sugar. That one must

be God's accountant. In the evening and the morning she arrives with his ledger books as he, stiffly, all wooden, stands in the stocks above the altar. She declaims his properties: butterflies, hoe handles, drops of water; she has kept note of rain ants and pans of milk, beads of sweat and leaflets to a tamarind tree; how many lashes will open the seam in skin and, not to overreach herself, how long she and Mère Marguerite would have to live to keep it all in order.

Ursuline man-o'-war Soeur de Clémy, though she is only a ghost, a remembrance, she counts the fingers on Bola's hand, as she'd counted Marie Ursule's—their weight and thickness and length—and she determines small weeding, picking up stones; then hauling bagasse, bringing water, growing bigger, tall, thin, broad-shouldered, slim-hipped, nine children swimming, water watcher, she says, counting into Bola's maturity, muttering her destiny. Her fingers on Bola's light and not there, sending needles through the little girl, giving her prickly heat.

The broken rooms of their ruins are full of their hovering. All that is left of their estate house is blanched white caking stone that breaks off at the touch. All that is left are impressions of rooms and windows and doorways, lice-eaten and gone. A door opens to a pool of fish, another to a mangle of hoes and green fungus, a window question-marks the sea. A certain corner that once had a piano is now full of dried sea fans washed up from some ambitious storm. There are the vain directions of walls, climbing only to fall down in pebbled ennui. The floors are what woodlice and water and sand moss might make of a floor, and then taken over by scorching heat again, dried to a white fragile powder.

This place is imagined over and over again. Each fragment belonging to a certain mind—a reverie, a version—each fragment held carelessly or closely. Which is why it still exists. Nothing happened here. Nothing extraordinary for its time. Two nuns held slaves like any priest or explorer or settler in the New World. It is the others, the ones they held, who keep the memory, who imagine over and over again where they might be. It is they who keep these details alive and raw like yesterday. They twist and turn in all imaginations to come, in plain sight or in disguise. This fragile place and its muscular dreams. Nothing really happened here.

Standing idle at the insubstantial window, Bola senses Mère Marguerite de St. Joseph, she smells her smoke and turns but no Mère Marguerite is in the room. Bola's eyes fall on the door and there is the shadow of a man-o'-war tipping away. They play a game, she and the spirit of the dead Mère Marguerite de St. Joseph. She tries to catch Mère Marguerite hovering and screams when she sees her shadow. Mère Marguerite, the one who hovers the most, has to cut her hovering in two to surprise the little girl. She changes her rhythm to fool Bola, she triples her hovering one day, doubles it the other and tells Soeur de Clémy to mutter to the little girl not to scream so much.

"Don't, cacao, scream so much, a thousand francs, Mère Marguerite de St. Joseph don't like it," Soeur de Clémy mutters in her ear but Bola doesn't hear so much as she sees brittle dust crumbling and Soeur de Clémy counting, "Seven bags of cacao by three-quarter so far will bring a profit of one thousand francs." Whatever Soeur de Clémy thinks she is saying, by now she is so full of additions that only figures mutter from her mouth. Other facts distract her so much she translates them into numbers.

These years were the age of counting, they were the age of expertise, it was modernity, the New World, little additions and subtractions, increments of stock marked the time, and Soeur de Clémy, Soeur de Clémy had always needed exactness, which is why she had joined the Ursulines. A little vanity to be in the world but mindful of her troth to God, modernity was the will of the Lord. And now she translated prayers into numbers and short phrases, sums for easier understanding. Holy Mary, three hundredweight rum, sixty poulets, mother of God, pray for us sinners. . . .

The Ursulines, in 1824, long dead, are airing and waiting in the resurrected doorway of their estate at Culebra Bay for Bola, as they once waited for Marie Ursule, muttering their piece. They are a story Marie Ursule once told Bola.

V

After Bola saw the sea, walking into a house was like walking into a wall, a barrier to the open, because this is what Marie Ursule had seen in her child's eyes, the sea, and a journey to be made that melts the body. She had seen the child in the sea. When she looked into Bola's eyes when Bola sang out her name "Marie Ursule, Marie Ursule," and Marie Ursule heard some urgency in the singing and ran to her, then when she looked into Bola's eyes she saw the sea.

"Is what you call me for?"

And the child would only reply, "Marie Ursule, Marie Ursule."

"Is what you call me for I say?"

"Water, Marie Ursule, Marie Ursule."

Marie Ursule saw water in the child's eyes. So much water she dabbed it away, but more and more came. It wasn't tears. It was the sea. "What kind of child I make, eh? What kind of child?" Marie Ursule lamented, dabbing the sea out of her eyes and almost drowning there herself. Seeing iron melt and dirt washed and nothing she could understand, whole islands sink and rocks and big mountains of ice and barbed wire and fences and stalls and tunnels and lights that were not lanterns or flambeaux. And cities she did not know were cities. There in the sea, in the middle of Bola's eyes, Marie Ursule saw skyscrapers and trains and machines and streets, she saw winters and summers and leaves falling in muddy roadways and on pavements, dams bursting and giving way and boats and pirogues crashed on shores and steamers on water far off and aeroplanes way up in the sky and she felt a lifting she would never know. Her heart came like water in her hand and her face splintered in faces of coming faces, and she knew that if it was the future she was looking at, then she was keeping this crazy child from it if she took her along.

"Behave yourself, you hear. Don't call me so much."

"Oui, Marie Ursule," the child said, stopping the sea.

Marie Ursule did not know what to make of this child she had made. The voice that came from the girl was as sensible as any big woman's. It often surprised her, and sometimes she knew it was not normal, this baby big woman saying "Oui, Marie Ursule," as if she were talking to a child herself and watching Marie Ursule's every move as if she did not belong to her and she was the mother.

In the days before the poisoning the child had cried incessantly. Though she cried without the sound of crying but with the sound of laughter, showing Marie Ursule the future in case Marie Ursule forgot to leave her behind. As if knowing what Marie Ursule must do. She had slipped

out of Marie Ursule like the full moon at the bottom of
an exclamation point, full grown. She had to live a full century and sit in a rocking chair blowing in the dust-kicked
wind, listen all her life that was to come of voices and
dreams and surfaces her fingers could feel; of faces that
would fall out of her thighs and stare at her in disbelief or
fear or love.

After Bola saw the sea and the shadow of the Venezuelan
mainland she knew what Marie Ursule took in her eyes for
strangeness. She remembered Marie Ursule saying, "What
you want from me, why you singing my name, eh? *ca ka fait
na?*" She remembered that she wanted nothing, just to see
Marie Ursule, just to see her and to tell her something that
she'd forgotten or did not know how to say when Marie
Ursule arrived. She loved Marie Ursule's face, the comfort
of its steady shape, since she felt her own face moving and
unsteady and when she felt her small face falling apart seeing Marie Ursule put it right, when she felt her fingers and
her toes melting and her eyes welling she needed Marie
Ursule to stop the water and to see her so that she would
know again.

"What you crying for, eh, *Ça-qua-pleur*? You want something to cry for, eh?"

She believed she could never live without Marie Ursule.
Who would dab the ocean from her eyes? Who would make
her forget what she needed to say as soon as she arrived?
Who could see into the other century that her eyes saw and
just wipe it away like no trouble but Marie Ursule? Because
when Marie Ursule came, no matter how rough she tried
to be, she could not help seeing the ocean welling and the
places that were to come. But even so she had no time and
wiped the waters away, saying "Stop the crying, you hear

me." And the child held on to Marie Ursule to stop the ocean that she herself could not see but felt, like all her small self splitting apart.

If Marie Ursule saw her eyes then she saw the Venezuelan Main too. She saw the big ragged map of the world. She saw something fierce in Bola, a need to strain the ocean between her teeth like a rorqual swallowing flying fish, xiphias and baracouta, she saw Bola swimming into the future until she was bloated like a sea thing. And though Bola didn't see as much of it as Marie Ursule, no, she didn't see cities and syringes and ships and windows of pictures, Bola understood it more like lust, a taste in the mouth and a need that hollowed the face in craving. It was not where Marie Ursule would arrive. Bola would go somehow.

AT THE FULL
AND CHANGE
OF THE MOON

~~~~~~~~

I

*To the slave population of the Island knowing how much
you all wish for receipt of those orders, which you have for
a long time expected, to release you from slavery and make
you free, I have great satisfaction in announcing to you,
that the Parliament of Great Britain has at last after a
great deal of trouble, completed the laws and regulations,
that have been found necessary on the great change, that is
about to take place in your condition; And the King's orders
which I have received to make known this to you, shall be
immediately obeyed, as soon as the Proclamation can be
printed and sent round the island. To prevent you however
from forming hasty and wrong opinions upon the subject,
and then meeting with disappointment, I think it right to
inform you, that no change whatever will take place in
your condition, until after next Crop time, and that when*

your slavery itself shall cease, you will still be required to work for a certain time, for your former Masters, but under regulations different from those to which you have hither to been accustomed. With these new regulations you will become acquainted before the time of your manumission. I have directed all Managers, Overseers, and Magistrates —in short all white people throughout the island—to explain such parts of the new law, as are most interesting to you: if you are not satisfied with what they tell you, you may come to me for explanation: but take care that you do not come in greater numbers than two or three together. I will not receive or speak to any body of slaves, either coming with complaints, or to ask for information, that may exceed that number.

I have now only to express my hope and desire, that you will not allow the receipt of this intelligence, to excite you to Acts of Insubordination, idleness or riot. You must recollect that you are still under the same Owners and the same Laws as heretofore, though they will in a short time be changed, and that it will be my duty (which you may depend upon it I will not neglect) to support those Laws to the utmost, and that any ill-disposed Negroes, who may absent themselves from their work, or advise others to do wrong, shall be selected as the fittest objects for severe example. Be peaceable, be orderly, attend to your work with increased diligence, and show by your good conduct, how much you value and deserve the blessings of freedom to which you will in a certain time be admitted.

Sir George Fitzgerald Hill
Lieutenant-Governor, Government House,
10 October 1833

This grudgeful news does not arrive at Culebra Bay. Its cheerless warnings, its jaundiced provisions are like so many other things that are eaten up in Culebra's coral tomb. Its authority is surpassed by the authority of Marie Ursule's act ten years ago when she woke up to the end of the world. It is useless to the two, Bola and Kamena, living at Culebra Bay; it floats in the air like the resurrected spirits of Mère Marguerite de St. Joseph and Soeur de Clémy. Even for those nuns it has come too late and admits too much besides, with words like *manumission* and *blessings* and *peace*.

To those *ill-disposed Negroes* who need this news, it is a slap in the face and more dreadful waiting. Sir George Fitzgerald Hill's news is for Mon Repos and Mon Chagrin, Calendria, Belmont and the fifty-six estates whose life now will be turmoil if he doesn't exert full control. The owners are outnumbered by those who are soon to be slaves no longer, and unrest will have to be put down severely. There have always been skirmishes with ragged and desperate Maroons, but now they may become more daring.

But Culebra Bay is arrested in rock, crumbling and calcifying. It is arrested in rain and wind, it is held by broken doorways and impressions of rooms, it is wreathed in sea spray and the separate business of its own beings and spirits. Culebra Bay is abandoned, a Maroonage of two. Long thought of as blighted by leprosy, Culebra does not receive the news. As Hill writes this notice to the few who can read it, there is a map on his desk. Culebra Bay is marked off there to the end of the island skittering off into islets and rocks. It has long been rumoured that the nuns died there of leprosy along with their slaves. For years, which have turned into decades and perhaps centuries, no one has been there. Rumour has turned into truth and truth into myth and myth into superstition. And it isn't leprosy at all but time. And what inhabits time, all fears and guilts. It isn't leprosy at all, it is the stroke of a pen designating a certain place on a map as a repository of all the mind's doubts and worries and malevolence. Maps are such subjective things, borders move all the time. There are encroachments and retreats. A map, like the one on Hill's desk, can only describe the will of estate owners and governors. Or perhaps their hopes. This map cannot note the great fluidity of maps, which is like the fluidity of air. Paper rarely contains—even its latitudinal and longitudinal lines gesture continuations. Paper does not halt land any more than it can halt thoughts. Or rain showers, for that matter. The best cartographer is only trying to hold water, to draw approximations of rocks, inclines, bays, depths, plains.

How many spots does Hill take in, in an off-hand look, as he pens his notice, how many spots of runaways retreating and encroaching; spots with sunken villages; leprous rocks; places where the Maroons are dangerous; where little by little the owners have given way to "ill-disposed Negroes." One year a ship's cargo of slaves is wrecked on the Anegada reef only to be seized and brought here from Tortola; one year several cargoes are condemned at Cuba and sent to Trinidad to be put out as apprentices. A map does not contain the dispositions and reflections that collect at a harbour, or what those people will do on arrival, which is to work out the way to Maroonages, the way to rebellion, or for that matter, the ways to docility. Nor the stories of those escaped from Venezuela walking over the waters like Jesus Christ or drowned babies; the rumours they bring back and spread of fighting with Francisco de Miranda and Simón Bólivar for South American independence. That is where a map succumbs to anarchy. Maps' inadequacies give out here. A map of this island of Trinidad is more and more like a map of the ocean then.

Hill writes his notice to hold the ocean back, commanding it to wait and be patient. He glances over the map, and his stomach turns queasy at the thought of Culebra. Rumour has it too that one of those nuns, the one who loved counting and multiplying, in this passion had a son by a slave. By the time Hill writes his pre-proclamation, blood is already commingled and paper will be needed to untangle it; also, sharp noses, in the future, will sniff out racial mixtures like wine tasters and gourmets. The nun's case was only more dramatic and disgusting than most because of her habit. Culebra at any rate is dead land now. At least there will be no petitions from there about lost revenues and compensation for slavery's end. All that remains there are some sea birds and coral dust and some contagion. He does not have to worry. Safely abandoned.

In his own cartography, that of longings and muddled sight, this is what Kamena told Bola, "The currents near this island is very strong and uncertain especially between this island and the Main. At the full and change of the moon the sea will rise four feet perpendicular. The northeast trades blow all year round. There is good anchorage at Englishman's Bay, Manzanillo, Petit Trou and Leychelles. There is shoals at St. Germain which makes a pilot needed. If you make this island toward evening and is afraid of running in with it, you must not by any means lay to but stand to the southward under an easy sail, otherwise the current which always set to the northwest or northeast will probably occasion your losing sight of the island and if it set northwest would perhaps carry you so far to the leeward that you should not be able to fetch it again. In going in to any of the bays to the leeward of the island you may go as near as St. Helen's Rocks as you choose and if going into Englishman's Bay, may go as near to the north point of that bay as you please. Vessels sailing from the eastward for the south side of the island must keep well to the southward, otherwise the current round Petit Planche which run always to the northwest will sweep them away to the northwest. To the southwest there is nothing to fear, till you come to Leychelles, except Culebra rocks."

This is what Kamena told her and this is what she marked down in her head. Bola imagines the reaches of an island, gathered from this fisherman and that runaway and that Maroon, from all of Kamena's wanderings and the stories he returned with, each corner of the island he doubled and redoubled to reach its interior, trying to find Terre Bouillante. Each journey ends in regathered hopelessness and hope. All his news was of shores and bays and oceans. All his maps were discourses for settlers. All his sightings buried in a terrible poetry. All his footings slipped over cliffs, sea skirts of creeping water whitened his toes. Each time he circled himself he returned with rags of stories, droplets of suggestions to directions, which he showed Bola, cupping his hands around them as if they would fall. He made drawings in the dirt, and positioning himself so that a certain wind flailed his paper-thin body at a certain angle, he asked her to look that way. Was it the smell, the smoke of Terre Bouillante?

They arrived at Culebra Bay ten years ago. It was now 1833 and he had not found Terre Bouillante or given up his search even if it only took him farther into his own mind. Sometimes without moving a step he thought that he could feel Terre Bouillante close. Sometimes in his sleep he discovered a way and awoke fresh and happy only to find himself at Culebra Bay. He was always hopeful that he would find Terre Bouillante again yet always fearful that if he left Bola alone she could not survive. Even the end of slavery, and Hill's notice which even so he had no way of reading, did not make him abandon the desire for Terre Bouillante or his searching.

He cultivated patches of wild tania and wild yams, as the Maroons had done at Terre Bouillante in his small time there, and he taught Bola how to gather water from the choked river running out to the sea. In some season he taught her how to catch crabs from the mangrove along the river. He bided his time until she grew up so that he would finally have no more obligations to Marie Ursule, already gone her way. But his mind was all on Terre Bouillante.

His brooding silences almost made them both lose the very act of speech. The nature of language became all directions and sighs.

Culebra was not the Maroonage he had wanted. He had not wanted the crumbling stones of this dead plantation. He had wanted some place without any signs of such things. He wanted peace. But as usual Marie Ursule had got him tangled up with these people. He had been willing to leave their presence, consider the debt void, just for some peace. But vanity would not let Marie Ursule leave it that way. He had begged her the first time to come with him and take the child with them to Terre Bouillante. She had said no, and only agreed for him to come back, if he could, for the child. She wanted to follow pain instead of peace. Not a day he didn't wake up in Culebra Bay and his heart wasn't breaking for Terre Bouillante.

First, when she could bear it he left Bola for hours, then

as she grew older, for days. His search for Terre Bouillante redoubled when she could fend for herself. His mind was so ragged, Bola grew ragged; half hungry, half fed, half thin when he could not find food, half fat when he did. He coming and going to get his bearings, she waiting, they passed years in his longing silences and his muttering confusion. When Bola told him that he no longer had to stay he could neither go nor remain.

She watched the Mainland across the water through the rain mist, and she learned the things he did not learn, how a trumpet fish sings, how seaweed tastes, how to swim like fish, how to suck stones for thirst. Bola watched the Main, she watched the skies, she watched the pelting rain, the steamy noons, the noons peaked in heat. Kamena came and went, leaving her things to remember until he returned. The outskirts of the nuns' dominion, into which he often disappeared, loomed clearer as days turned into months. As months turned into years. Beyond those outskirts the world itself had disappeared. The world of planters and masters and slaves and soul-breaking labour. And of news and proclamations.

II

Between the spectres of the nuns and Kamena's frail charts to Terre Bouillante, her waking is like sleeping. Often the distinct scent of something else more alive made Bola set off for the outskirts, the land horizon where she saw Kamena disappear and where he warned her not to follow ever since they came here.

The outskirts are a semicircle ringed with short hills and thick growth. An old riverbed has left a white wash of stone through the thick growth, leading to the sea. The bed is wide and blistering to the eyes when the sun is high. In the rainy season the river tries to come alive and find its usual way to the sea but it is only a muddy trickle now. In the dry season the stones are hot white and Bola loves the feel of hot pebbles under her feet and stoops to put a warm stone in her mouth to comfort her hunger. She walks the length of the riverbed, stopping where it browns into mangrove undergrowth. There are crabs there, big blue ones, and she hears the breaking of alligators against the mangrove roots; the heave and thick splash of murky water farther along where the alligators dive and where the mangrove remembers a river still and sends roots to the air for food.

When she was small she could not even make out the last place in the semicircle, let alone arrive there. All she could make out was orange turning to green and white heat where the old riverbed is. And then, all in her mind was her mother whose name was Marie Ursule. And fleeing from Mère Marguerite and brushing the dust of the Ursulines out of her hair and eyes, she often thought of following Kamena but could not recall at which spot he had disappeared so that she might go too.

Only gradually did she come to see the outskirts' semicircle as more than its orange cloud turning green and then brown, or come to see the glare of the riverbed as the warmth and food of its stones. Gradually, as one does when one grows, earth finding its acreage, water its fathom, things finding their edges, their angles, she felt herself humming into a kind of clarity. The awkward bone-jangling meditation of adolescence.

Every year, as the outskirts came nearer and nearer into view as more than magic, more than conjuring, the gauze and webbing of Marie Ursule's spell fell away. Bola's own angularity pierced through. Turning into her own self, the outskirts witching into the world, her memory would fade of the things that happened before. Until Kamena arrived again, reminding her with his urgent face. She felt tired from his face and at times wished that he would stay away forever, find his place and leave her to hers, but no sooner would she wish this than she would miss him, violently, and his desire for directions. She resigned herself to seeing him come and go, each time returning with less of himself than before; leaving pieces of himself in each trace and gully he wandered.

Picking up stones and broken trees to keep pieces of the crumbled house together, planting wild tania and greens, bringing water, catching fish, growing tall, thin, broadshouldered, slim-hipped, seeing her blood, she walked into the intelligence of her muscle.

Rounding the semicircle, the other horizon is the sea, and this is where Bola spends most days now. Going down the riverbed to its mouth open to the sea, she feels the desire of the river drying to the ocean, pebbles giving way to broken shells and sand. She can reach the sea. And the rock out there seems another land, her own, where her circle is all water and not an orange horizon where Kamena disappears, or the still faint hovering of the Ursulines. Rather the rock's horizon, its circle, is the sea, and when it rains it is the colour of the vermilion air that morning when Marie Ursule was afraid the morning would come too quickly, the morning when Bola and Kamena left Mon Chagrin.

When Kamena returns again, gaunt and worn through, he tells her, "Hold this for me." Telling her a measurement,

"Five days long in any direction from the crabland should get you to Terre Bouillante if you are sleepy. You must be famished and it must be after the rains come and count out twenty or so macaques, five parrot heartbeats, the green ones, and sixty-five feathers, that is how long it takes." And then he falls dead away in front of her, faint from walking and grieving and measuring his way to Terre Bouillante. And when he wakes up and asks her what did he give her to keep and she tells him, "Five long days in any direction, five parrots' heartbeats and sixty-five feathers..." he cannot make sense of it. "Hold this for me," he says again on returning, "the second balata tree next to the mahogany whilst a yellow-crested bird trills, not sings but trills, and it must be eleven o'clock."

"Hold this then, the sun must be on my left eye when I am facing the immortelle tree next to the ridge at Morne Diable."

"Hold this for me then." His next visit he arrives triumphantly—"If a agouti cross me in the track and my lamp blow out in the wind and my water is low, then and only then is Terre Bouillante." Bola holds all of his signs and repeats them once he wakes up, repeats them to his sad sad face that cannot decipher his own calculations. Each story she holds for him takes a story away from him and each story gained burns him to a chimera.

"Hold this for me," he said lastly, leaving blue tracings, scintillas, gold gleams, parings and russet scrags forever in the air. "Do we arrive already empty, gut of everything already, knowing no remedy will ease the drift of our soul, how heavy, how like the sea our tears is; some of us does not recover from the sight, the wound of our heavy black bodies sinking in water." "Hold this for me," he said, his cheeks emaciated from lack of water and his joints whistling like reeds, "———".

With that Kamena had left her here for good. It might be years since she'd seen him last. Even Mère Marguerite de St. Joseph and Soeur de Clémy and their dusty centuries had faded, their estate crumbled into its superstition; its boundaries of leprosy, air, bitten coral and crushed conch shells had been spat out by time. Kamena had turned into a skeleton searching for his Maroonage. The last day she recalled of him, he was burnt up with walking and dried away with crying, starved with remembering. "Hold this for me."

III

The first time she saw the whales she burrowed into the sand like a crab. She heard their breathing as if they would suck the whole ocean of air, as if the wind would go out of Culebra Bay and the almond trees and the palms shrivel.

She waits and waits in the rain, looking for spouts, and the rain mists and it clouds. She swims in the rain to a rock out in the sea far from land and looking back she cannot see this island now in its rain dress. She found this rock running from Mère Marguerite. Mère Marguerite who could not touch water any more though water was how Mère Marguerite and Soeur de Clémy had come here but now it hemmed them in. Her rock was the one place Bola could come to escape the Ursulines, who as she discovered had no control of water. They evaporated once she ran past the foam, once she swam to the rock breathless. She would look back to shore and see them helplessly waving. She would swim out in the rain to stoop on her rock, looking for the Main. Or what she thinks might be the Main. Perhaps that is where Kamena goes when he leaves her. Perhaps he has found a land bridge. Every time he leaves she thinks he has gone for good.

She wants to swim to the Main. Now in the rain, the ocean sand kicked up enough to make a path, she thinks she will walk across the water to the Main. The sea rising, her dress is like water and her legs like seaweed and the cold does not matter and with only one hand she holds to the rock as the water lashes her and pushes her out to the Main. In the rain she will disappear.

Looking back to the island it is in mist and rain and cloud and does not exist therefore. She cannot see the shore, the broken house, the door, the bell, the cow tied to the tree. She cannot see Kamena's road or hear the sucrier singing under the flower bushes. And she cannot see the Main except in her mind. So she is alone in the water like a boat and a shipwreck and if she lets go of her rock she will swim and drift down the Main, out of the Golfo de Ballena and up the Orinoco, the Rewa, the Rupununi, the Demerara, the Mahaica, the Essequibo. She alone in the Golfo de Ballena floating, down to the Main.

When it rains the sea rises ten feet in open water and when from the shore it looks like heavy seas out here, she sees calm steady motion. She dips her head into the ocean and becomes seaweed. The sea is always changing and so is the sky. She is never tired of drowning in both, the days when clouds bunch up on the horizon, lying in for the evening, making doorways and windows, and if she escapes Mère Marguerite de St. Joseph she can walk through those doorways, break the horizon sleeping on her rock.

Bola retreated into the sea the way one retreats into the bush. Fled the way one flees terrors, craving joys. The sea's billowing mountains and crinkling ridges became as well known to her as any territory is known by its travellers. She plunged into its wide ways, its hesitations when waves crested, its untouchable crystals and soft diamonds.

The whales' breathing was as magnificent as Marie Ursule. She followed Kamena's discoveries and directions, where to anchor, where to land, where to make for come evenings. His accounts of bays, of indentations, of promontories, she navigated and swam in her mind, making her way to the Main.

The truth is she did not want to leave Culebra Bay, just to navigate the passage around the island and up the Main. She was already taken by the bell chords of trumpet fish and the endless breath of whales. She was already taken by the circular sky, the perpetual blue, the incessant night black. She was already ravished by the shock of red birds and by sudden silences when the sea steamed. In the midst of dust and inhumanness, in the midst of closings, she had succumbed to tastes and smells and the sharp graze and cool sting of the body.

IV

After many years she knew that she had been the only living thing at Culebra Bay. As stories fail, Mère Marguerite de St. Joseph powdered and drifted and her voice faded, Soeur de Clémy lost her numbers now and then, looking worried. Kamena lived in his own directions. The nuns' banisters and windows crumbled under the touch of her hands. Bola heard the Ursulines less and less and the world fought its way in more and more. The boats. Footfalls breaking down the cattle grass and mimosa tangle. Cutlasses cutting tracks into Kamena's outskirts. Footprints cracking new sand. The noise of living coming closer and closer. The horizon at the outskirts cut itself into a road with flame trees and tin-roofed shacks. The outskirts narrowed to particular shapes, and the semicircle of hills was conquered by vegetable gardens and goats and chickens scratching for seed.

People had drifted here little by little looking for a way out, looking for a life away from the estates and the years of indentureship that they were locked into even after slavery ended. These were people who needed to see the sea when they looked up from planting a yam or feeding their chickens. They needed to sit under a shade tree on the dry hills, listening to their own breathing, and look out to the ocean hourly. These people needed to glance over their shoulder at any moment and see the vast blueness that would relieve them.

So, beginning in 1834, the year slavery ended, more or less, they began drifting toward this semicircle gibbous to the sea. Some drifted knowing no one would follow them to Culebra Bay, not waiting to finish the six years' indentureship that the proclamation of emancipation said they owed still; some barely dragged themselves to Culebra Bay with their last will, gasping when they saw the big water. None of them questioned that they found Bola there or asked what her life might have been before; they did not talk of their own lives, let alone look at others'. They had all arrived for the same reason, and Culebra was their newness and their youngness and to find Bola there, a young woman full of life, knowledgeable about the sea and the dry river, was only a good sign to them that they need not question. Eventually all stories come out in their time and they all had stories and those stories would ease out when they were cooking or looking for firewood, or when fanning a half-dead fire or gathering grass for a goat that one of them had straggled in with or balata for a red monkey tied to a tree. There was enough time in the future for recounting but all they really wanted to do was go on, advance into their next years, which had to be sweeter, and were, just by the fact that they were at Culebra Bay.

And someone who looked like Soeur de Clémy's son, half nun, half black, cleaned out the boiling house and built a stone house on the path along which Kamena had carried Bola. Boats came across the Gulf more frequently, fishing within sight of Culebra. But rumour can last centuries and then more. Culebra remained a small place. Its reputation for leprosy and its remoteness kept it so for the next fifty years. That suited those who had wandered there. They wanted to be alone; any disease was better than more indentureship. They didn't want to see another estate and they didn't want their children to see it either. They hated cacao, they hated coffee, they hated cane. If they could pass this hatred on in a chromosome they did, their hatred was so physical. They took it as a matter of pride not to work for anyone.

The outskirts settled into a village around Bola by the sea. Soeur de Clémy's son, or the man Bola took for him, lived on whale blubber and whale oil and whale bone. He had watched the movement of the whales until he noticed that it was simpler to watch Bola. She sensed the whales days before they arrived, because she had lived there and had come to know the breathing of the sea. Nowadays she could only see two nuns drifting in the air if she looked up quickly or listened with her head in the water, listening to trumpet fish and whales' breath. She could only see them if she thought steadily of Marie Ursule and a vermilion morning long ago. But the voices of real people broke her senses until only now and then she would come upon the Ursulines suddenly hovering and whispering over some old rotted piece of wood, which was the doorway and some stones, which were the hearts of the nineteen others.

And last, worst, and best, Kamena never returned after a while with agouti and lime. He never returned looking in her eyes for the way, the sign to Terre Bouillante, the directions he had begged her to hold, the days when he would shake her in his grief and weep for her to tell him, the days when he cursed and loved Bola. Not returning with a tamarind or balata or chenette to coax the secret from her, the secret way to his life and his new beginnings. He never returned to the days he kept her company with his heart beatless in his hands and his face so shadowy she stroked it into existence else he would fade, his head spinning, his hands trembling and his mouth in a fever. He must have finally left his body now, she thought, where his eyes and his brain had been. Marooned. She had watched him year in year out circling himself, leaving in the rain, going to find Terre Bouillante, returning without it. She had learned that searching was useless.

Whale-watcher they called her, because no one could undo her from the sight of whales, nothing distracted her gaze and no one could swim as fast toward them when they arrived or hear them so long before they surfaced. But what they did not know was that she was trying to warn the whales away as well as tell them to come get her. On seeing whales, she blew Marie Ursule's name into a pink conch shell and remembered that vermilion morning.

When she first saw the ocean she knew Marie Ursule would have seen its tears and said, "Hush up, hush up," to comfort the soaked face of the earth, "Now, what you crying for, you want something to cry for, I'll give you something to cry for."

Now she was trying to tell the whales, "It is shallow here, here are the new people and the boats and here they will rip your sides open and no one will carry you to another shore where you can breathe. No one. Not even Kamena can do that."

When the sea turned like that, when the water was turquoise and full like a belly and when the weeds were so plentiful and the fish indescribable and everything was pregnant and the sea full like only the sea, Bola breathed into her shell like another whale. "Stop now, stop now, you will frighten them off," screams the man who looks like Soeur de Clémy's son. And she breathed harder and harder standing on her rock out in the sea, blowing all day long. Long after the whalers had caught the whale, long after they had dragged it tired to shore, after they had sliced it open and the blubber had gone to the boiling house; long after a ship's keel had been greased, long after.

———— ～ ————

When the village of Culebra Bay fully arrived it was almost the middle of the century and Bola had survived the ruins of Marie Ursule and Kamena and the spectral Ursulines. More than survived, she had thrived waiting for their shades to pass, their enchantment to subside, their bitter dealing to be slaked, if not cured. She was not faithful to sorrow only to a muscular yearning for everything her eyes touched. What her eyes touched she craved, craving raw like a tongue, and pinned to one look, one shadow, one movement of an almond leaf, one wave, one man, one woman with a fish basket, one moment. And as soon forgotten. She moved to the next lust, forgetting the one she'd just hungered for and thought she would die without. Lust for anything she saw, any bird, any passage of air, any cut of landscape in a look, any food, any stone or flight of birds, she would see just what they were and covet them, coveting their shape, their thickness, their redness, their saltiness. And lust for her own flesh. She would knead her soft thighs and smooth them in her fingers for hours.

And lust for the men who drifted down to her from the village that had settled on the outskirts. She liked them for the way they walked or the way they sang. The one who could not see she liked for the leaning of his head, the way he heard everything and his grey eyes watered. And the fishermen for their skin—burnt, singed from the sun and spray—and the banana keeper for the flame of his cutlass and the sound it made slicing and sucking the sticky milk of the stem. She loved the smell of one of them so much she became sick with a fever and hallucinations, so much she lay down and imagined it for two days when he had left. So sick with his scent she had to tell him to leave so she could savour it. She only took note of her senses and was uncomfortable with those who wanted to stay too long.

Bola always looked down at her swollen belly in surprise and as if it was not something she had lived with for nine months, but forgetting, all of a sudden looking down and wondering what she was carrying, forgetting it was her third child, it was her fourth child, it was her sixth. The fathers soon vanished or were forgotten too. Going back to their tin shacks with their wives because Bola had neglected them; going back to their vegetable gardens from which they had seen her on her rock, looking for whales. They vanished in their fishing boats after she had lain there with them, her legs wide open, her wet dress tied around her waist. She forgot them when they walked beyond the flame trees, beyond the outskirts of her thinking. They were often forgotten when they turned their backs momentarily. Living so long by herself she had developed a self-centredness, a fascination with only her own thoughts. She appeared distracted, which was her charm, yet intensely curious. She viewed everything with a curiosity, though that only lasted until the next thing came along.

And if the children born to her took more from her, or from Marie Ursule, whom they did not know, or from these lovers, it was nothing to her, she just gave them what she had, which was her senses all tuned to their pitch, tuned as greed or slovenliness or mystery or idiocy or curdling charm. If they took some benefit from her it was her intensity at peeling her skin to see if it was black inside or hitting herself on her rock to see if she could have sex with it. Or her curiosity as she walked on the same spot for hours to see if she would go anywhere, then stood in the sun to see if it would come down and cover her if she prayed. If the language describing their life was her lusory idiom, it was not because she gave it but because she gave it by blood without thought of gratitude or remembrance. Without hopes— because *hope* was a word for the ignorant and Bola was old before she was young, and in the world as flour is in flour or pebbles in pebbles. Not for hope but for being, and for the things that dropped out of her eyes, which she could not see but felt. Feeling was all. Her senses were all.

Bola would be ninety years old and still as candid as a child, easy to pleasure and quick to pain and grief just as soon forgotten. She felt everything, the light and the door handle as much as the scar on her lover's face or a stone's middle or the jerk of a flea, an ant's intention and the bleeding tail of a lizard, she saw a smile coming before it arrived and she reckoned a wave's proposal long before the sea. Suffering would skip her generation, she didn't have the patience for it. She only knew it like something welling in her eyes and singing, "Marie Ursule," and she only knew how to put it from her mind.

Bola filled the semicircle with her children, discovering her hunger for people after the drought of her years with Kamena; then gave them away or kept them, depending on a whim. Depending on which one had something written in her face that said *cloth* or *iron*, depending on what first came out of their mouths, sighs or grunts or singing, depending on how fast they walked she let them go about their business because every child wasn't a child but had its own life and its own way and its own age.

Bola was not one for sadness. When the children came to her crying like mewling birds, she told them, laughing, "What you have to be sad about when you en't even live yet? What you sad for? a green mango, a tamarind seed? a hole in the sand? What? What when you have a good life and you have food and if you don't have food you can suck a river stone? What? When you can breathe air and drink water? You lucky."

So she gave the serious-eyed one to the serious-eyed man because it must have been his: the girl who was nine and looking out, serious-like, to Curaçao saying, "Boto, bayena, awa, mama awa." That one who said she could iron clothes and put a fire out.

And she gave the boy who liked golden things—sunlight and coins and yellow yams and butter—to the man from Venezuela whose skin was golden with the merest breath of Angola and who passed his hand across cloth as if he were taming it, and who spoke Spanish dropping it like a stinging waterfall. She gave the boy to his love of things with a texture.

The boy who ran away she gave to running away because she couldn't comfort him, she couldn't still the fright in his eyes, she couldn't warm his hands, she couldn't fatten him or stop his wasting away. He loved things too much, she told him. He would sob when the sun fell into the ocean. He followed her furtively along the beach, rubbing out the imprint of her footsteps in the sand. His fear of the ocean was consuming. He searched the beach for her footsteps, stepping into them so that he would be safe. Taking his own path he felt nauseous and dizzy, thinking the ocean would suddenly lash out, slip the sand from under him and drag him in. She felt him behind her, felt his distress. When she turned he would be gone, but the print from his feet would be where hers should have been and it would be as if hers only just started but from nowhere. No matter how suddenly she stopped and spun around looking for him, he was not there. Only his footsteps ending and running away and hers always beginning. He grabbed her painting of the Main to see if she would follow him, and ran to the interior, the place that used to be Terre Bouillante, finding without looking what Kamena could not find, to make a generation.

The one who was born just when the rain falls and falls and falls until it is nothing but mist, that one left at fifteen

with a man from the Guaripiche who sold her to a wag-
onload of loggers; she always walked with rain streaking her
face, and when it rained Bola remembered her as the one
who wanted to come out of her belly so fast she left without
her little fingers. She left like a going river. She would live
for ever and ever, rematerializing along roads where there
is forest waiting. She will hike to towns, bringing necessary
rain and floods.

The ones Bola kept grew by themselves without her
assistance and came and went and gave her a rocking chair
to sit in the windswept dirt and to chuckle, but that was
years later.

She gave the one who dried her milk to a woman who
walked by with a fish basket full of red fish and who made
the sign of the cross as if she too could see the crumbling
nuns and Marie Ursule's conjure. They looked at each other
shaking and became the kind of friends who know too much
about each other; the kind of people who are wary all their
lives and drink from the same cup to make sure, or never
drink from the same cup and never leave their belongings
near the other one's hands. The woman with the fish basket,
misinterpreting Bola's simple curiosity, took all she had
on a boat to Bonaire—the fish basket and the child—and
watched the seas for Bola's coming, never telling the child
about her beginnings. The woman with the fish basket
counted the waves and forbade the child to go near them
because waves were like Bola's eyes and she'd seen them
plain as Bola's mother and she was a woman of smaller
needs so understood them less.

Bola gave the one who loved dolls to the madhouse; and
the one who cried incessantly she made in the dry season
and milked his tears for water.

One never arrived and made Bola's belly empty and bloated for long years. That one pushed many others out before their time and sat in the cloaked blood of Bola's belly, jealous and grudgeful, until Bola washed her out with salt water and lime just like any fish.

One was taken by the hurricane of 1875 on a joy ride of his might-have-beens, entangled in trees and galvanized roofing and wooden steps and bhaji bush and karili vine. He split and spun all over just like any bit of rain or rag of land.

And the last, Augusta, was as blind as her father with the leaning head (though not from her eyes but from her ambition), and she learned her father's way with sounds and surfaces. She could tell a name by a footstep, and she stood over the washtub all day for the love of the scrub board's grit. She would catch cold easily, which gave her an audible speech from her chest. She, Augusta, had a boy who went with his eyes half closed to a great war.

TAMARINDUS
INDICA

~~~~~~~~~~~

*T*amarindus indica. He sat under this tree every day. A tree perhaps brought here from Africa in the seventeenth century. Probably brought here by his great-great-grandmother, as a seed in the pocket of her coarse dress. Probably held in her mouth as a comfort. Perhaps then germinating in her bowels. How the tree came to stand in his path he really did not know. And if it had been his great-great-grandmother, she would have brought a silk cotton tree, its high wing-like buttresses webbing out in embraces. His great-great-grandmother, however, had not passed down into memory but he had heard that silk cotton blew all the way here from Africa and that is how he thought of any ancestry before Marie Ursule, who was his great-grandmother.

This tree grew daily in purpose. It was brought; set down in his path. Or perhaps he was fooling himself again, fooling himself that any piece of the world could be arranged with him in mind; fooling himself that he had a specific heading or that he was in the middle of all actions, important.

He sat on the ground under the tree's shade each day. He had counted leaves made of fifteen pairs of leaflets, rarely more, sometimes less, fifteen pairs of leaflets as small as the nail on his baby finger. Smaller. He was noticing minute things. A sliver of blue glass between his bare callused toes, a piece of gazette paper gone black, which he used to insert in his shoes. The flower of *Tamarindus indica,* smaller still and pale yellow, not enough for a show; all the show was later in the pods he mashed open, which looked like some brown jam but was sour.

He sat there each day after his walk in the burning sun, when the sun was heavy on his back as a sack he carried, the sun a burden and a relief in the wood he had grown of his life. *Tamarindus indica*—finally shading him from the stout relentless sun which always proved too much for him in the end.

And so the next day his walk would have to start all over again. And then he would have to sit there under the feathers of *Tamarindus indica* and count how many leaflets on this leaf, how many leaves on this branch, his face in a stroke-like sweat and his penance unpaid. He wished the tree did not stand there, as much as, returning from his walk, he longed for its shade. Because if, when he saw it, he felt relief, then that meant he had not done with what he owed, and if it were not there, it meant he would not have the relief to fall under it and recover to do his penance over again.

It was a fitting tree to hear his confession and take his penance since such a tree must have come in his grandfather's cheek or in his broken toes. More native to India, such a tree would have travelled this way. Yes. Such a tree, which had seen to it that it did not wash itself away in water or tears, but waited until it was spat out from his grandfather's mouth, or passed from between his legs, its seed an indigestible stone. This was the tree, *Tamarindus indica*, from which he had to beg a forgiveness to which he had no right.

Misconduct! he mumbled to himself, sweat and the sun ironing what was left of his black suit to a shine. Misconduct. The man tell me to clean his knife, get his water, clean his clothes, dig the pits. Misconduct! So is not me and he climb the hill on Damieh together? Is not his foot in mud just like mine, why he tell me to shine his boots, clean his knife? I not tired too? Force-march back to Jericho, one whole day and the fever fighting me in the desert and I must get his boot when we both sit down. I must dig shit pits. Who more misconduct? The man have no mind! I poorly with the fever coming and he need his clothes clean.

"Misconduct, my ass," he mumbles each day to the *Tamarindus indica,* since no one else will hear him. No one wants to listen again to the story and anyway all who knew it have passed away and those who remain think that he is off his head.

It is dry and hot the morning they rout the Turks on Damieh Hill. The unexpected cold at night chills him, his leg wrappings seem meagre and the paper in his boots rank. He has been cold ever since he boarded the ship and left home. He hasn't known whether to take his boots off and rub his toes or leave them hurting in his boots. But all turned to unimportance when they received the order and the knowledge that the Turks were trapped between their lines and the assault was to ensue. The Second West India Regiment, posted in Palestine for the past five months doing labour services, advanced up the hill at Damieh like real soldiers.

He had come all the way here to serve the mother country, Great Britain. After all the official entreaties by the governor of the island, whose impassioned letters to the Colonial Office assured it of men, though of colour, willing to fight for Great Britain, the Second West India Regiment had received condescending assent. Men who were young and strong and of intelligence no matter their skin. And he was one of them, marching and doing their aimless drills across the parade grounds in case they were needed. And he was not feeble like the Indians all sent back not fit. He was in his physical prime, boarding the ship first to Great Britain then to Palestine. Him. Private Samuel Gordon Sones of the Second West India Regiment. The name of his grandfather, Rabindranath Ragoonanan, was buried under illegitimacy of some kind or another, and any Indian traces in him were sun-sweated to tightly curled hair. The name and the physical signs lay dormant and unattended, unremembered, as those traces were both unimportant and a liability.

Rabindranath Ragoonanan had arrived a man-boy on the *Fatel Rozack* from India almost at the same time that Bola saw Culebra Bay turn into tin shacks and flame trees. No sooner had he found his legs to stand up, after 113 days at sea, than he was bundled off to the vast plains of the Caroni to work the cane fields. The expanse of cane overwhelmed him. The whistling and rough soughing of the stalks and leaves took over his hearing, big as the waves he had just departed. The flat unending plains, waving green turning to blue with cane, made him know that he was here to stay. His gaze never surpassed them, he could never look far enough.

Many years after, he wandered into Culebra blind, heard

Bola's shell-blowing and headed for the sound. Blind, because fire had taken out his eyes, caught in a razing cane field, a flaming stalk had lashed him across his face, running for his life. It was the way he carried his head that Bola loved. He was waiting for sound because he could not see. All his direction was sound, all his life was sound because he could count on nothing else, except perhaps the feel of something on his face, so much is bound up by seeing. He ended up at Culebra because it was where some sound took him. On his road there he took all paths away from the glutted noise of coming big towns; he listened for air with space in it and he listened too for the sea, which had first brought him to the island. Though he was a man of interiors; of the heavy rains and long floods of Gorakpur where he was born, which had driven him to the port of Calcutta. As if swept down by a monsoon among the other debris and the things monsoons turn into other unrecognizable things, covered in mud and useless, Ragoonanan had been pushed and rolled and dragged to the depot at Calcutta to be sent indentured overseas.

He and 224 others, most in destitution, some in ambition, boarded the boat under the immigration scheme to feed the cocoa and cane estates of Trinidad abandoned by Black labour after slavery. He was a bit of rag by the time the *Fatel Rozack* set out and he was probably only thrown in by the inspectors at the last minute in anticipation of the casualties along the way, perhaps as a goat for the jharay to rest bad luck on instead of on the more robust. One hundred and thirteen days on the sea and he had arrived thinner than he began and scarcely able to walk. And later then the fire had scorched his eyes and he had brought his lashless stare to Culebra Bay.

Another generation had erased Ragoonanan from the

face of Private Samuel Gordon Sones of the Second West India Regiment. Not deliberately but by sheer force of the tin shacks, the flame trees and Rabindranath himself; as if, not seeing, he did not see himself. Settled into the outskirts he learned another language and another race, and in his own mouth he cursed his own beginnings because if not for that he wouldn't be here. Rain put him in the foulest mood. He felt like a muddied rag sitting at the mouth of his damp shack. He remembered the monsoons, he begrudged not loving them, which, had his circumstances been different, he might have done; but were it not for them he would have still been in Gorakpur. So it did not matter if his daughter Augusta, by Bola, a woman twelve years older than he, obliterated the rest of him in a man who came round with an instrument for pulling teeth. A black man, with grainy hair, whose name was Sones, and whose name Augusta took, preferring it to Ragoonanan, or Mon Chagrin which was all Bola could offer of anything like a last name.

When the Second West India Regiment first disembarked at Liverpool, Augusta's son had kissed the ground, taking a handful and putting it in his pocket. He felt the wet remains of it hit his thigh as he moved up the hill with his regiment at Damieh.

War! he roars under the *Tamarindus indica*. War. I went to war for them. Misconduct, my ass. But most days he just does his penance without a word because the sun is so hot it doesn't take a word. Breath has to be rationed, and besides it is nobody's business what his penance is for. It is between him and the *Tamarindus indica* and the furnace of a sun that makes his skin weep.

When he returned in disgrace he looked at himself in the mirror and said to his own face, "You is a English man?

Take that in your arse then." He put on his black English suit
with its vest and his white shirt with its stiff starched collar,
his black English shoes and white socks; he tightened his
tie to his neck and set out to walk the length and breadth
of Culebra Bay, beginning at precisely eleven-fifty and ending at one-thirty back at the tree. He chose the time when
the sun is most fierce; only this could burn away his shame
and loathing.

He showed himself no mercy. His collar ate into his neck
and he did not carry a handkerchief to sop his brow. Now
the suit is frayed. For the first few years he had bought a
new one every year but thinking after a while that this vanity
was why his sin was not expiated, why each year he felt more
and more criminal, he'd worn the same one now for nine
years, patching it where decency required and leaving the
sun to iron the sweat and dirt into the seams. He had grown
thicker, more dense than the young man who had climbed
with hands and feet up the hill at Damieh, slower than the
young man who had shot into a fleeing Turk and, pausing in
shock, was swept up by shouts and the running frightened
inhuman screams of the Second West India Regiment, under
the terrified command of Captain Michael De Freitas.

It was not that he hadn't noticed little by little or that he
did not know his place, and yes he would be humble in that
place. *Yes sir* was not a hardship. Yes sir, no sir. That was the
result of his birth. But a man could rise. A man could strive.
And he had been let into the Second West India Regiment,
proving that men of colour were improving their situation
and would be repaid for their duty. It was the public contingents that he was let into and they were just for Blacks and
Indians, but no matter, his mother had said, a man could
rise above all this. His mother had encouraged him to think

himself a man above what Black men thought they could be in those days.

His mother, Augusta, was above what a woman could be. She managed his birth and the world and managed to make a son who would rise above himself. Augusta Sones built a parlour up on the roadside, selling fried fish and sweets, doing washing in the back of her shack and so, little by little, built up her son and put shoes on his feet and sent him to school. Whenever Sones, his father, came to pull teeth with his pliers, she took a few shillings from him and tied it in a knot and put it in her bosom, then lifted her dress and bent over her washtub so that Sones would give her some pleasure for herself until the next time he passed through.

And his grandfather, Rabindranath Ragoonanan, had not been less a man, given all that had been done to him. He asked for nothing, wandered off following this or that sound and returned to sit in the doorway of his shack, singing prayers and ghazals and welcoming various Hindu gods and goddesses or cursing them out of his house as the case might be. He was far away from them anyway, they could not hold him or exercise any power over him and he was far away from the pandit who was still in touch with them. He was a poor labourer who could not labour any more, but the fact that there was life at all in him made him worthy. And in his shack even Shiva and Kali and Lakshmi were lodging there only by his beneficence. Where were they when the monsoon deluged him toward the lice-stricken depot in Calcutta, where were they on the vomiting ship? He'd cried when they delivered him on land 113 days later, but his faith was stingier, smaller, and the burning cane that took out his eyes took the rest of his devotion. So when he sang prayers it was for the sound, not for any faith.

In her ninety-sixth year Bola had laughed aloud in her delirium when she heard that her grandson Samuel was going off to war. Rocking on the veranda, her eyes blind, her body as robust as when young, her face collapsed around her gums and her hair patchy and balding, she laughed big and rippling as if she had heard something fantastic and absurd.

He had been afraid of her ever since he was a boy, because when he came home she would always grab him and go through his pockets like a bullying child, looking for candy. And she would slap him if he didn't have any, and if he did she would steal it and warn him not to tell. Then she would go back to her rocking, rocking, endless rocking, and all alone talking to herself, then every now and then she seemed to catch up precisely with whatever conversation was going on around her. He felt that she could read his mind when he was a boy.

Her chair was in the yard near the clothesline and she would rock there after sweeping the dirt clean leaving lines from the broom crossing themselves and making arrows and swirls, and he would play around her drawings, destroying her lines and brushing her feet with his stick. He did not know what to make of her. Senseless his mother said, senseless, she had lost her senses and he was not to interfere with her. And so, like someone who had his senses, he provoked her, happy that there was an adult whom he could mistreat, until she reached for him and grabbed him to her and rode the rocking chair on his toes and looked him square in the eyes, her own eyes emerging from their glaucomaed grey, and said when he screamed, "Don't cry. When you're wicked you can't cry. Who will hear you?"

He left her alone after that, playing far away and glancing toward her every now and again to see if she was about to attack or if she was still there, sitting in her chair, rocking in the middle of nowhere, the dust swept clean around her, her occasional pointing at the sea, her internal conversations lifting her arms in delight, and mumbling, her sometimes singing, "Pain c'est viande beque, vin c'est sang beque. . . ."

So when he heard her laugh as he was going off to war dressed in his khaki breeches and leggings, he spun around, forgetting that she was still alive, his face contorting in worry. He felt an urge to pick up a stone and fling it at her but her old warning that if you hit your mother in life your hands will remain in the air in death and you would not fit into your coffin, that old warning stopped him. "Old Ma, shut up!" he screamed instead.

Rocking and chuckling to herself, Bola, the grandmother who had lived in two centuries, was living somewhere else already, though every once in a while she would catch the voices from where her body was and laugh. So they could not know that she had not heard a word as to substance but had heard a voice to help her trace her way back to where she had left her body.

When she heard it she was down by the water many years ago. The man-o'-war birds were coming in to signal to her that a ship was coming, or a whale, and far away she saw the spray, so picking up her dress tail with one hand and grabbing her shell she ran, hitting the sea in a splash, she swam to her rock and stood there blowing and blowing to tell the whales, to hitch a ride, to warn them of their coming death, to talk to them with her own air through the shell, calculating that they knew the sound of air, they understood the language of water which she needed to know.

"Don't worry with her." Samuel Sones's mother pulled his eyes back to her own. "She old and gone." But he suspected his grandmother's laugh and remembered it now, sitting in the relief of the tree.

Old and gone, dropping all her pieces of conversations and laughter. She lived now in the best of places, where everything happened at the same time. Her days were full of all her living, everything she had done and seen and heard, all her children and her childhood and Kamena and the red birds and the blind man and the golden man and the man whose scent was too sweet and her mother, Marie Ursule. All happening at the same time. In all of it the present was small and just a part. She saw her daughter Augusta and took her for Marie Ursule; her grandson Samuel she took for the son who flew off in the hurricane of 1875, saying to him, "I thought you gone, boy." Sometimes she thought that she had the path to the present cleared up, when Augusta and Samuel spoke long enough or high enough for her to hear them. But if it was dew light she mistook them for Marie Ursule and Kamena. Sones heard her singing sometimes. Marie Ursule. Just these two words were her whole song. But only sometimes could she leave the water and the nuns and the trumpet fish and all her living to hear something heaving like a coming whale.

~

He was twenty when he went away to England in the year 1917. His mother, Augusta, insisted that he be baptized the Sunday before her left. They went to the water, his grandmother trailing them, with a small crowd for his baptism. All the people were in black and the preacher broke off strips of water, blessing Sones. His mother wore a blue robe and held an umbrella. She had finished Sones' white camisole the night before and he looked regal. He clasped his hands and swallowed chunks of sky and cupfuls of land as the preacher dipped his body back into the water. His grandmother Bola sucked her teeth when he came back up from the water, her face sour like a lemon, saying, "Foolishness, that don't save nobody."

Sones was twenty-one when he returned in disgrace. Sent back for misconduct. He had spent another two years in the military jail at St. Joseph, suffocating in the hot dome half buried in the fort's hill. They let him out as if they had forgotten him. He heard a steward wondering aloud who he was and what he was doing there. He had been so quiet, stewing in his own flesh the whole time, the steward had not noticed him. When he was released he lingered outside the jail for many hours not knowing his direction, then walked home to Culebra, where his grandmother still sat in her centuries and his mother already dead of consumption.

"Waiting for you, boy. Your mother gone." Bola precise when she was lucid.

"Gone where?" he asked, refusing her meaning.

"Gone where people does go, where else?" she said as if he was stupid. Then she went back to her rocking and he to the small shack and the roadside stand to weep. Late that evening he noticed her stillness in the chair still rocking and went to give her food. Her shell was in the firm grip of her hands and her body was stiff, her face strangely had only now really fallen into its age and Samuel Sones for all he cared was alone in the world. If he had not shouldered Bola's own coffin onto a bullock cart and made his lone procession through Culebra Bay, past the flame trees, halting at the tamarind tree in recognition, and taken her coffin out to sea himself, he would have believed his eyes when he returned and found her rocking in the swept dirt.

"Waiting for you," she said again when he arrived home after her funeral. "Your mother gone, *oui*. She not strong. She catch cold easy."

He ignored her ghost, he did not trust her confidences and went about his business and she continued her rocking and her searching for the breath of whales. She lived her life as she'd always lived it, swimming and loving and birthing children, sending some off in the ocean and off in the world and keeping some. She continued her skipping from the hovering man-o'-war nuns, she continued her waiting for Kamena's return and she honed her shell-blowing, warning whales off the coast.

"Englishman," they began to call him in Culebra Bay, out of admiration that he had been abroad and in the Great War, and behind their hands in derision as he had been sent back for misconduct. He explained nothing, and some malevolence visible in him told them not to ask or laugh when he was present. But as if asking them to be cruel he began wearing his English suit everywhere. To market, to garden, to drink, to the river, to stand in the roadside stall reduced to a few dried-out provisions from Augusta's usual plenty. He stood there in his suit, offering weevil-eaten flour and ants-liquefied sweets left there since his mother. Once or twice he tried to sell a fish that he caught, but he had become so belligerent no one came to buy. As if inviting their scorn he didn't speak to anyone personably. He was abrupt, formal and dismissive. A man inviting ridicule and determined not to have any comfort.

This tree, which was hard and brown, whose fronds he remembered for the stinging childhood beatings he received from Augusta, he hated and loved because it gave shade, because it forgave him and punished him for being an Englishman.

He had had it in mind to disappear into the English countryside with a milk-white woman. To stand like a man who was on the edge of a book page, overlooking a field and a milk-white woman. She was in a small book he had borrowed from Captain Michael De Freitas when they were both small boys and De Freitas lived in the village of Abyssinia down the road from Culebra Bay in a big house with his mother and father, and De Freitas shoved a school book through his iron fence for Samuel Sones to notice him. Sones left off rolling a tin can to snatch the book like a jewel. She would have a blue ribbon in her hair and wisps of hair across her face—he had seen her in that *Reader*, a milk-white woman going a-milking in the English countryside. Or he had it in mind to find someone called Mary. "Oh, Mary, go and call the cattle home, and call the cattle home across the sands of Dee." Yes, twice, call the cattle home and call the cattle home.

But he had seen no milk-white woman when he finally arrived in Great Britain, and no countryside. He had only heard men barking in another language and all he was aware of were his ears trying to understand. His only sense, it seemed, was his hearing, because he did not want to make a mistake and his other senses were already overwhelmed. His eyes overwhelmed by smallness where he had expected greatness, his mouth overwhelmed by rations, and his nose overwhelmed by the stench of other men sweating their fear.

The events of it, the actual events and what things looked

like he could not remember. The moment they were loaded again onto the ship at Liverpool headed for Palestine, he became senseless. He was just part of a senseless mass of physicalness. He lifted his body like others, he ate like others and he dressed like others and he wanted to do that because if he thought for a moment about himself alone he became weak, his chest and arms would sweat and his mouth turn dry and stink.

Washing linen and cleaning latrines, digging trenches and refilling them and running to the beck and call of anyone with less colour than them, the Second West India Regiment was sent to Palestine and Sinai for labour services along with other Black soldiers from the other islands. Anyone with less colour than they could spit and they would have to clean it up. Their encampment smelled of night soil and disappointment.

One night he wrote home to his mother, "We are treated neither as Christians nor as British citizens but as West Indian 'niggers' without anybody to be interested in us or look after us." The letter arrived but his mother never opened it, nor could she have read it if she had, but she kept it nailed to her stall, pointing to it and telling everyone of her son, the soldier, in the Great War.

The others in his battalion wanted to fight. They quarrelled each night about the back-breaking work they were doing, although they were not allowed to do combat against European soldiers because of their colour. He grew smaller and smaller inside. He wanted to go home. He wanted to get through the days.

When they were called up to fight the Turkish troops on the other side, he sank on his bunk, sweating, and thanked God that it would not depend on his own will to move but the surging upswell of the regiment, the sheer energy of these men wanting to be a credit and to prove the British Empire wrong.

He could never remember what really happened then. They routed the Turks on Damieh Hill and even that he was told. His body was so liquid events fell through him. The only thing that he remembered was the stunned Turk whom he shot by mistake, and felt wicked after. All he could remember was a body trying to give in and the steep climb and the mud or dust, he could not say what. Whatever it was he was burdened in it and his boots were wet and hot and his toes itchy. He did not think of himself as a person any more, and his plans to return with stories of his heroism were taken over by his fear.

After the battle they marched for days toward Jericho and a fever made his remembrances more blurry. His nose was running and his eyes felt like blisters and he wanted to sit down. Sit down in his yard where his mother combed his hair and his crazy grandmother sat rocking in another world. And someone kept pulling him up every time he tried to sit down. Someone kept barking at him and by now his hearing was gone too and his head wrapped in his shirt as they used to do when he was a child and got an attack of fever and delirium. They would soak him in bay rum to sweat his fever and wrap him in cloth and put him to lie in a warm corner of the room, and he would hear rain and he would hear night and he would hear the wind, as if they were breathing. He would see the flame tree dappling on the curtain as the sun was falling. And he wanted to cry into his mother's lap but they kept pulling him up and making him walk.

Once he lay down hearing feet pass him by, stumbling over him, and he turned his face to the ground and licked the dirt of the road and realized that he wasn't home but on the road to somewhere where something should be waiting for him and he hurried to his feet and kept going. Feeling thin in his clothes but suddenly invigorated he pushed forward, jostling other men in many stages of pain.

Tamarindus indica. The tree under which the remainder of the world passed him by. He did not see the arrival of his cousin Cordelia Rojas by small boat from Venezuela. He didn't see her, with her small grip and her hair pulled back severely, walk up the beach to begin her new life, going toward the shop that had now taken over all of his mother's business. He would not have known her anyway. Her grandfather, Esteban, was only a rambling song in his grandmother's mouth. It came out in inconsequential verses about a man who loved gold things and who wanted her blowing shell. A man with a grip of coarse and fine cloth who had a silver compass. At first Cordelia Rojas came toward him wanting directions, not suspecting it was her cousin, but noticing his delirious walk to the tamarind tree she hesitated and went another way. She could not see her grandmother Bola then, rocking in her chair in the swept dirt as always and forever.

Four years later, in 1929, when they sank the oil well "Magdalena" five miles away in Abyssinia, and the spout of oil could be seen and felt in Culebra Bay, Sones did not look up; when the warm black spray rained on Culebra for two days, and fear that the uncapped well would explode spread, Sones sucked his teeth in derision. The transformation of cocoa pickers to oilfield workers made no impression on him, not even the emptying out of Culebra Bay to Abyssinia in search of money and modern houses. In the years to follow, the deaths by fire and mishaps in the oilfield and the growing dissatisfaction of the workers did not concern him. The strike of 1937 passed him by. When the policeman was killed and the army marched on Abyssinia and Culebra Bay to quell the rioting workers he found himself in the middle with a bloodied head among bloodier ones, only because he was walking to his tree. Even the lashes he received from the soldiers, their bullwhips whipping left, right and centre, didn't disturb him. He waded through them to his tree, his suit dripping blood. "War," he said, "war."

Small years and then decades passed him, the whole march of villages to Port-of-Spain and San Fernando looking for work. He did not notice that he was now alone. And the importation of workers from Grenada and the small islands, and the migrations to the Panama Canal and all who did not return from there. He sat impassively as boats ran aground on Culebra coral. In the deluges of water he saw fishermen disappear, he saw storms and four hurricanes between 1939 and 1952. Through all of it he made his way to the tree, which had also withstood what was immaterial.

Him. Private Samuel Gordon Sones. Next to his name in the war registry was, "Sent back for Misconduct." Not "Unfit," "Unfit," "Unfit," as was written against the names of Indians, but "Sent back for Misconduct."

De Freitas. De Freitas was a minister in the government now, a minister of water. And Samuel Sones had thought of killing him many times in the years since. But in the end of every plot he made, he ended up with himself to blame. He ended up with that stinging moment of recognition of his colour and his dreams. "...because who send me to them people' place? Who send me to be in their business?"

He had trusted De Freitas, ever since he had first seen

him. A lonely boy, just like him. A lonely boy behind an iron gate, whose loneliness Sones took for friendship, but which was really envy. Envy that Sones could walk about on the road in his bare feet rolling a discarded can if he wanted and Sones could kick a rag with other boys and Sones could take a stick and whack puddles of rain water collected in ditches after rain fell. And though Sones envied De Freitas his iron gates and his orderly flower garden and his crisp clothes and shoes even when it was not Sunday, De Freitas loved and envied the way Sones could turn away from the gate to some other child calling him and break into a gurgle of a laugh, forgetting De Freitas standing there.

But Sones trusted De Freitas if only because De Freitas had shown him his book and therefore another life, and had given him a round orange marble to play with. If only because he spent as many curious hours sitting against the fence peering in at De Freitas's world of silence as De Freitas spent looking out at his. There at the fence he grew to know the real value of things. Those reflections coupled with his mother Augusta's dissertations guided him. "I didn't lift up my skirt for you to be a old 'rab. I didn't suck salt for you to come out like the rest. I e'nt come out of the gutter for you to put me back here. I e'nt stand up on the street whole day selling nuts for you to sell nuts too. I e'nt buy you good clothes for you to jump in canal with them. I e'nt make you for you to dead on the street on me. I e'nt make you for no knife fight. I e'nt make you to get kill. I e'nt make no ragamuffin. I e'nt make no criminal. I stand up over scrubbing board for you to make bad? I stand up over hot stove? I take the meat from my mouth, I deny myself, I walk bare foot."

In the endless stream of Augusta's tongue which always

began in "I" as if she were God, Sones saw more and more what he wanted to be. And what he wanted to be was De Freitas, who had a father who owned a cocoa estate and leased land to the foreign oil company and a mother who always smiled, a mother who spoke harshly only when she called him from the fence away from Sones, a mother who, when Sones observed her, unaware of him hovering at the edges of the road, played with De Freitas and laughed with him and gently held him, a mother who could afford tenderness and who was not washing, ironing, selling; a mother under whom he, Sones, could be a boy without anxieties, a boy who did not have to amount to much but who could simply, with the effects of his shade, glide into manhood as if it were his skin and his island.

When Augusta noticed her son's friendship with the De Freitas boy she encouraged it, sending Samuel with a cloth-covered dish of mangoes or pomme cytheres or pomeracs for the boy. Hoping the De Freitases would throw a little kindness to her son. She made Sones dress up to go talk with De Freitas, she asked him constantly what they spoke about and if the De Freitases had invited him in behind the fence yet. Sones became uncomfortable and didn't always go to meet De Freitas but sometimes shared the mangoes with his other friends running past De Freitas's house, only waving at him. He showed De Freitas how to pitch marbles, he digging three holes on his side of the fence and De Freitas doing the same on his; they sucked mango seeds white and sometimes De Freitas would sneak out a pretty tin of wafers, which Sones ate not wanting to eat because it would spoil the prettiness of the tin. They often stooped together against the fence in a friendship sweetened by green plums, sweet candy, salty tamarind balls, joints of sugar cane, pulpy cocoa seeds or velvety chenettes, rocking on their heels enjoying the tastes on their tongues like an unspoken world.

De Freitas went away to big school in Port-of-Spain and Sones saw only glimpses of him when he came home, taller and leaner every July, and more and more reserved. The last time they talked through the fence they were fifteen and there was not much to talk about. Sones knew that De Freitas was expected home, given that it was the end of the school year, so he lingered along the street with De Freitas's house until he saw him and De Freitas yelled, "Aye, boy!" out of habit, before realizing that perhaps he had nothing to say. Sones hurried over to the fence smiling and they both stood there awkwardly for some moments. Then Sones said, "Well, anyway, boy, I gone," and took off in a brief confused sweat.

Sones finished the elementary school in Abyssinia, walking the five or six miles each morning and afternoon. When he was done with that there was nowhere to go except helping the teacher to clean the blackboard and standing in front of the class taking out the talkers and those who moved their fingers from their lips when the one teacher was absent from the classroom. Augusta didn't want him helping at the roadside shop; he, she said, was not made for that. Only on Saturdays she made him stand there counting people's change out loud so that she could show people what a bright son she had, and when the roadside stall was crowded and he was warming to the numbers she would tell him loudly and chuckling, "Rest your head, child, rest your head now. Go and lie down. All your book-studying and you still want to help your poor mother out. All you see what a good child I have?"

When Sones saw De Freitas in his uniform in 1916, he adored him. He wanted a uniform just like it. He read slyly to his mother from the gazette paper that men were being mobilized for the war, hoping that she would let him join up. "But people does dead in war!" Augusta told him and cut the talk short. Sones pined away to go to the war and sat sprawled in front of the roadside stall, looking like a 'rab who was going to turn into a no-account, until Augusta relented.

He'd seen De Freitas's face when they were flying into the flanks of the Turkish troops. It was as frightened as his. He was certain that he would not recognize his own face, nor would he know what feeling was passing over it. He had tried to convey some sympathy and he was sure that De Freitas acknowledged him, remembered him as the boy who used to pass by and play with him. But the next day and the following, on the march to Jericho, De Freitas was as cool as any other officer. De Freitas had received his commission, joining up in the merchant and planter contingents, the whites. It was a shock to see Sones and that same look of sympathy as if he was still behind his iron fencing and Sones on the outside, free. He avoided Sones until they arrived at Jericho.

Sones was among his group, their dehydrated bodies struggling for one more foot of ground; De Freitas himself, officer or not, was weak with exhaustion. He went over to the group, they tried to stand up straight. Pointing to Sones he said, "Soldier, fill these!" handing Sones a string of officers' water canteens. "When you're done come back and get the boots."

Any soldier in the regiment would have understood the orders and those beside Sones understood, any soldier would have moved quickly to comply but Sones stood there drooping and dumbfounded. The others became uneasy when Sones did not move and one of them made an effort to

rouse him. Sones brought his eyes to De Freitas's, lunged at
him, knocked him down with a ragged bruised fist then fell
on De Freitas in exhaustion.

Lovers passed him. *Tamarindus indica.* Some who liked
his fine suit, some who wanted to strip him naked, some
who only wanted his baby because, dour and disagreeable as
he was, he used to be handsome. Some thought that he had
money when he used to change his suits each year and even
after he stayed in the same one they took this as the eccen-
tricity of people with money under their mattresses. Lovers
lingered, walking slowly past him at his stall or calculating
the time that he made his walks, waiting at the bench under
the tree, dressed in yellow or pink, in red polka dots or
white cambric, and smelling of violet water. These passed
him long before he came to resemble something filthy under
a tamarind tree. His cuffs frayed and gluey from mopping
up every liquid that came out of him. And even after that
some thought that maybe they could fix him up like a house
or a water tap, brush him down like a horse, because they
knew that he would be faithful. Some thought that they
could fix up his roadside stall and make a go of it. Some
even thought that they could get used to his ghost of a grandmother rocking in her chair. But they all failed. He was filled
with so much self-loathing every time he remembered the
Second West India Regiment, he tried to root out that small
place inside him that had led him to it. Root out that small
pain that never grew any bigger but was like a tablet of poison. He had knocked De Freitas down. It wasn't an insult
that he could just pass off. Yes, he had knocked him down
and had wanted to kill him right there and then. Yet killing
him would not have been sufficient because the man had
insulted him and he understood that the insult would stay

with him no matter if he knocked De Freitas down or killed him. And he understood that it was his fault. All of it. He deserved it for pushing himself up and thinking that he was more than he was.

He sat there through another world war and he crowed for the enemy. In August 1940, when the Germans tried to cross the English Channel and the Luftwaffe bombed London nightly, Sones was gleeful. *Tamarindus indica*. He walked back and forth to this tree through the sweep of nationalist ideas and speeches toward independence from Britain, the lowering of the Union Jack and the lifting of the blood and the earth. He sat through small children stiffly starched and sweating in the hot sun, waving the Union Jack to the motorcade of the vanishing Queen. None of that could soothe him. He had already disappointed himself too much, nothing could repair him. He laughed at the speech-making, he knew that in the end it was not grand plans that ruled the world but some petty need of some individual, some small harassment that made things go bad.

He could have picked a flame tree, cooler and at least colourful, an orange one or a red one; he could have picked a poui, again indescribably coloured, and soft, when the petals fell; he could have picked a mango tree, the rose or Julie, sweet at least, the fruit and the smell would have calmed him, but no, he had chosen *Tamarindus indica* with its sour fruit and spindly dry branches, its unnoticeable flower and its dusty bark. He didn't move from the tree now, because some days he just couldn't make the walk or some days he thought that he had already done it. Some days he in fact did the walk many times.

He grew flabby and thin at the same time, like an old man. Fidgety and narcoleptic at the same time. Dropping off to sleep and jumping up, remembering his way again. From where he sat he could clearly hear his grandmother laughing in another century. Her hand fluttered on a shell in her lap. And he wished that he could go back before that laugh—that laugh that had filled him with uncertainty and nervousness and opened a dread in him. He wished that he could return to the time before that laugh, just before he came home with the news that they were going to the war, because before that he was a young man in his stiff starched khaki pants and shirt; a young man who could have stayed home and married a girl and made many children, he could have become...And yes, he remembered...Well, he recalled....He recalled nothing. Nothing but the hope of going to Great Britain, going home to the mother country. He recalled nothing but the plans he had made right away when he touched De Freitas's reading book, when he kept it and thumbed the pages smudgy. That was his departure, and the laugh of his senseless grandmother.

A SUDDEN
AND BIG LUST

~~~~~~~~~

Cordelia was fifty and didn't know what had come over her. It was 1953 and, for no reason at all that she could admit, a sudden and big lust had overtaken her. It had burst in her mouth like a fat orange, the gushes of juice bathing her chin and splashing into her eyes. Looking down at her hand rubbing soap into a skirt, she wanted her fingers kissed. Each one. One by one. She wanted her palm kissed, then her inner elbow, kissed, then the fat of her inner arm. Her appetite startled her when she passed a mirror and looked at her eyes and looked at her figure. She saw a woman who wasn't finished with the taste of her body as she was supposed to be. She lingered there at the mirror, seeing a woman who must have been planning for many years against her own plans.

She was married to Emmanuel Greaves. A quiet, decent and devoted man. Her second cousin twice removed and two landfalls, though neither of them knew it, because of a great-great-grandmother named Marie Ursule. Marie Ursule could not have imagined Cordelia or Emmanuel. Though she might have glimpsed them in the fat moon body of her own baby or heard tell of them in the sound that a baby makes, which is nothing and full of every possibility. Still in a blushing morning long ago, she had no time to imagine Cordelia and Emmanuel. He came from people who lived on fishing and therefore silence, and Cordelia from traders in cloth and so, smooth talk. Their grandmother and grandfather were half brother and sister, Bola's children, a son by a Venezuelan trader and a daughter by an unremembered father, given away to a Bonaire fishbasket woman. Emmanuel Greaves from the Bonaire side. Cordelia Rojas was the Venezuelan side, the reckless side, the side that began in the love of a bumpy-faced red man for Bola's pink shell, blowing. That was where Cordelia's own mother, Gloria, as if disinheriting herself, got the story to fling in her face of a waywardness. A waywardness that had been passed down and passed down by blood and was responsible for the child Cordelia threw away, with the help of an old woman in Socorro, before her long journey to fifty years and life with Emmanuel Greaves from the Bonaire side.

That was the waywardness returned in the woman whom Cordelia saw now in the wardrobe mirror and who was asking for release from her sentence of abstinence, but Cordelia could barely remember her. And so this woman startled even her.

She didn't know what had come over her but her skin felt as if it was bursting all over and only the close touch of skin back on hers would hold it. Trying to put her finger on it, she felt like flesh deep down and red and she never felt her own flesh before but now there was something there that wanted to swallow everything.

One day, just so, looking out her window she saw a man short and thick, yes, she knew him as Kumar Pillai, the man who fixed ice-cream freezers, he was walking home, wiping sweat from his neck all thick and black and short, and she wanted to reach out and grab him, put him between her legs and swallow him up. She never felt her flesh like that before, and then Yvonne, the seamstress from the next street, came walking the same way, her legs luminous with flesh and her feet bare and Cordelia wanted to bite them, suck them up into her mouth and bite them, she wanted to run her fingers up Yvonne's dress and slip them between her thighs and squeeze.

She pulled herself in from the window and did not look out for days, but the ice-cream-freezer man and Yvonne were all she thought of. Then she began to notice smaller things: how she buried her mouth in the face of a mango and how she ate and passed the food through her cheeks and under her tongue and how she wanted to put her hands in the pot full of hot rice and how between her legs was always wet and how she broke into a sweat each time she thought of the window and what else might be outside and soon she couldn't keep from the window and the ice-cream-freezer man and Yvonne were not enough and she noticed every bit of open flesh when a woman came down the street barefooted or a man stretched and yawned so that his belly was showing under his shirt; she noticed every tongue wiping itself on a word and every slip hanging and every hand smoothing a dress hip and pinning clothes to a line, and sweaty arms coming home from work didn't bother her as they used to but made her hot and want them strapped around her legs or folding her breasts.

You wouldn't think that just a few days ago she was a woman who had grown children who came to visit with pitying in their eyes—how old their mother was, how

without anything like wanting to caress flesh or feel her legs
wet with desire. She was a woman with a husband who
had mounted her every night until their last child was conceived; every night until she knew his skin as if it were her
own, and held him like she would her own elbow if it
were aching. Every night she felt like taking his little face
in her hand and washing it as if he were a child with a cut on
his cheek, writhing in pain. She sent him off to work every
morning with his food carrier and watched him run for the
lorry to take him to the oilfield.

Emmanuel Greaves. She had liked the sound of Emmanuel
but not Greaves. And she, Cordelia Rojas, had married him
because she liked the name Emmanuel though not Greaves,
but liked Emmanuel because he was steady and she knew
that every morning he would wake up when she woke him
up and wash his face and hands and take his food carrier
from her as she stood at the door with it, and run up the
road to catch the lorry taking him to the oilfield. She knew
that he was a man with nothing else on his mind except that
duty. That this made him stand out from other men and that
he was a man who needed a purpose such as this. Come rain
or come shine Cordelia Rojas knew that this man would
rise in the mornings, take his food carrier from her hand
and run to the lorry for the oilfields and every woman
around would say in their minds, "Cordelia girl, you have a
man"—in their minds, because Cordelia Rojas spoke to no
one and tolerated no conversation that was not necessary.
Good morning, good afternoon, and how much a pound
for the fish or meat and how much a yard for the cloth, but
nothing else.

And with Emmanuel Greaves working in the oilfields
in Abyssinia, Cordelia Rojas could buy fish and meat and

ask the market women in an imperious tone, "How much you asking for it?" and turn away if she did not get a satisfactory answer. She could feel cloth between her fingers at the Syrian store and ask the Syrian woman for ten yards of anything, looking at her straight in the face. Cordelia knew cloth just like her great-grandfather Esteban and her mother, and even the Syrian woman, probably the richest woman in Abyssinia, could not sell Cordelia overpriced cheap cloth as she did the rest in town. Cordelia walked into the store sometimes just to remember her family. Anyway the pieces of her family that she wanted to remember. The texture of cloth reminded her of them. Thread crisscrossed in fineness and roughness. Even how cloth had appetite, gobbling up tables and eyesight, going on for ever over the plane of a room, tumbling down outside and stretching far into the distance.

Like her grandfather, Rafael Simon, she took a deep breath and smiled as a span of cloth opened between her arms, she loved yellow yams; like her great-grandfather she loved the glimmer of anything, anything shiny. He had seen the pink-pearled shine of Bola's blowing shell and loved her just to get it from her. He had seen the glow of the pink-pearled insides and followed it up Bola's black arm to the soft of her neck. Stepping out of the fishing boat with his grip full of cloth, he had made his way along the beach and reached his free hand toward her. He had spoken a different language, 'Pañol. Then he had opened his grip full of cloth to show her and eased the shell from her hand. He was a red man, mixed, with a bumpy face and only his grip of cloth made him beautiful.

Cordelia could also afford to pick and choose who she talked to. She had Emmanuel Greaves build a fencing around their house, enclosing the chicken coop and the rose mango tree and the starch mango tree and the guava tree, so that no one would step on their lot of land without ringing the front bell and waiting until she made herself decent to answer. No one could surprise her in her nightie or without her slippers or eating with her hands. When the bell rang she would send Emmanuel Greaves out in his white merino to see who was there, then she would call out in her best voice to him, "Who is there, Emmanuel?"

On a Sunday if she was expecting no one but someone rang the bell she would sit behind her curtain and say nothing to the intruder, making sure that they knew full well she was sitting behind the curtain watching, but that she thought this presumptuous of them, because on some special Sundays early in their marriage she used to take the time to enlighten Emmanuel Greaves on how she wanted sex from him. Not mounting her like a goat and twisting his face as if in pain, but first that he should put his mouth on her down there and then work his way up.

On those Sundays Emmanuel Greaves got up first and Cordelia lay in bed waiting for him to finish cooking. Smoked herring in tomatoes and onions with thin slices of bread, piping hot tea with fresh cow's milk, that is what Cordelia Rojas liked on a Sunday morning. After she ate, Emmanuel would bring the white porcelain jug and basin that Cordelia bought with his good money, filled with warm water and vetivet bush, and bathe Cordelia Rojas from head to foot. Emmanuel bathed her slowly as she wanted. Cordelia knelt on the floor and Emmanuel caressed her with the cloth in warm water and vetivet bush.

Sunday mornings were like this for Cordelia Rojas and Emmanuel Greaves. Emmanuel wiped Cordelia down with the same concentration as he greased bolts on the oilfield pipeline. He loved Cordelia and still could not believe that she had married him out of all the much prettier and much more talkative men in Culebra and Abyssinia. Cordelia would kneel on the floor on Sunday morning and Emmanuel would softly pass the warm cloth on her whole body, her neck, under her arms down to the thick of her waist and in the creases of her open legs. Here he would pause until Cordelia moved him to do the small of her back and the line between her buttocks.

Cordelia tolerated Emmanuel's bath both as a lesson for him and as the obedience she felt she deserved for marrying Emmanuel Greaves. Kneeling on the floor she would forget that it was Emmanuel and take his small stroking touches as if he were a supplicant to her sainthood. She closed her eyes and breathed deeply, blocking out the smallness of Emmanuel's hand where she wanted large hands, his quick breathing that interrupted her saintly reverie and made her think of a little panting dog. But still she insisted every Sunday that Emmanuel do this. When the water grew cool, Emmanuel would run to the stove and refill the jug with hot water. Cordelia hated the water cold. She made Emmanuel rub her with the vetivet bush, holding some between her palms, bringing her palms to her nose and breathing deeply. Sometimes Cordelia knelt there for hours after the bath, clutching the vetivet bush as if praying. Sometimes, in the middle, her lust, or what she'd tamed it to, would come to a stop. Cordelia knew she twisted it around to stave off bad things, she'd tamed it, squelched it thin until she could not have it. So sometimes in the middle of her Sunday she stopped and prayed for this terrible thing to go away. And prayed for Emmanuel to go away. And it was as if she tasted the aftertaste of something that in the middle was good, but regret and bad feeling came at the end. As if at the end she had some knowledge of herself that she did not want.

Emmanuel would then stand outside the door and after a while begin to call Cordelia's name. When Cordelia went into this trance Emannuel didn't know what to do. He couldn't think what he had been a part of but it made Cordelia more mysterious, so mysterious that though at first it excited him, it frightened him, and Emmanuel couldn't take so much mystery so he began to call Cordelia in his Monday-morning voice. "Cordelia! Cordelia Greaves!" And after a while Cordelia would return, from where Emmanuel did not know, but he didn't like Cordelia going anywhere he didn't know about.

Outside the door, which is where he always stood on a Sunday waiting for Cordelia to emerge from her trance, he said in his everyday voice, "Look here, Cordelia, I don't know what kinda stupidness you doing but come out, you hear me!" It annoyed him that Cordelia would stop him from washing her and go into a trance. It felt unholy because he always planned throughout the Sunday bathing to lay his hands on Cordelia and jump into her body like a bucking goat and satisfy himself. After all, if it was that she was teaching him about sex why did she have to go and get holy? It didn't seem right. It spoiled everything. And even when he said, "Look here, Cordelia," he knew that he could only use this tone while Cordelia was in her trance.

The Sundays when Cordelia was not in her trance she showed him where she wanted him to touch and lick and how slowly she wanted him to put himself into her. And these Sundays he tried to please her and hold on to himself as he slipped away into Cordelia and tried not to annoy her by jerking fast up and down. Cordelia liked circles and not thrusts and he felt small lying on top of her and he felt smothered when Cordelia took over and lay on top of him and he felt harmless then too. He felt Cordelia was so great and nothing he could stand up to and Cordelia's desire was suddenly not for him, he felt. He felt Cordelia became aloof and used him like a stick to make her way through her great lust, feeling out all the spots that made her breathe heavy and racing to the ones she knew would make her come.

Cordelia liked the room dark so she would not have to see Emmanuel's face, she would not have to recognize the man she was riding as her second or third cousin twice removed who went to work on the lorry each morning and whom she had chosen because he was steady. She had chosen him because he was certain and because she could live her life as she wanted with him. He would bring home the money and she would feed and clothe his wiry body and give him sufficient children and one day she would live her own life when she had taken so much good care of him that he would never try to tell her anything.

In these moments Emmanuel felt Cordelia leave him— if he ever felt Cordelia there. He felt Cordelia leave. Her lust overwhelmed him. And Cordelia who never took Emmanuel for her equal rode him toward her lust, handling him and making him fit in the gullies and places in her body. She made him as tangible as she needed. She needed to break her own body open and wring its water out toward the ends of the room so that she was not in a room and not riding Emmanuel Greaves but riding the ocean's waves, her flesh coming off like warm bread in her fingers and floating out to sea. When Cordelia rode on Sundays it was the only time that she did not have order and her legs wide and liquid carried her to another shore.

The weeks in between Cordelia's Sundays were normal and for twenty-five years she raised Emmanuel Greaves' children and cleaned her house and kept the neighbours from her business.

~~~~~

At twenty Cordelia had taken a boat from Venezuela to this island. Watching the bilious sea she had willed herself not to throw up. She was going to marry her second cousin twice removed, though she did not know it yet, she'd only thought that it would be any man who would yield to her charge, but she had envisioned her husband as a man who could take moulding and a man who would not resist her trying to lift herself up and a man who would appreciate her high colour and worship her word.

Emmanuel Greaves was a decent man, besides not liking mysteries. Emmanuel Greaves would not see her cardboard suitcase with her few flowered dresses, he would see her manners of a lady and the uplifting that a woman of her colour would bring him. And she would make Emmanuel work hard and she would fix up a house for him and his children and he would be overwhelmed by her rightness and her beauty, which was not beauty at all but colour. Cordelia Rojas was a red woman who strapped her hair back with clips and grease and water to show off and hide her origins all at once. The red in her from her great-grandfather, the black from Bola.

Taking the wind on the water across the Bocas de la Culebra, she imagined one day a piano in her living room with a photograph atop it of her children and her husband standing and her seated in the centre. She imagined other photographs of her children in different stages of their childhood, in their best clothes, their hair greased back like hers. Their confirmations with prayer books in their hands. Their graduations, their marriages. She imagined tea sets put away in glass cabinets and doilies on the back of her velvet sofa and chairs, she imagined armchairs varnished and polished and a large wooden dining table where she would sit at the head. She imagined white lace curtains and stone steps coming up to her mahogany wood front door.

She had her gold chains, her mother's wedding rings and her bracelets wrapped in a cloth tied around her waist and that was to be her beginnings. It was the same cloth she had tied around her waist to conceal the swelling of her baby and that was to be her reminder. Since a woman could not by herself take over the world or act as if she had her own will, Cordelia would find Emmanuel Greaves and he would be her hand in the world. Her children she determined would marry upward if not in colour in money.

The whole night of the journey by sea Cordelia imagined her new life. It was a small boat with smugglers and traders and higglers and Cordelia Rojas, whom the others suspected of leaving something behind, a baby perhaps, blood in a room with an old woman. Whatever it was, they had left more; she was merely a beginner. They had cheated on everyone they knew, without meaning to and meaning to, because life was like that. You'd start off innocent enough but circumstances forced you to see that the hardscrabble place you were born in had to be got out of else it would choke you to death. So if you found your hand on someone else's wallet or their food or sometimes their life,

well, you had to do what was hard. So they understood
Cordelia throwing the child away and stealing her mother's
rings even if they did not know anything for a fact. The fact
is her mother had seen her steal the rings and brooch and
had walked up behind Cordelia without her seeing and she
had whispered in Cordelia's ear, treacherously and with no
disappointment, *"Lleválos! Y ojalá no tenga que mirar-te la cara
jamás. Si pudiera te mataría. Desaparece de mi vida!"* Take them
and never let me see you again. If I could get away with it I
would kill you. Disappear from my life!

Some of them waited up, watching Cordelia Rojas,
waiting for her to fall asleep so they could loosen the cloth
around her waist and empty out her possessions, but
Cordelia didn't sleep and they had to admire that. She must
have had a knife, they reckoned, a knife that she would use.
They had to admire the imagined knife and how this red
woman, girl, would use it.

Cordelia saw the sun coming up on her right shoulder just as she thought her eyes would not hold out and
she would have to surrender to sleep and complete poverty.
Just as she saw the sun, she saw this island rising in a point
with a long sandy beach at the bottom. The sun was only
a quarter up over the sea and she straightened her dress
out and stood up from her small suitcase, patting her waist
and wiping a hand across her face from the continuous
spray. She was ready to leave the boat and go live what she
had dreamed all night long. Already she had Emmanuel
Greaves, already she had babies to make up for the one she
had had to lose. If the treacherous waters and the slimy
thieves of the Bocas de la Culebra did not take her that night
nothing would, and anything that would had to come from
her own insides.

Cordelia stepped out of the boat when it came to shore at Culebra Bay and vomited all that was left of Venezuela, all that she had wanted to throw up in the room with the old woman in Socorro, all that didn't come out with the child, she threw up on the beach, everything, everything came rushing out of her. When she was done and her insides as empty as the sea, gripping her suitcase she wiped her mouth and walked to the main road in Culebra Bay with not a word.

There were man-o'-war birds wafting in to shore signalling a light rain. She cut through the flame trees, passed by a man in a black suit under a tamarind tree and made for the first shop. She might have stopped to ask him the way but he was out of his head, shouting, "War." If not so single-minded that morning, she would have heard her great-grandmother Bola saying, "Waiting for you, girl." A pink shell, tendered in her direction, fluttered to the sand as Cordelia turned and headed another way. She stopped for a minute to find other bearings and then walked toward a small building with people lined up outside. At the shop she asked about lodging and was given to another old woman, who watched her suspiciously through the smoke of her clay pipe and gestured her to a room at the back of her house.

Cordelia slept like a child. Several times she woke up to the feeling of being in a strange room but she could not lift her body up to leave. Someone else seemed to be there weighing her down. She tried to move but couldn't. For a moment she thought her mother was there. Then there was the uncomfortable feel of her father and a bolt of cloth falling in her small room at the back of her mother's shop in Venezuela. She dreamed the last look her mother gave her, a look of pity or jealousy or both. She could not raise herself from her sleep. Eventually she succumbed to its heaviness, until somehow she stopped dreaming and slept so soundly and emptily that when she woke up she did not remember her dream. She remembered her plan, a plan that was without her family or anyone down the Main, and rose to do it.

At the shop she found work quietly copying the accounts into an exercise book for the shopkeeper, at times cutting pig tails and salt beef and keeping the shop clean. And after a while the shopkeeper left her to the shop—a red woman was a showpiece and a draw for customers—and he stayed in the bar, which was the other side of the shop, and where the men and certain women came to drink and gamble.

The shop is where Cordelia Rojas met Emmanuel Greaves. A small wiry man who came to the shop to pass through to the bar but instead stayed and sat on the bench near the bags of rice, drinking a grog and looking at Cordelia out of the corner of his eye. He would jump to help Cordelia with a side of a pig or cow or a crocus bag of sugar, and when his presence seemed useless he would buy some small item and go home.

Other men came to the shop, passing ostentatiously into the half door of the rum shop. Other men, red men who thought for sure Cordelia with her colour would want them, married or single. Louder men, men people listened to, men who made jokes, men whom women called "salt-fish" because they were so sweet. But Cordelia didn't want a man who was already made or a man who was too forward. She didn't want trouble, she wanted a good life with a sure man, a man who would take direction, not a man whom she wouldn't see for days, not a man who would spend his wedding night in a whorehouse, not a man who would squander her and her good plans. And not a man who could pull colour on her, so not a red man, a dark man, a man she would reach down for and lift up in order to make herself greater, a man who knew she would prevail in all matters because she had the intelligence that colour gives and the command. She noticed how weak those red men were, how they left everything half done, everything except their liquor, how they left their shirts outside their pants and how their faces were always slack in a smile. When the time came she knew that it was Emannuel Greaves whom she would leave this village with.

Emmanuel had travelled to Culebra with his two big brothers. They had travelled many places before they landed at Culebra, hearing on the sea about the work to build roads to Abyssinia where a British oil company was going to dig a well. They came wanting to leave the sea. Their hair was tipped with orange from the sun and the salt water. They wanted to be smooth men, men with cash in their pockets. They had spent time in Aruba and Curaçao but they wanted a bigger island, an island with an interior and wonderful cities and people migrating from all over. An island like that would have great opportunity. So they landed in Trinidad, bringing their little brother with them.

As they walked three abreast up from the sea and cut through the flame trees to the village of Culebra Bay, an old man in a torn black suit charged at them shouting, "Soldiers! Damieh!" They fled Samuel Sones, laughing at themselves for being frightened of an old man. Sones gave chase for a short while then turned, bedraggled, heading for his tamarind tree.

The brothers laid roads to Abyssinia, roads to Arima, roads to Point Fortin. They saved their money for a good suit and a pair of shoes each, then the two eldest went to Port-of-Spain. Emmanuel stayed in the village of Culebra

Bay tarring the gravelled roads and sitting in the rum shop each night listening to men talk. He was not ready for the city, he was not as forward as his brothers. He had seen Cordelia Rojas arrive with her small grip and he was rooted to her shadow.

When the oilfields opened up five miles away in Abyssinia and all the men got work, Cordelia decided it was time to marry Emmanuel Greaves and move there. She washed her hands of the pigs' tails and went to copying out the accounts and when Emmanuel Greaves arrived that Saturday evening she looked up from her copying and told him he was a good man and a woman like her needed a good man to marry. Emmanuel stuttered that he was glad for the opportunity and that she would never have a painful moment in her life, and then he said, "I love you, Cordelia," and Cordelia smiled her only smile since he had seen her.

It was the most important moment in Emmanuel Greaves' life. It was the most glorious thing that would or could happen to him. Cordelia could do nothing, nothing that would ever betray him, nothing that would make his devotion lessen. He had sat there near the pig-tail drum, drinking grog and expecting nothing more than to sit in Cordelia's presence and have her tolerate him. This was his whole aspiration. And so when Cordelia proposed to him he was taken aback. He had been prepared to sit there in the brown light of the shop, rice dust and rich rank perfume of pigs' tails covering him. He had understood that a man like him must apprehend pleasure through other means, other ways; from distances, smells and gratitude, but not from accomplishing anything, not from actual acts. He was used to doing without, he was used to being one of many chil-dren all clamouring for their mother's or father's lap or hand or voice, or look; all waiting for something special, an extra piece of meat or an extra dumpling or piece of bread. He was used to the luck of it and more used to the lack.

He was well equipped in being forgotten, and to tell the truth he did not mind it, he did not hold a grudge, he thought that it was as life was. To tell the truth he welcomed it. He could not bear to be so frontish as his friends. And even among those he called his friends, and God knows his presence with other men was not sufficient to qualify them as friends, he was so withdrawn and unpushy that he was the man they depended on even though they could hardly recall the last thing that he said or the sound of his voice. No, he did not mind.

Eugenia was Emmanuel's grandmother who had been thrown into a basket of red fish, in a hurry. She slithered around with the fish until her takeaway mother booked passage by boat and landed on Bonaire. Eugenia kept the fish alive and fresh with her gurgling, and the sight of her burbling and laughing in the basket, resplendent among fat red fish, made the village where they landed think that it was a divine coming. Though nothing happened after, no great thing, and Eugenia lived a perfectly ordinary life doing the perfectly ordinary things that people do. Perhaps she could not hope to better her glorious red coming, it had been so royal.

She led an almost dull existence, full of children and plates to wash and her yard to be swept, and just sitting or walking; it was as if the elaborateness of her birth had not happened. Perhaps if the fishbasket woman had told her about her real mother, Bola, she might have made something different of herself, she might have interpreted her life differently. As it was she forgot her power to keep dead things alive. Everything depends on memory.

But since his grandmother was found in a basket full of fat red fish, her cheeks full of milk, providence would float Emmanuel, as it had floated her, and he would be thankful for anything. Nor would he have any bad feelings if things went wrong. He was a man who was satisfied with life and never expected a wonderful happiness.

So ordinariness was part of Emmanuel Greaves' destiny. If destiny is part of any story. So that moment in that evening after Cordelia washed her hands of pigs' tails and went to copying the accounts, and that evening when Emmanuel Greaves' foot landed on the doorway and landed in Cordelia's glow; that moment when Cordelia said almost gravely, "Emmanuel, you is a good man and a woman like me need a good man to marry." That moment, the dust of the shop's interior turned golden, the old cans of sardines, the jute sacks of flour, the brown paper wrapping and the counter top turned golden; the evening black itself coming into the open doorway coiled and rolled golden. Emmanuel was bathed in gold dust and light, his face wrapped in his own smile, there could never be a moment as pure as this in his whole life. All his life to come, this moment was his beginning and his end all at once. It was more than he could have imagined. Cordelia had enveloped him in gold light and she had released him from ordinariness.

It was all that could happen to him and more than he expected, though in the next twenty-five years with Cordelia he would slip back into himself. And it was himself that Cordelia wanted. She did not want him transformed into a man who thought too much of himself. She had watched him, she had determined that he was what she needed and that while she could spread a magic over him he was humble enough not to be vain. He would do as he always did, steadily, and, perhaps even passionately, he would remain ordinary.

They moved to Abyssinia, leaving all the red men with a sour taste in their mouths, not the taste of Cordelia Rojas. They envied Emmanuel, who they imagined was going to taste that full red woman all by himself. But no one would taste Cordelia until her fiftieth year, which only made the taste of her stronger and sweeter, the smell of her dearer.

Cordelia made him three children, Hannah, Gabriel and Alicia. All ordinary. She washed them and oiled them and taught them their place. She never allowed them to leave the fenced yard except to go to school. She never allowed them to go outside without shoes or socks. She made them listen to the radio on Sundays to the children's show, then they would go into the back yard and play until late afternoon. On Saturdays she had them whiten their shoes and hang their washed clothes on the line. She taught them how to iron and fold and she taught them how to boil water and go to the shop for messages. She sent them to school and took them up in their lessons every night. The last, like the rest, left home for England's National Health Service in 1951. She had taught them the ordinary things they needed to know so that their life would hold no mistakes or mishaps. She had made sure that nothing hard came to them. She would never walk up behind them and whisper their downfall.

Not a day went by that she didn't remember that. Over the years it was all she could do to put it aside for even a moment.

She'd been given the room at the back of the store when she turned thirteen. It was not really a room but a large cupboard for storing bolts of cheesecloth and jute and anything that her mother did not want in sight. Her mother,

Rafael Simon's only daughter, had said she didn't want two women in the same house. "Two man rat," she said, "can't live in the same hole." And she'd given Cordelia this little room.

Later, placing herself square in the small doorway, it was here that Gloria accused her daughter of bringing men, of being a *puta*. It was here that Cordelia became more and more afraid to sleep when in her sleep she felt, sensed, the door open and someone looking at her. When one night someone reached out to touch her in her sleep and a bolt of serge fell across his hand she saw that it was her own father.

Her mother ran to see what the noise was and discovered them returning the bolt to the shelf, her father's eyes pleading and threatening at the same time not to tell.

That is when she decided to leave with a boy from up the Orinoco River. A boy who made them a shack with wood and tin and one day got tired and left to make another girl a shack. Cordelia by that time was pregnant, and someone who saw her sitting miserably on her miserable mattress with the door wide open told her where to go. But the *abuela* needed money and Cordelia didn't have any, so another month went by and she took a long cloth and bound her belly in so as not to show, and thought of how to get money. And there it was. Even though she had vowed never to go back. Her mother's store had money. She knew where it was kept and how much. She had meant to take only what she needed but as she stood over her mother's bureau drawer she became angry and dangerous, unconcerned with being caught.

She took her time, taking everything, the gold bracelets, the rings, one with a ruby and a thick silver one, and the brooch with many small stones. She took enough money to pay the woman in Socorro and then to buy food, and

enough perhaps to entice the boy from up the river back to
their shack; but then she thought also of more, leaving on
a boat for an island, the one her great-grandfather loved because it was pink and pearled and a woman there had given
Rafael Simon to him, a boy who loved shiny things; or perhaps she could take a bull cart into the interior. Perhaps she
could steal a few yards of cloth, put it in a grip and sell it in
the interior.

She heard someone enter behind her and knew that it
was her mother. She stuffed the brooch into her bodice
and was about to turn around when her mother came up
quickly behind her, whispering. Cordelia turned, almost
pushing her aside, and walked across the room. She hesitated at the door, wanting to say something. What could she
say that would bring them close since close or far it had to
be. But her mother's look was unforgiving and unexplain-
able, terrified and contemptuous. So there was nothing to
say or else the rest of her mother's life would be unlivable.
If her mother admitted that her husband, Cordelia's own
father, had tried to touch her in that way, she could not survive it. They both knew that was why her mother let her
steal the rings and the money, so that Cordelia could go
away and not crush her mother's life in the truth. She left
the bureau drawer open. Her mother moved to close it and
Cordelia left, meeting her father on her way out. He was
quiet and secretive.

The *abuela* in Socorro said the child was too big and
asked for more money. Cordelia gave it to her, begging the
child's forgiveness because she couldn't take whoever it
was any farther, she couldn't take whoever it might be with
her. Lying on her back, in and out of pain, Cordelia decided
on the pink-pearled island of her grandfather.

The pink-shelled island of her great-grandmother was quiet. Here Cordelia could start anew. Culebra was all that she had heard. Its rose sun, its coral dirt hills. Those first days she slept, it rained a light rain, a very quiet rain. The kind that Bola loved when she would swim out in the smoky green sea to her rock. Cordelia loved the swelling and heaving of the grey-green water. She loved the sea whatever its emotion, whatever its whim. She went looking for the nuns' place deluged in chiton and other dead coral. Rafael Simon had described it so many times she would find it even as it was now, dwindled to an impression. She saw the madman again shouting, "War! Friends, war!" Avoiding him she found a dry riverbed covered in tiny pink open shells; bluish at the base, they shimmered pearly. The fine rain had filled them all with lucid water. She felt like drinking from them, tasting the salt and the pearl of her great-grandparents' desire. Her great-grandfather Esteban would often take the boat to Culebra, just as she had, with his grip of cloth. This man loved gold things and things that shone and he wore them on his fingers and on his neck and that is why his son Rafael Simon loved butter and thread. Bola's children would gather around him for what new plaything he'd brought. Sometimes it was a long paper ribbon or a bell or a mouth organ. He would always hold out something shining. Once it was a compass. He said it told of directions. It skittered off his hand like a crab. They would run off to play with whatever he had brought and he and Bola would go to her shack to hover in their pink love.

Cordelia licked the shells, feeling the last warm blood of the *abuela*'s deeds fall out of her as if she was peeing in the cool ocean. Sucking the delicate shells, her tongue running smooth over their pearl she was comforted that she had arrived at the small country of her blood. Here her grandfather Rafael Simon was born to Bola the shell blower and Esteban the cloth salesman, and here she, Cordelia, had abandoned all her own weeping mornings.

———

And then, in her fiftieth year, Cordelia burst from her own seams. She had gone to her window with a sudden remembrance of pink shells and Culebra Bay. She had not meant to remember. All her years had been taken up with ordering her thoughts. The vigour she had used all these years to contain her memory, to clean her house and maintain her children, had turned on her. She was greedy for everything she had not had.

What she had not had was the enjoyment of her body clear and free. Her father had terrified it, her mother had found in it an enemy. The boy from up the river way had put a baby in it and dressed it in a kind of passion that had felt hurtful, burning and unfinished. The woman in Socorro had loosened the baby from it. She had long since done opening her body to Emmanuel Greaves, she had only done that long enough to make Hannah, Gabriel and Alicia. She had done it in that purposeful way of hers. Then she had moved Emmanuel out of her room.

She said to him in the same way she had told him of their marriage, "I am finish with this now. I am a woman who just want to live her own life. I give you a home, I give you children. I am finish now." He had accepted that her word was final after a few attempts at putting his foot down for which Cordelia abused him, reminding him of how she had brought him up. If not for her where would he be? Who would he be? He could not bear Cordelia's resentment. He gave her her privacy. In his spare time he retreated to the rum shop five miles away in Culebra Bay, where he had first met her.

Cordelia had lived in her body as in a never-ending bitterness. She did not know the meaning of it beyond these uses it had been given, the uses that she herself had put her body to. She had not looked at it clear and free, ever; nor in any curious way had she considered it as needing some simple caress. Some gesture not designed to lose or take but to awaken. Simply awaken. The hints and scents and allusions of her skin had been insinuated into a coarser sense of the body. She had given up on whispers as anything but treacherous. Love was that miserable bed with the doorway open and the Orinoco boy gone. Just days before she crossed her fateful window, seeing the world new, she had been tired, weary. She had felt some energy leaving her or some weight, and her next turn at the mirror refracted a voracious ardour.

She wanted the man who fixed ice-cream freezers to set his tools down and cool her. She wanted the seamstress to take her around her waist. And so she contrived to have them both. Since her lust was a secret, its boundaries were as wide as a secret's. Everything in it was forbidden, just like a secret.

Kumar Pillai, the ice-cream-freezer man, was only too willing when Cordelia touched his thick belly and rode him right there on the kitchen floor. He was not a man like Emmanuel, so Cordelia didn't feel holy or charitable or restrained. He came at another time in her life, when restraint was not a part of her quest. He was not particular in any way. Cordelia had merely seen him by coincidence, just as she was finished staring into her own eyes in the wardrobe mirror, seeing her great lust unshadowed, and then turning to open her window she had heard his calling-out call and

her eyes landed on his thick belly and his black slicked-back
Indian hair. They landed on his dark Madrasi face almost
blue in the midmorning's hovered light, they landed on his
fingers rough and callused and she wanted to nibble them;
they landed on his thick legs which she knew would have
short tight rings of hair darker than his face. And it was just
the extension of her thoughts from the mirror to his face.

He had caught her when her body was deciding to listen
to its own logic and all the objects in range of her senses
would now be their outcome. He was for no purpose but for
her happening on him when her body was remembering its
manner and course. And all around him was the midmorning
light, the Indian laburnum in her front yard spraying yellow.

Kumar Pillai did not know that every other afternoon
from now on he would lie on his back on Cordelia's kitchen
floor, his rough hands being licked, his hips salty and slippery under Cordelia's. He did not know that he, Kumar Pillai, who had never put his head between a woman's legs and
boasted about it, would become a convert. He could not
know that Cordelia would choose him just because she had
seen herself in a mirror moments before and decided without deciding in her usual way, decided purely and anonymously that he might taste her lust; and because he looked
as robust as her feeling, bursting in the midmorning with
Indian laburnum showering his head, his hair smelling of
coconut oil and jasmine when he came near; when she saw
him, long before he saw her, and took her look as asking
for his industry and asked, "Madame, you have a ice-cream
freezer to get fix?"

She contrived for Yvonne the seamstress to come to the
house one afternoon to measure her for a few dresses. One
afternoon which like all afternoons was slow and sleepy

with everyone having the heavy sleep that afternoons make
with the sun after lunch. A few dresses, which a seamstress
could not resist in the middle of a month when business was
scarce. A few dresses for Cordelia Rojas, who had always
had store-bought clothes as a sign of being well off or sewn
her own white cotton with frills on the tail and embroidery
on the sleeves. That afternoon and many other afternoons
to come when the sun made Yvonne the seamstress sweat
and she came fanning down the street into Cordelia's house,
Cordelia moved her curtain to see Yvonne's approach, noticing the flush of small sweat on Yvonne's neck and breasts
and the mark of wetness under the arm of her no-sleeved
dress. She noticed one bead of water gather all the rest and
make a river through talcum powder toward the path between Yvonne's breasts when Yvonne entered the door saying, "A glass of water, do please, Miss Cordelia."

Cordelia felt the bead of sweat on the tip of her tongue
as Yvonne the seamstress patted it away with a handkerchief. She watched the handkerchief smother the water and
move away again, Yvonne bending to put her bag down and
ask if she could sit for a moment. Cordelia wanted to dip
both her hands into the seamstress's bosom and lift her
breasts to her lips.

The seamstress took Cordelia's hesitation at the request
for water as maybe she shouldn't have asked. Perhaps she
should have waited, said good afternoon. She was about to
feel that she had overstepped when Cordelia smiled and
hurried toward the big pitcher of iced water already lying
on the side table. She handed the seamstress one of her best
glasses filled with water and a starched cloth napkin and
watched her pour the water into her mouth like swallowing
liquid diamonds.

Cordelia beckoned her to the bedroom. She brought out bolts of cloth from her closet, Sea Island cotton and linen and lace and satin and brocade, all colours—taupe and mauve and red and aqua and royal blues—which she threw on the mahogany bed and watched the seamstress pass her eager hands across the bolts breathlessly. She watched the seamstress feel and heft the material, rubbing it against her face and scrubbing the satin to show it was real. The seamstress caught the hem of all of them together, pulled them blooming to the length of the bed to set them off and savour their colour and texture. She lifted and hung them to see how they would fall, and then her eyes fell on Cordelia's body lovingly to see what she could make of such riches.

"You is a woman who would look good in them cloth, Miss Cordelia."

The seamstress contemplated the roundness of Cordelia's hips, the full pelvis, and the legs, and swallowed at the way a tight skirt with a fishtail or a kick-pleat would hug Cordelia; how a V-necked bodice with no sleeves, an off-the-shoulder or strapless would look just sweet.

"Miss Cordelia, when I done with you, you going to look so good it wouldn't have man good enough for you," the seamstress said, forgetting herself again and that Cordelia Rojas Greaves was a respectable woman and you couldn't bring no backstreet talk to her. But Cordelia laughed a backstreet kind of laugh and the seamstress joined in, remarking to herself that Miss Cordelia wasn't so prim as people believed. She began draping various pieces of cloth over Cordelia, figuring out the styles, working out the cut and design, her hands brushing Cordelia and patting here and there, and Cordelia on impulse or design herself draped a piece of brocade over the seamstress offering her the cloth saying it would look better on her; Cordelia laid the brocade where the seamstress's hand had mopped with her handkerchief, her own large warm hand lingering there and moving over the seamstress's shoulder. Soon they were like young women together playing with cloth and laughing and Cordelia could not remember the last time that she laughed with any woman and she laughed louder.

She offered the seamstress a little drink, a little lime punch with ice and just a little rum to take the heat out of the afternoon. And the seamstress accepted and sank into Cordelia's wicker and velvet chair and sipped on her lime punch and when she was ready brought out her measuring tape to measure Cordelia for the beautiful dresses she would make.

"*Pero*, a little cake first," Cordelia said, wanting to prolong the moment and slipping into a language that she hadn't used for many years. "*Un poquito*, Miss Yvonne."

"No no no, Miss Cordelia, girl. Where I going to put it? You don't see my hips? Not like yours, you know."

"What! What! look at these hips, Miss Yvonne, don't try to mamaguy me," she said, smoothing her hands across her own hips and thighs.

"Miss Cordelia, you have a figure. Don't worry about that at all. I always admire a woman with a figure like yours. You is a dream to cut cloth for. You is not no stick. You is a full woman with a good figure. Believe me, I know woman when I see woman."

With that she rose, staggered to Cordelia and embraced her with her measuring tape. Cordelia loved the feel of her close, her arms around her waist. She smelled talcum powder and *My Sin* perfume as the seamstress took measurements, patted her and moved to her hips then the length of her thighs and where she wanted the dress to hit, here, or here, or here, touching Cordelia and Cordelia grasping the seamstress's hand and moving it, here for the brocade, here for the linen and the kick-pleat to start here. The V-neck to here and the boat neck with the V to the back down to here. Yes, here.

Then Cordelia asked if it was more accurate to measure naked and the seamstress agreed and they began all over again as to where each measurement would reach. Cordelia parted her legs and the seamstress fell into them among the brocade and satin and Sea Island cotton. And on the afternoons when Cordelia was not slipping over Kumar Pillai she was sweat wrapped in bolts of cloth with the seamstress.

Even decency could not dampen Cordelia Rojas's greediness. From his old room in Culebra Bay, Emmanuel wrote to his children in England to come and see what a fool their mother was making of herself, come see what a shame she was bringing on him. They came in shock to beseech her or put her in a madhouse. But when faced with Cordelia's still imperious face and her reminder, "You come from between my legs. Don't come here and tell me what to do," they blanched and demurred into their usual childishness. They took their poor father with them to live in Ladbroke Grove, London, where Hannah ran a small West Indian grocery store. On Saturdays, Gabriel took him to Walthamstow Market to feel at home among other West Indians. Alicia, who gave up nursing to become an artist, breezed in now and then to take him to the pictures.

Violence did not exhaust Cordelia's desire either. Women came to her door with big sticks, searching for their husbands purely on the rumour of Cordelia's ardour. She met them at

the door, insinuating, "I could ever want your husband?"
They felt caressed and fled.

When a religious revival came to Abyssinia with a boy
priest who many said could give absolution for sins and
was the mouth of God, hard-working people washed their
hands and feet and bodies and dressed in their most regal to
attend the revival. Cordelia passed by the revival thinking of
going in when she heard the inspired voice of the boy. But
changed her mind, remembering suddenly of Kumar Pillai
visiting tomorrow and Yvonne the seamstress whom she
should hurry to catch before she came up the road to the
revival. As she passed, Cordelia brought a lush silence across
the revival tent door, a longing deeper than God, which held
the congregation and even the boy priest in thrall.

PRIEST

The dark was like the dark of any morning anywhere. He could see coal greyness lighting the east. It was no time to pray, because he had no more currency there, but he said prayers anyway in the faith of his boyhood. The Pentecostal murmuring, "Thank you, Jesus, thank you, Jesus," hummed on his arid lips. His body melted the unusual frost of the early morning, which gathered in his armpits and on his forehead. He smelled the nicotine on his fingers and longed for a smoke. The man next to him breathed in gasps. It was morning, but dark still. Nothing was anything yet, nothing had coalesced into any shape. He liked this time of day, like him it was indeterminate. He was waiting for the sound of a car.

The road wasn't a road yet. There was no place to really hide except in the morning itself. Anthracite and hawkish, its flecked light strafed the dark fields down the road from the camp.

He heard crickets or whatever insects lived here. Stars, the Southern Cross, the Dog, would soon dim into the greying morning. He wished Eula would hurry. He heard a car but it went by fast, its headlights stunned him and he prayed for transparency. Some guard coming on shift. Shit. The car turned, came back heading straight for him, he was stiff with intended movement. It was Eula. She almost hit him.

He said nothing when Eula screamed, "Fuck you, Carlyle!" He hadn't heard his real name for a long time. It shocked him more than her anger. Only his family called him Carlyle. To everyone else he was Priest. Her scream resounded in the car. He figured it was best to keep quiet until they'd driven away from the dead wasteful country of the immigration detention camp outside of Gainesville, past the point at which the electric wires made sense and finally added up to a city. Jacksonville, Florida, he hoped.

So he only said hello when she picked him up. He didn't even introduce Adrian. He sat in the car silently, getting angry but biding his time.

"Fucking bastard! This is the last time, you fucking bastard!" She was driving too fast but he didn't tell her anything. He had already threatened her—that was how she'd ended up driving the several days from Toronto to the barren fenced-in camp where deportees like him languished, waiting to be sent home. What he had on her was family, a kinship that he took liberties with. And her passport.

One year ago, she'd lent him her passport to get across the border at the Peace Bridge, and he had come to see his wife, Gita. He had crossed from Buffalo into Canada with no trouble. But getting back into the States was more difficult. So Eula had driven him from Toronto to the bridge at three in the morning and he had pretended to be a woman, using her passport. He had promised to throw it away and she would report it lost, but he had kept it as insurance. Just in case Eula or his other sister, Sese, thought she could let

him go and forget him the minute he crossed the bridge.
They were ashamed of him and fearful of their good name.
They didn't want their name in the newspaper. They didn't
want to be embarrassed. Assholes, he thought. Who the hell
in a big country like Canada would recognize their name in
the newspapers? Who the hell knew them? Who would be
scouring newspapers, looking for their name? Stupid.

He knew she had given him the passport not just because she was frightened but because maybe she loved him,
because he was her brother and because she saw him as a
tragic man with everything against him in life. Yet even if he
knew that, even if that were true, he still had to hold on to
the passport in case he was wrong about her and she feared
him like the rest, then he could use it later.

He called his sisters from time to time from Florida or
New York, just to hear the jumpiness in them. They didn't
want to hear from him but they wanted to know that he was
far away and never coming back. He wanted to make sure
they were still afraid of him so he called them just to hear
their nervousness, just to be sure that if he needed anything
they would be there for him. So he'd called her to say that
he still had the passport and would she come and get him—
he had been picked up in an immigration raid. It would only
take a few days, a week, rent a car, wait at a certain place at
the same time for a couple of days and he would never ask
her for anything else again. Then he told her he still had the
passport. Hearing her pause on the other end of the phone.
"And bring Gita."

So she had come, and brought Gita with her. Gita was in
the back, waiting for him, so he pushed the man who had
come with him into the front seat and he climbed in the back
next to her, embracing her. The car was hot. When he went

to say something to her Eula screamed, "Fuck you, Carlyle." The car was silent. What should have been a conspiracy of greeting and relief was tense silence. The air in the car was so hot that the stranger sitting beside Eula wanted to open a window but was afraid of the woman gripping the wheel, her mouth set in a pout, her temples tight to bursting.

They drove in her silence for a long time and it wasn't just a silence but a balancing and tightening. Sometimes Carlyle seemed to fill up the car with his side of it, sometimes Eula's anger engulfed it. The air shifted as in a bottle, turning first this way and then that. He would win since he'd brought them all here. He would break the bottle with his own brand of anger as soon as he felt Eula lose hers. It would probably be the last time he could call on her because somehow he knew she wouldn't do it again. He felt she had come to say something as much as she had come because she was threatened, and she didn't care if there was a stranger in the car. She hadn't even looked at the stranger or noticed the resemblance. But Carlyle knew that he'd have to turn wicked anyway, because Gita was there and the man was there and they had to know who was who.

She was driving so fast that sooner or later they would all die, or some highway police officer would spot them and that would be the end again. Though it was dark outside, and they were on a road with no light, only the yellow line down the middle and the reflectors on the side to guide her. The sound of the road, cracked and rutted, could be heard every fifteen seconds as it hit the wheels flying over. "Stop the car," he said quietly.

"Fuck you, you bastard. This is the last fucking time you pull any shit on me. Never call me again because I will kill you just like this."

She had been waiting for the sound of his voice to explode again. She pressed the gas harder, her eyes almost closing.

"Okay, Eula, stop the car now."

"Don't fucking threaten me again, you hear me?"

He was getting tired of her or frightened of her and he didn't like it whichever it was.

"You think you're crazy? Well, I fucking crazier than you, you hear me? You think you alone can be crazy? Let we see who more crazy."

He could hear something in her going. It was the same thing in him. Moments of rage and depression, moments when all his chest came loose, and he knew that she was serious. As serious as when she'd stuck that safety pin into his side when she was little. Stuck it in him until she could only see the curl of its end, and when she began to bend the curl open he could not scream out because he was touching her and he didn't want his mother to know, so he stopped, all his blood rushing to his skin in a heat and his eyes watering and he couldn't reach out and pinch her hard enough because she just kept twisting it. So he knew that he couldn't stop her. Not by doing anything to her or threatening her any more.

He leaned toward the door, reaching over to Gita in the beginning as if in a caress. Then he opened the door and pushed Gita's face out.

Gita started to scream as wind and dust broke into her mouth and the heat of the road and the heat of the exhaust singed her. Gita's face that just a moment ago, despite the anger in the car, had been expectant and wanting Priest to notice that she had come because she loved him and she had come all this way to be with him whatever. He said nothing, just held her face out the door, close to the fast-moving ground. The door knocked her head and she looked at him but he was not looking at her. She as always found affection in his hands even though they were trying to kill her.

The other man opened his mouth but nothing came out, and for two minutes the car drove on, the woman at the wheel determined to outlast Priest, and Gita begging for her life with no sound coming out of her mouth either. Eula finally slowed and stopped, got out of the car and walked away down the road in the direction she had driven from. She looked back, seeing Priest now standing outside of the car, holding and kissing Gita. Gita, barely standing, crumpling under his kisses. It made her stomach turn. He would have done it. She knew he would have done it and that's what separated her from him. She was ruthless in another way. He knew that she would not stop for him. She no longer cared if he was alive, but she would stop for Gita.

She walked back to the car, detecting streaks of early light. She had had enough of highways now. It had taken her four days to get here. Four days because Gita couldn't drive, four days of cracked highways and slabs of broken graffitied concrete marking cities. Pills and coffee helped her to drive almost steadily. The rims of her eyes felt like wire. They had only seen the outside of cities, the scarred backs that cities turn to highways—Detroit, Cleveland, Pittsburgh, Washington, a huddle to the east—sprawled in grime and smog. She had not thought that they would look so old, so worn down. She had expected some lure, some sweet smell. Most of the people she knew from back home preferred American cities. They said they loved the raw at-your-throat ways of these places. She passed them with a nervous fear at their largeness, their spillage. She was afraid of them. She preferred the clean coolness, the slow reserve of Toronto. These cities were like mounds of

refuse, scourings and dregs. Bridges seeming to lead nowhere climbed over the cities, even the concrete seemed
rotted to her, the steel underneath weeping brown stains
down the side. The one time she'd been to New York she'd
felt as if harm would come to her any minute. Where others saw glamour she saw something so cold and corrosive
she didn't want to stand on the streets. After Washington
the road eased out into less frequent bursts of dross as she
headed south. They ate at the gas stations and rest stops,
some spaceship-like, some dingy and small, along the way.

Her head was ringing as she walked back to the car. She
looked at the three of them waiting and felt that it was she
against them. If he asked her for the keys she would kill him
on the spot. Her head was ringing, the whole long ribbon of
road she had driven to get here kept repeating in her brain—
the long-haul trucks, the silver cylinders of milk, fuel, waste;
the whoosh, whoosh drone of the thousands of vehicles she
had passed. Her mouth tasted metallic and dusty. She was full
of bad coffee and pills. She got into the driver's seat again,
waited for everyone else to get in, and drove in silence.

Somewhere along the way she felt rather than saw the
man beside her in the front seat. Carlyle's doppelgänger, his
double, only much younger and she thought, what fucking
obeah was he working now; a younger him? More of him in
the world? Jesus Christ. He was sitting behind her as well as
beside her, the bastard.

"Don't ever call me again." That was all she said. Carlyle
understood, but he really didn't believe her. He figured
he'd give her a few months, she'd forget.

Yet he knew people, there wasn't one that he couldn't
make out. Everyone wanted something, and when he found
out what it was he knew that he had them. So maybe he'd

used up his papers with her. "Free paper burn" as their mother used to say. All his time used up, all his ease, all his leeway, all the rope she gave him; but she'd forget.

Yet he knew that he could also miscalculate, any trouble he had was because of miscalculation. He'd go one step too far and bring the whole house crashing down. He felt that moment in himself. That moment when he made it go wrong. No matter how much money he had, twenty-five thousand, fifty thousand; the moment would come working on a bet, in a gambling house or a new deal, and he would blow it. A moment of sheer confusion would follow months of clarity. Or something reckless in him saying, *Fuck it*; the good life wasn't for him anyway, even though that was what he had stolen for, that was what he had beat somebody up for, that was what he had scared his children for, that was what he had smacked Gita around for, that was what he'd cut his best friend Icepick for, the good life, and when it was within reach he said fuck it. He couldn't hold on to it anyway, he wasn't made for it, he was made to trawl the bottom of life, so fuck it. You couldn't turn bad things good.

But that moment pissed him off all the same, because it was the one moment that he didn't have under control. Shit, the one person he didn't have under control was himself. He could feel it coming in him. Those were the times, when he swung around suddenly and hit somebody or drank a whole bottle of whisky or shot himself up with heroin or threatened to kill whoever was near. Or there'd be the other times when everything was going right and he felt high and he was laughing and joking around and then he would see himself in a mirror or a shop window and he would feel like it was someone else and he would feel like breaking it. He would see his eyes and the sink in his cheeks where his teeth were missing and the one cheekbone higher than the other and all that imperfection would make him hate his face. It was the same imperfection that made people trust him. His face was strong, hard, and vulnerable at the same time, and perhaps it was handsome. He didn't feel any love for anybody, he only felt like having them—friends, lovers, anybody—having them like you would have bread or money or marbles. He watched them to see if they loved him and what they would do for him if they did.

———

When he was sixteen he walked into the only gas station in Terre Bouillante, not a mile from his house, stuck a pen-knife in the manager's face and asked for all the money. He bought a shirt, a pack of Broadway cigarettes, a box of Plume matches, a chicken roti, an orange-flavoured Solo sweet drink, two Guinness stouts, which he stuck in his back pockets, and a switchblade—a better knife. Then he ran home and sat on the back steps. He heard the police at the door, heard his mother wail and scramble to shut the door so that they wouldn't take him away. He sat there cool as ever but inside him he wasn't cool at all, he just couldn't move, inside he was molten red and terrified.

So he sat looking cool. Two policemen came through the house and on to the back steps and grabbed him. His body went rigid, his knees seemed to lock and he felt as if he could not walk, so they dragged him and stood him before his mother for a moment. He thought that she was going to embrace him when her hands descended on his face but instead he felt stinging slaps raining down on him and cursing and spittle from her angry screams.

It astonished him. Nothing all day had astonished him, not anything about his behaviour, not his sticking the penknife into the gas station manager's face, nor his taking the money, nor the cold burning of the stout down his throat, nor the coughing when he tried to smoke the Broadways one after the other, not even standing under the lamppost the night before, his left foot up against it, staring at the closed doors of the gas station, the dead motor car of the owner to the side, the rounded gas tanks, the cans of oil and the daily newspapers behind the glass, the thought forming, and deciding that he would rob the gas station. But his mother's hands knocking his head from side to side and her face so angry he did not recognize her—that astonished him. So much that he felt tears wetting his cheeks for the pain as well as the betrayal. She beat him and beat him, calling him a shame and a disgrace, pushing the policemen aside, beating him until her own body was tired. His thin neck dangling over, his head wilted like some dying dahlia in the rain, the police rescued him from his mother and took him to the dodge for boys.

She went to get him two weeks later, dressed in her one good dress, her hat, dark glasses to shade her pink sore eyes and her one good pair of shoes that weren't cut back to ease her feet. His mouth was white around the rim and his feet were bare and she made him walk ahead of her. "Thief," she hissed at him, the sun sizzling her albinoed skin. He felt her voice like a prod directing him. "Thief! You want to come and bring shame on my family? You want to make me have to hang my head in this Terre Bouillante? Damn little thief!"

Here was Eula now, driving him through Florida, hissing at him too. He felt the same helplessness and the same sudden vigour, exhilaration, at having done something that someone else had to worry about. Walking down that little street thirty years ago with his mother behind him, he apprehended a certain kind of power in shame and in violation. He no longer had to answer, he was singular and beyond reproach now because he had already done what he did and his mother had to fix it because of something in her that was no longer in him. Shame.

Why should he be ashamed? If only his mother knew that it was relief that he felt, relief at not having to appear good to anybody. He felt like a stick, solitary and dried brown or bleached brown, of whom nobody expected anything but for him to be a stick, and so he could be himself. Her words hissing toward him suddenly didn't reach his ears, suddenly they only meant her acknowledgement of him. He walked home, becoming more and more himself, becoming calmer and calmer but inside himself so excited he felt like jumping up, something like electricity running through him, something like water too, electricity and water, and he was burning in the middle of it, bright like something so hot it was white.

He no longer had to do anything inside the tight line of shame he had felt around his head, the waking up in the mornings ashamed, washing his feet and his face and his mouth ashamed, putting on his clothes ashamed, eating whatever little there was with his head bowed, ashamed, and walking up the street like a good boy going to school, ashamed. An enveloping sense of shame wrapped around them all, and there was no cause he could point to for all this shame, and he didn't understand it and he didn't want it.

It was the tightness of Terre Bouillante, the pervading secrecy that seemed to wrap itself around the small town high in the hills, still obscure to plain sight more than a hundred years since it was last a Maroon camp. The town where everything new was viewed with suspicion. Beginning with the road that sinewed its way up the rise during the time of Bola's son, his grandfather Sayman, who had stolen her footsteps and her drawing and run to Terre Bouillante.

In Culebra, Sayman used to follow his mother along the beach, rubbing out her footprints, but he would not go to the sea to watch sunsets with her. It made his heart hurt when the sun plunged into the sea. He would sob and run home. He was a boy who had a great love of everything and that made him afraid. He ran away and found Terre Bouillante without even looking. The noises of machetes far off cutting out land drew him. He had heard sucriers' sweet whistling just as Kamena had. He had found a half-starved family on a mule cart with a girl just his age (a girl who later became his wife) and a baby and a mother and a grandfather and he had gone with them to Terre Bouillante.

It was a quiet place, a place where strangers remained strangers for decades until the last person who knew them as strangers died. The building of a store or the coming of electricity made Terre Bouillante nervous. They wanted to go on as they were, farming up the terraced mud hills, toting water to the steep inclines. The uniform latticed shutters of Terre Bouillante's houses did not even open for a breeze. Its voices never rose above a faint sound. This is what the boy who ran away from Bola had loved, everything closed and secure, everything private, never the wind or rain or rush of water or circumstance at any moment taking your very breath away.

When the government cut down large tracts of the forest around it, Terre Bouillante felt naked. Even though sucriers flooded banana trees in thick yellow-black clouds the people in Terre Bouillante thought they detected their sounds vanishing. Its past as a refuge of runaways left Terre Bouillante with a dislike for modernity, a dislike for flashiness, for surprise and quick emotion. All things were cautious there. Even love.

Something of the one who stole Bola's footsteps remained in his family, his need for and yet disappointment with love. How love can never be enough, how the fall of the sun into the horizon made him weep even though each day it would return, how each moment his mother, Bola, spent in her own life he sensed her singularity and therefore his loneliness. His wife, thirteen children later, died of exhaustion. Sayman had drained her of love. Even his children looked watered down, their colour paling gradually to albino. The last of them was Carlyle's mother, her eyes so sensitive to light she stayed more often in the cool dark rooms of the house, the louvres shuttered.

So this need to test love, to probe love, to break it open, to see how far it would go, to examine it like the line of the horizon until it disappeared, was Carlyle's possession. And the secrecy and reserve of Terre Bouillante, where everything was about to be interrupted, everything about to be discovered, was his prison. What had taught Terre Bouillante to survive kept it from living and Carlyle felt it stifle him.

He had skipped school for the month before holding up the gas station. He would take his shoes and his white shirt off and walk in the dirty canal water along Richie Street. He would sit on the bridge at Moree Junction and plan to have his own life. He'd cussed a woman walking by for no reason at all, loosened his tongue on the words *cunt* and *pussy* and shown her his small ox-blood penis, asking her if she wanted some. In the evenings, when schoolchildren were out and school was over, he put his shoes back on and his shirt and stopped wandering and went home and ate and washed the back steps and picked up the paper in the yard and cleaned the drain as he was supposed to.

But now he didn't have to do any of that any more. He could be the boy he'd made of himself, pitching stones at people walking below the Moree Junction bridge.

His mother could have the tense worry of wondering what was to be done. His sisters, his brother. He watched them scrambling to explain him. He watched them with more shame in their faces for what he had done and he discovered their new fear of what he would do. He took to standing behind doors and frightening them, or walking into a room so quietly they did not hear him come in. He took to not coming home until he felt like it and he didn't pretend to go to school any more. He sat on the back of the bench across from the Savannah playground around the corner from their house and he smoked as many Broadways as he could gamble for or wrestle from any badjohn less bad than he. He whistled at girls he grew up with and knew because he wanted them to know this new him was dangerous and not the same. And he stayed out on that bench long past midnight, when the whole street was asleep, smoking and thinking and getting used to the dark, which he was determined not to be afraid of any more.

The bench became his and he could tell any other badjohn to leave it because he had his switchblade, which could open fast. He could sit on that bench and be visible and invisible at the same time. He tested his invisibility by saying quietly when someone was passing, "Good night, Mr. Holder." His voice, gentle and threatening, as if walking out of the dark and the quiet and the smell of lilies and green bush bugs, would startle the passerby and make the warm flow of air turn tepid.

He did everything to make himself hard and everything hardened him eventually. One day the police raided his bench and he sat there waiting for them while all the others ran across the Savannah and through the tracks and back yards, skimming drains and canals, shoes flying and fowls scattering before them. But he sat there, sat on his bench, brazen and sullen until he felt a knee to his stomach that made him retch and taste the oil of blood in his mouth. He had nothing on him, no cards, no money, no bits of paper with numbers or signs, so they beat him until his face was swollen and then let him go. He staggered home and sat on the cesspit retching blood and trying to control his skinny shaking legs. His mother stood at the kitchen window watching him and offering him no help until he relented and came inside.

Days later he woke up in a kind of bright hot light with someone murmuring prayers to him. It was his own lips saying the small prayer that he knew from lunchtime at school. "Bless this food O Lord...for these thy gifts we pray...." He lay in a light and saw only the shadows of his family move over him saying things he could not understand, he understood only the prayer his own voice murmured in his ears. Opening his eyes he saw only white light and his small knowledge of his prayer book revealed heaven to him. Delirium made this meagre knowledge grand, and once again he experienced that aloneness and sanctity he had felt walking down the street ahead of his mother. A compact holiness and purpose that made him feel that the beating and his sickness were wholly directed by him to arrive at his way in life.

For months after, no one recognized him as the boy with

the switchblade on the bench. He emerged from his injuries and his illness with a faith in God no one in his house had ever lived by. The Easter revival in the Savannah field across from his bench now drew him. Dressed in his white shirt again he sat in the front row, seduced by the exhortations from visiting preachers. Sometimes he stood tall at the back, his by now six-foot figure looming and opening its arms as if to embrace the whole crowd.

He disappeared from Terre Bouillante, travelling with the revival throughout the island, Blanchicheuse, Grange Village, New Road Town, Longdenville, Golden Grove, Belfield, August Town, Jackson's Seat and Galina and Abyssinia and Culebra Bay. As the revival progressed across the wet lands, the lands sprawling with arrowroot and cassava, undulating in cocoa and tonka beans he received the gift of tongues. White-clad women and black-clad men, heads tied in yellow cloth, waved in the heat glow along Sunday streets to the prayer clearings and the churches to hear the young man who could speak to the spirits. And in some places a solitary woman with an umbrella waited in hope for a transport, her faith getting her the five miles to the Savannah; or a small boy, sent by his father, looked back to the long road he had come, a small moving bundle against the vast rain forest and endless road. They came to hear him. These people tired on hard work, and generous to every living thing, would take Carlyle in, feeding him and babying him asking only for his presence in exchange for his gift and his light. They fell in love with his boyishness. He played in their yards with their children until meeting time, when he seemed to know all the suffering of their life and appeared older than they, and turned into an instrument for their messages to God himself.

In Culebra Bay he was kicking a ball along the beach with some children when he saw two man-o'-war birds circling above. They headed toward shore, signalling bad weather coming. Looking up and then back to where his friends might be, he saw an old woman sweeping the sand. He stopped to laugh at her useless task, thinking that she was an old woman out of her head, but realized the others did not see her when they kept running up the beach as if she were not there. She stopped her sweeping, looking up, her eyes making four with his. The man-o'-war birds dipped as if to touch her shoulders. She waved a hand at them, shooing them away, then she pointed him to a rock out in the sea and when he turned back to her she was a glimmer, some air shape he had mistaken he thought, because the day was so hot and the sea wind whipping up sand.

In Abyssinia he saw an elderly woman pass by the door of the revival hall in the glow of two lovers, and for a moment the light of her rivalled his own as he knelt before his congregation speaking in tongues. For a moment the congregation paused in its incantations and looked back wistfully, watching Cordelia Rojas walk by, burning. Cordelia, black with passion, moved by like a wave. In the wet-lipped quiet she left behind, the congregation saw their slight souls. For a moment he almost stood up to follow her, knowing that she was going to happiness. But she passed quickly, leaving a darkness like a lamp going out, hurrying to her own passions without so much as a look for him.

All this time his family had not heard from him. But they had heard rumours of him becoming a boy priest with the revivalists. His brother Job had travelled to Carapichaima to see what he was up to and had seen him dressed in gold and white robes and shouting something in tongues to the sky.

A chorus of people answered him with the same sound and moaning, and Carlyle was crying and kneeling until the ushers drenched his body in water to free him of his lightning hold on God. Job took the news back home, sitting in the small living room re-enacting Carlyle's performance and gift.

"Ma," he said, "you would not believe is the same boy! You would not believe!"

"Is God I pray to for that boy," his mother replied, "God." There were others to pray to but she had gone to the highest of them.

The family felt relief and a small sense of pride that Carlyle had pulled himself up. They didn't have to worry about him any more and went back to living quietly and decently and hand to mouth.

———

"Good night, Mr. Holder." The night as usual was pitch dark, it had darkened since five-thirty, since the sun dove headlong into the houses up the steps across from the Savannah. And the breeze was soft across the field with a brief smell of rain. And his voice was even sweeter with invisibility and Mr. Holder jumped, thinking that he had heard a spirit, and walked briskly on.

The revivals were over and the revivalists had gone home to America, and their praises and promises to take him with them to Atlanta, Georgia, and Tulsa, Oklahoma, had not materialized so he had come back to his bench on the corner and his chilled voice in the dark street. "It have a lotta money in that," he told his badjohn friends, who took to calling him Priest. "A lotta money I was going to make if I did only get to go to America."

He didn't mind being called Priest as long as it wasn't a joke and he made sure it wasn't a joke by grinning knowingly and saying, "Yeah, man. I is a priest. You don't understand what you saying there. You telling the truth. I could make God snatch you any time."

He could not tell when his feeling of the gift became a burden but night after night of talking in tongues and feeling wet through to his soul had made him sober again. All those people wanting him made his head tired. He would fall asleep kneeling there in front of them and feel washed. He had been washed as if washed to return to his life—or as if all life was the same with him now. The gift was the path of extremes: the mud ground was the bench, his hands raised to the sky were the blade. He could step out of himself and see the boy walking ahead of his mother, his brown head perfectly spherical, gathering himself out of the world and out of the rules. He could feel himself in his own orb of light standing against the lamppost with its superfluous glare, planning the robbery. And then the act, whatever it was to be, done like any other act, like eating or pissing or walking in a circle, like touching rice or putting his hand into hot bread. As if all materials were the same and just an extension of his own body, the knife in the manager's face or his voice's healing gifts.

So then there was no reason not to return to the corner and his bench and his switchblade. Especially since he wasn't going to go to America—to Atlanta, Georgia, America. They would send for him, they said. They would tell of a powerful young man so blessed by the spirit of Jesus. He saw no contradiction in going back to his life on the corner. In him it was the same source of energy and vigour, the same calling to be singular and alone, and his time with the revival had confirmed his power and his command of his own being. He was outside the strictures of a street or a family or a building or other expressed powers. He was a free man now. Nothing stood between him and the acts he was to perform.

His family received him with silence and fear, at first concluding that he had changed and then understanding, when he spent all day and night on the corner, that they had the devil living with them. They heard him racing through the house one day, blood drenching his face, reaching for the cutlass in the kitchen to go chop whoever had chopped him. He looked like a priest, crimson and single-minded. And they were almost trampled in their own house by his host of hooligans draping after him. He crossed his mother's body shelling peas on the kitchen floor, he swept his brother Job aside with a fierce look and he jumped the five back steps in a leap heading to somebody's heart. His mother wailed getting up, spilling and scattering the shells from the bowl of her skirt, the peas falling and skittering like a rain of pebbles across the flowered linoleum floor. She ran after him but he was gone this time and her hands, which could otherwise astonish him, hung over her head as if his blows were now descending on her.

Self-defence they called his rage cutting the other bad-john's ear from his face, leaving it hanging on a string, and manslaughter they might have called it if he had not heard his mother wailing and swung around to see what was the matter and swung again finding the badjohn running and screaming to his side of the Savannah, and hearing the sirens he thought the sound was still his mother screaming from some pain.

He dropped the cutlass, needing to go home and rub her

back for her and bring her her favourite sugar water with a taste of rum. And then needing to sit on his bench calmly and figure out why he was bleeding and what the consistency of blood was when faced with various stages of air, various lengths of exposure. And when he figured that out and when he took his mother the water and the rum from the flask under the bedspring, then the police could arrest him. Picking it up he sat there turning the cutlass this way and that, watching the blood coagulate, and it might have looked threatening to the police waiting but it wasn't, he was just checking the dullness or shininess of the blood over the blade and if the one enhanced the other or if it really had to do with the light and angle of the sun.

It was becoming habit that after a rage he would return to piety, but his was not penitence but a kind of justification. His rage was absolution from piety and his piety absolution from rage.

He had grown too big for prisons not to hold him, and he hated the anonymity of their barracks, the inconvenience of swabbing WCs and the piddling undifferentiated food. He hated being controlled, and in prisons someone was always controlling you, someone with a key and a bull pizzle. He planned never to be caught in a jail after his nineteenth birthday, which was the second of June 1959, the same year his mother gave birth to Eula, her last.

He was sitting on his mother's bed, playing with Eula's fat pleated legs, putting his finger in the creases and shaking her skin. His mother was dreaming, remembering the one who ran away with his mother's footsteps. Remembering, not dreaming, because he was sitting on the bed beside her, she felt him there, so she was between sleep and wake, remembering and dreaming. Dreaming and remembering the one who ran away with his mother's footsteps, because at that moment she wanted to ask him a question that she could not remember or bring to her lips. The one who ran away, the dream says, cannot bear tracings or impressions, he cannot bear his mother's pictures or footprints so he walks behind her, scratching them out. Stealing over her shoulder he sees her fingers tracing a far shore in wood black and roucoo. He worries why she is always thinking of places he is not, why is she always fingering maps he falls into, why she never draws his face and why if he follows her she is always planning to leave. He cannot bear leavings. The boy is running in his daughter's dreams. The boy is sitting on the bed beside his mother, dreaming of her father running away with his mother's footsteps. He sees his mother dreaming of a boy who is his grandfather running away with his great-grandmother's footsteps. And in the dream the grandfather grabs his mother's paper and runs, thinking she will follow, and runs and runs and is himself leaving as he runs into the dreams of his daughter who his grandson is sitting beside, she, watching herself dream. He runs and runs to Terre Bouillante without even looking, where he will make a generation who will not remember him except in dreams of augury. He will make a generation who will be a boy and a little baby—a boy pinching the fat of the little baby's legs—and who will break apart, what little is left of them, in a car on a highway in another interior. He runs in his daughter's dreams, he runs so that he makes nothing, leaves nothing behind.

His mother's eyes opened from their sleep and it startled him because her breathing did not change rhythm and he did not hear the sound of her eyes opening. She stared at him, finding him as vulnerable and close as when he himself was a baby, finding herself still in her dream of a boy who was her father who stole his mother's footsteps and ran to the interior and made a generation of which this boy, Carlyle sitting beside her in her sleep, is one, and this baby, who is gurgling and whose leg is about to be pinched and bitten, is one.

"Why you so?" she asked him, "Why you do what you does do?"

Was it the baby that made her ask him, had she read his mind about taking that fat baby leg into his mouth and biting on it? It was a wordless moment, less full of words than full of what passes between people and which has nothing to do with words but with recognition.

And he, closing his eyes from her and opening them again as if to seal some wound she had seen, some opening he no longer held open to her, he answered honestly, confused at first, as if he really should have a reason that was coherent, and then, searching himself, finding that indefinable shame in the air they breathed, that impenetrable skin that seemed so tight on him, he said, "I don't know." He was not hiding what he knew or saving her or saving himself; there was no time for cunning and it seemed to him no time or need to lie either. It was the truth as he knew it, and his mother understood that it was the truth. She dozed off again as suddenly to rejoin her dream of a boy afraid of leavings and tracings and impressions, a boy stealing his mother's footsteps and her paper drawing. She dozed off again then, parting the century back, leaving him playing with the baby.

He would come running home with a fowl under his arm or a pair of shoes or money all crumpled up as if it were dirty and he didn't want to hold it. And when the house was hungry he thought that she would love him for it but she sat on a chair at the window nursing the baby and telling him to take it all away. So this wasn't what she wanted him to do either. He had resolved, after they'd talked and he had sat caressing the baby, that perhaps if he did a kindness within his means she would be pleased. But no. So he went on with his life, turning on her sometimes. When she told him that he could not expect food from her house he walked into the kitchen and threw the full pot of food out the back door. If he couldn't eat, then no one could. And when she locked the doors against him, he broke the kitchen window to come in. Only when his brother Job, who usually said nothing, raised his hand to him did he realize that they were finished with him.

Well, perhaps, he thought, he was finished with them too. He had come back to the house on instinct but whatever was between them was gone, he had come back to the house first for their love and then for their fear and he knew that fear would always work so he need not come back. He could loom over them like a tragedy, they could feel him even if he didn't sleep there, even if he never spoke with them again. He had crushed the frail house of where they were and he could reach in at any time and move them.

~~~~~~

They heard that he had a child with a girl over in New Calcutta, that she was fifteen, that the child was half Indian. It was a year and a half since they'd seen him. They'd stopped locking the doors, thinking that he wouldn't have the face to come back again.

That April, he came into the house carrying the baby; behind him was the fifteen-year-old girl with a face both shy and bold at the same time. He gave the baby to his mother and introduced the girl as Gita, then he went out and bought a large can of milk powder, brought it back, told Gita to help his mother, and disappeared again.

The girl hovered by the bedroom door, waiting for his mother to say something, and when the mother said "Girl, go in the kitchen and take some food for yourself," the girl smiled in relief. "And make some tea for this child when you done," the girl heard as she looked around to find the kitchen.

One morning, a few months later, Gita came to his mother's room to say, "Ma, my papaji come for me to go home." A small greying man stood at the front of the house. He looked as shy and bold as Gita, his cutlass and a crook stick under his arm, his dhoti swathing his waist. She didn't like the look of him, she wasn't sure that she trusted his quiet, but it was his daughter.

"Don't ill-treat this girl," she told him. "Is not she fault."

He looked at her long, then nodded. "But I will kill that boy' cunt if I see him," he said, still nodding.

Her usual heat to defend her children rose but then it subsided and she handed him the baby with sudden intimacy. She pushed the hair out of the girl's face and straightened her dress. She asked the man if he wanted a drink of water as if he hadn't just threatened her son. He shook his head no and took his daughter and left for New Calcutta. She watched them walk down the street, the girl with her head bent, the man holding the baby awkwardly. She wanted to run after them and offer them food, she wanted to take the baby back, she wanted to erase her son from their morning walk down the street, she wanted to erase his touch from the little girl's body and the man's shame.

Whether he was inspired or not, they called him Priest. Only his family remembered his real name. And even he had grown so much into Priest that for a moment his real name was unfamiliar when he signed the paper that would take him to an orange-picking job in Florida. His real name, Carlyle Desrosier Childs.

He had no intention of picking oranges. He had his best friend Icepick's address in New York in his shoe in case he was searched and he had a little money there too. He felt the paper like a stone in his heel growing heavier and more noticeable. He hoped it didn't make him limp. He knew the stone was only in his imagination but he felt it like a secret about to betray him each time an official looked at him.

This group of men herded together at the airport at Piarco, their pants short of a length, their jacket sleeves ending above their wrists, their jerseys worn out at the navel, their hats from another decade in America, he had no intention of sticking with them. No intention of picking anything, tomato in Sinaloa or strawberries in Watsonville or grapes in the Coachella Valley, none. Or of cutting cane in Clewiston, Florida, none. Or doing the circuit with a raggedy horde of poor people like him, none, of travelling up and down the fat belly of America with sticky red hands, cracked fingers or stinking clothes. He was going to America to make some real money. He intended to get rid of them as soon as he got off the plane. Their small plans of sending a little money home or buying a length of cloth or buying a hog or a cow or a piece of land, he didn't want any part of. He wanted to swim in life, he wanted a lot of it.

"Stop talking shit." He silenced a row of them on the plane. His stomach couldn't take even the soft indiscernible air pockets. A man with gold teeth sucked them at him and said, "It en't have no badjohn on plane, bredda. Is America we going you know. It have free speech there."

This just encouraged the chorus of voices he didn't want to hear, some other stupid argument about America.

"What wrong with you, Gold Teeth?" someone said. "It have better badjohn in America than anywhere."

"Them is joke badjohn in America. You ever hear about a man name Priest?"

"Yeah," the chorus replied. Carlyle's stomach did a lurch and he kept quiet. He wanted to hear about himself. Suddenly he was not angry with them for being there with him. "Priest cut off a man's ears and keep it round he neck. Now, that is badjohn. It have anything like that in America? Tell me? You think they could beat that?" He listened for more. How these men had heard of him he didn't know, but he was flattered, a celebrity among them and they didn't even know.

"Cheups"—one of them brought back—"American soldier-boy do worse than that in Vet Nam. If Priest was to go to America they would do for he backside. Big badjohn does come small in America."

The rows of seats went quiet as they all contemplated their position, their muscles' softness and the weakness of their myths in the face of America. If their best badjohn wasn't good enough, who were they? All frightened for a few minutes at the little threat they posed and the uncertainty of what was to happen to them when the plane emptied them all out in the orange groves.

Priest among them was happy. Let any soldier-boy American try him. He was looking forward to it.

"Priest is not just any badjohn," one of them said, recovering himself and rescuing the rest of them. "He have the gifts. He is not no ordinary person. He does deal with the devil. That is why he does get through."

"Is true," the gold-toothed man agreed, needing to be rescued from their feelings of sudden weakness. "Is true, yes, them American en't know anything about *obeah*. That boy does talk to God and the Devil same time."

"Yeah, man. That boy could preach to God and the Devil at the same time, so they say."

They took swigs of rum out of bags they had brought on the plane clandestinely and enlarged the myths of Priest and badjohns they had known. They anaesthetized themselves against the America to come, which had become too large and, really, all they intended to do was make some money and come back home and if they worked hard enough and were well liked they would go home and wait for the next season, sure to be called. They sometimes drank too much and forgot or drank too much and chafed against their small-ness; shouting loud in the street about killing someone or loving someone; they only felt destructive power over their girlfriends or children and mostly that was sufficient for them, to slap a woman's face or break her jaw or pinch a child until he trembled and cried. But here on the plane going to America it was all they could do to control their awe, their fright, their small hands.

That was Priest's first and last trip. He spent a few weeks with a bag on his shoulder picking oranges and then he walked away the first chance he got. He'd ingratiated him-self with a foreman, let the foreman beat him at cards just enough and bet him a ride to town on a Saturday night for a drink and some whores. One thing, he had a way with him. His disquiet wasn't always on display. Otherwise he laughed and joked a lot and liked the life. He made himself loved.

He was playful, if you could imagine playfulness in a wicked way; as men are playful, so the others never quite saw his rages coming because it didn't match the signals that they were used to. Not that it didn't make sense to them. His rage made sense to them as the ultimate of what they could do, so in that way it wasn't unusual; it was just the way he mounted from calm to rage that they couldn't always predict, the trajectory or the exact result.

The foreman was in the back. The foreman wasn't dead. Well, maybe he was. He'd made him drunk and then hit him and when he could throw him out he would. He figured he'd drive an hour or so, then leave him at the side of the road, then drive on. By morning he could be somewhere else with the foreman's green card. All the labourers' talk about getting a green card and here he was a fucking citizen already. He laughed aloud, looking back at the lump of a foreman, his green card and his citizenship. He would do this, then he had to get a trade, get to New York and Icepick, get a piece of something to sell, maybe he could take the foreman all the way to New York with him, keep him drunk, take him all the way to New York City.

It was days and days before he arrived in the city. He had ditched the truck and the drunk, maybe dead, foreman. He didn't look to see if he had killed him after all. He'd heard his head or some part of him, perhaps his boots, knocking around in the back but he simply parked the truck off the road on the other side and walked away, ran in the other direction. He hitched a ride, walked, took a bus and then a train with the foreman's money.

When he arrived the city was in daylight and it might have been two days later, maybe three. The city was all he had expected and more. Its rusted iron bridges, boarded-up buildings, its crowds of people, its noise, all glittered to him. Its stink from dirty roads and human skin, from cloth and metal and dust and concrete. Even the way it made him feel, that he was choking or lost or too small, he loved it all.

He realized no one looked at him, no one knew him, but more, no one looked at anyone, or if they looked he could not see. It was a different kind of look, different from the one in his town. Quicker, slipping over his face, measuring him up in just that quick moving look. And hard-bitten but with a sense of dangerous lightness. He knew that Icepick would show him how to get along for the first.

They'd been badjohns together, turning out different corners in their small town, different streets, and hiding in the same brothels when the police were looking for them, passing through the same country villages charming and knocking up girls, sometimes the same ones. Somehow they had known not to fight each other, not after that first fight on the corner when Priest gouged Icepick's face with the cutlass and Icepick gave him a cut to the forehead. They knew that if they fought it would be unlike other fights; neither could predict the outcome. And so they didn't, because one of them would end up dead and in his heart neither could decide which one. So instead they became friends, drank babash together and fucked together in the same bed and beat up other men together and stole money from working girls and grew marijuana for a time up in the Arauc Hills and lived just like businessmen, buying gold chains and gold watches. And for both of them none of it was for anything but the momentary pleasure of it, none of it was for anything but the beautiful look of gold against their ebony arms and chests, the polo shirts and straight-legged pants, none of it for more than the adoring gazes of women and men envying and loving them.

When Icepick opened the door of his dingy cubbyhole of an apartment off Flatbush, Priest didn't recognize him at first but he saw that cut-out hole in Icepick's cheek and felt like licking it. They gave each other a dangerous grin and couldn't stop saying each of them, "Boy, is you? Is really you, boy?" Each seeing the commerce the other represented, each the threat, each the daring and each someone to watch his back until it came down to the two of them again.

Icepick looked a little older, a little worn down. He saw Priest, fresh and new and, in the end, younger and harder, if only because New York had made Icepick older, sharpened his cunning, made his eyelids droop to dream his intentions instead of showing them and letting them escape, hitting sidewalks and cabs and giving away his play. Priest loved the look in Icepick's eyes immediately. He had to have it. He loved intangibles. "New York City, boy. You in New York City," Icepick said, grabbing him through the door.

~~~~~~

Priest was forty-five now and running was just part of life because everything went a certain way. Impatience. Impatience made him skip all the steps in between. His game wasn't wired to wait. That was for people like his brother Job—waiting for some big shot back home to give him a break. Always wanted to do things but not get his hands dirty. So Job sent him money to invest in the business as if he didn't know that the business was selling drugs. Job didn't want his name dirtied. But he wanted his money all right.

Job had put him on the plane, saying "Good luck" but looking as if he'd meant "Good riddance." They were never close. Job was his younger brother but he seemed older. He seemed as if his life was settled. His life did not flutter around in his chest like Carlyle's, looking to burst out or to break him into pieces. He would live happily, marry happily, even die happily perhaps, he would feel the ground under his feet steadily and not as something illusive. Good riddance, he would think, and hurry back to Terre Bouillante to live his life without his older brother, the point against which he'd compassed himself since he could remember. He had even dusted his hands after saying "Good luck" and turning to go. There were countless letters from Priest asking him for money. He would walk around for a week with the letter burning in his pocket, then send him what he could. One day he stopped opening the letters, saying good riddance to them too. Though he imagined their contents, he imagined big-brotherly advice and inquiries. He imagined what he had needed from Carlyle—how to play cricket when he was a boy, how to catch fish in the ravine, how to run over the hot mud springs up behind the village. In his reinventions he almost opened the letters but tracing Carlyle's writing on the envelope only reminded him of the things that really happened. It reminded him of the sombreness deep inside him, which Carlyle had caused; all the things that he had missed doing because his mother watched him so carefully for signs of Carlyle. She put him in charge of guarding the house against Carlyle's raids and searching out towns and rumours for indications of him.

Job in fact had missed cricket, he had missed kicking a rag, tightened to a ball, from one street to another, he had missed straying from school. He had missed burying his face in the orange-pink flesh of stolen mangoes. All because of Carlyle. He had in fact lived happily, married happily and would die happily after he left Terre Bouillante, taking his wife and his children to Caracas, where he worked on an oil rig out in the sea. Until Carlyle left he could not have left. He had to stand guard. Even after Carlyle had left for America, even after he had stopped opening his letters, he still stood guard, waiting, anticipating Carlyle's usual kind of return, throwing life into fear and unhappiness again. Job left for Caracas still feeling tethered. In Caracas, though, no one would know him or his family or Carlyle and so he would be happy.

Priest believed in nothing. That was the simple truth. He believed in nothing. Which is why his departures and his pursuit of the most intense feelings and acts were so radical, so deep and so honest. The truth of life was perfectly clear to him. Nothing was made, every new morning was clear. His only challenge was inward. He had not been disillusioned or had some bad experience that he could put it all down to. He had simply seen the world and that was that. And he understood how slippery every moment was and he liked the thrill of it. Slipping from the knowable to the unknown, walking from one street to the next, being different all the time. In one afternoon he could slip from one personality to another. Why not?

⌇

He looked at the back of Eula's head now. There was still no talk in the car. Though he couldn't say that she had ever wanted anything from him, she used to love him. He had counted on her ever since she didn't cry out when he pinched her fat baby legs, or the other time, but he knew her resolve was deep when she decided. Fast and wicked like his somehow. When she stuck the pin in him when he tried to touch her, looked at him without blinking and rammed the pin into his side. He could see the crush of her jaw tight over her skin and he pulled away in pain not saying a word himself but thinking that she was as wicked as he. "Wicked little child," he would call her and she would laugh, giggle and carry on her playing with her doll or her mud dogs which she made in the back yard and lessoned and schooled in behaviour. She would gurgle and then make her eyes like pins stabbing him. He felt her watching him through all his rages. She was the only one not frightened, the only one not taking him seriously. She just watched him as if he were performing. She was fascinated and curious to see how much more he could do.

After the fight on the highway, after he'd given her fifty kilometres to cool off, he had launched into a stream of a monologue as they travelled—Gita and the doppelgänger intervening with grunts and giggles. But all the talk was directed at her, warning her not to do anything stupid again or else she would be the one paying, not Gita. He was saying, Do that again and I'll take this car and leave you right here on this road. Only he wasn't saying that. He was saying, "That is my good, good sister driving this car. My best sister." He was really saying, I'll hurt you too.

Eula had not heard the voice of the man next to her but she refused to be curious about him. Though she became more and more conscious of him, a sweat coming off him that she didn't like. She opened her window to let air in. Glancing in the rear-view mirror she saw Carlyle, his rawboned face, his chin jutting out, his eyes half closed, his eyelids slow to open. He was an angular man, slender and wide-framed all at the same time. When he walked he seemed to jangle, yet his limbs gathered into their own fluidity, a kind of grace. It was no more than Priest's science at work, to double himself and pretend he was someone else. The boy beside her had the same face and body only he was darker, his face smoother and his eyes were not yet secretive.

Priest had tried to make the doppelgänger talk after a while, tried to make Eula cool down by saying, "Eula, you ever see anything so, look at this boy' face. I just meet him in that place just so. Eula, this is family, man, look at him."

Eula hadn't said anything, just pressed her foot on the gas harder, the faster to get rid of them.

"Eula, you real ignorant," Priest said from the back seat, "I find a family we don't even know about and you, you can't even be pleasant. You just ignorant. Boy, talk to Eula, tell she who you is, man. Curaçao, you know, Eula! He don't talk too much English. Adrian he name, Dovett. He from Curaçao. You ever hear about Curaçao, Eula? you know where that is? Little island right off of Venezuela, there. But you ever see a face so. He bound to be we people."

He wanted to carry on as if it was all normal but she wasn't having it. Perhaps, she thought, this was his normal life. You could go from trying to kill someone on a highway to making pleasant conversation. Fucking madman.

"You too fucking ignorant, Eulalie, fucking ignorant. You can't even say a word to the fella." He was back to normal as if all that had happened was that she was discourteous. And he kept this talk going in her ears until she dropped them off. "Gita hungry, Eula. You have no heart, you can't just stop and get her something? Jesus!" He had just almost killed Gita. "She heartless, boy," he said to the doppelgänger, who still could not form a word out of the last several hours, which he was grappling to understand. All Priest had told him was that he had a way out, someone who would come at a certain time, and he'd paid the guards already and they'd just walk out like it was nothing, like they were in their own life and on their way to somewhere casual.

"Eula, why you treating Gita so. I tell you she hungry. Stop na. Boy, let me tell you," he said, touching Adrian at the back of his neck. "Boy, we going to make money, big money, take what I tell you. Them son-of-a-bitch in New York en't know it yet but I coming back with vengeance. Me and you we go fuck them up."

Adrian wanted to turn his head to say something to him but he felt transfixed by the woman at the wheel, as if she were willing him not to move. He could speak English but when he was nervous it deserted him, leaving him only *papiemento*, and sometimes it was convenient not to speak it. He wanted to say to the woman driving—look, I don't know this man, I look like him but I don't know him. I just wanted to get out of that place. But nothing came to him, just a thin sweat filming his face.

"Whappen, boy, you lose yuh tongue? Ay ay, don't let Eula frighten you, boy. That is my sister, man, my good good sister." Carlyle sounded jovial, happy to see her, joking with her as much as with the doppelgänger. As if nothing had happened, as if he hadn't tried to kill someone.

She wanted to fill her mouth with spittle and fling it at him. She gripped the wheel to stop herself. Now she only wanted to dump them on the side of the road. She wanted to get rid of them. She wanted to drive the car into a ditch or she wanted to be back in Canada and not here with them.

And he, he was holding himself off his next rage. He was

euphoric, he had a boy to show around, a boy who looked like him and was him already. A boy who would give him back the years since he came. He and Icepick would train him good. He was happy and what had happened earlier was not odd to him, nor was the expectation that his sister would simply fall into ordinary talk with him, ask him how he was doing, greet Adrian like family, perhaps take them all out for a meal. Why wouldn't she? "Eula, you too damn ignorant. You was always so." His logic lay in him alone. He made up the rules and he understood them. There wasn't some normal life that he was outside of. He wanted to live good, and living good meant playing too, and playing— well, certain people come to harm and certain others don't. He liked the heat of a blood fight, feeling another person's heart beat when he touched their arm or face, a glowing beating as if he were close to their being born or dying. He would put his fingers to his neck to feel his own heart beating in his throat hours later.

He and Icepick sold everything. They sold watches and coats and soaps and cheese and boots. They sold women, they sold smack, they sold ecstasy, they sold magic mush-rooms, they sold themselves as mules with loads of cocaine running down America and back. But they didn't rule the roads as they had ruled the corners where they came from. Other people did. And their game was small sometimes, purse-snatching or beating up drunks.

Icepick had been to jail already in America. Attica, he said, "Attica, boy," shaking his head and laughing with a kind of experience. Priest liked the sound of the word when Icepick said it, "Attica." Like some dream place where it was all tough. Icepick said he was there for the famous riots but he couldn't have been, because he wasn't in America yet. He wasn't there until two years later and it might not have been Attica at all but he too liked the sound of the word. He had been in some prison though because every morning he jumped up as if jumping out of his skin at 5 a.m. It would take him a few disorienting minutes to figure out that he wasn't in jail.

In the beginning when Priest moved in with Icepick he would jump up too, sensing Icepick, and Icepick would collect his face out of its disquieting dream and chuckle, shaking his head saying, "Attica, boy, Attica." Later he would say to Priest, "Boy, never pray to be in a jail in America. It not nice at all." He would leave it at that, knowing that neither of them knew how to do life straight anyway and some kind of jail was inevitable.

One thing changed between them, they no longer feared each other as much, there was no audience of peers to watch their performances, no women to impress and take, no juveniles to emulate them, no reputations to protect. Here in New York between the Blacks from here and the ones from Jamaica and the Puerto Ricans and the Mexicans and the ones from the Dominican Republic and the Russians and God knows who else, between everybody else scuffling for a living, they had to watch each other's back and this made room for a lifelong friendship. "You is my boy," one would say to the other, "You is my man, man." "Any time you see you need anything, don't even ask me man, just take it." Now they were looking for security, a more steady thing, and Adrian was a sign to him.

He'd be back on the street now. He just had to be more careful in future. It was stupid to have got picked up for nothing like that—driving too fast, that's all. The cops had stopped him, searched him, taken his fake green card and his car, and dumped him in the INS detention. This always happened to him, some stupid thing would have him in the hands of the police and some cunning thing had to get him out. He couldn't call Icepick, who was in the same situation, so he called his sister and he called Gita. He needed a new green card, a new identity, and one for the boy, Adrian, he'd discovered in the detention place, and life would be perfect.

There were always men and women who could make borders invisible. He was one of them. You only needed money. There were men and women who could change a passport from male to female and back, use it three times over, multiply it and subdivide it. There were always people like him who lived on the corners and in the seams of towns and cities. Most people lived in the damp and hungry interstices of real life. Most people lived with their bellies in their mouths and nothing but their hands covering their privates. So there was always room for creativity, virtuosity— long wails of trumpets in their stories, pirouettes in their journeys. Bobbing and weaving his mother called it, bobbing and weaving, dipping and diving around big people and bigger life.

Already he was calculating what he would do with this boy. How he would send him back and forth from Miami to New York to pick up the stuff. He would bring Adrian in with him and Icepick. He would trust him, he was family. The doppelgänger wouldn't rob him, he knew this just looking into his face. He knew what Adrian would do because he had read his face as well as he had read his own. It was God-sent, this double of his. He could figure out without thinking what he would do because they were the same. His own mind had conjured him, if God had not sent him.

The first time he'd seen Adrian something grew in him, live and electric, every idea he had bloomed, became twice its size. Priest was forty-five now. Adrian, half his age he figured, must have been sent to give him another play.

Eula stopped at a roadside chip truck, got out of the car, and wandered up the road until they were done. "You not hungry, Eula? eat something, man," Priest called out to her back as she walked away. "Boy, that girl stubborn, you hear me."

Since she was small she'd known that he was someone to watch but she had let something else get in the way, compassion, which she thought that she needed to give, like performing some exercise she was bad at, building some muscle she never used, not for him and not even for herself. He had just called at the right time, when compassion was her experiment for the month, and then Gita called too, so she went, taking Gita with her because Gita had begged her to, and she was here now and had to get back in the car and drive this strange set of people somewhere and, please, go back to her life.

When they were done she started the car again. They were just outside of Jacksonville. She had stopped just to stop him from talking in her ear. Walking up the road she had tried to figure out why she was here. Not because he was her brother any more, not because they shared the same mother and the same sisters and brother, family, but in the end she supposed it was out of that somewhere, out of the sea of them drifting every which way. No reason at all to help him, none left. He didn't need help, he needed people he could use. And she, her false pity brought her here, thinking he was somebody to be sorry for, somebody who meant well but had got fucked all around. Well, it served her right for being so high above him, like she could save him or he needed saving. Eula to the rescue, feeling superior to him.

The whole Gita business was her fault. It was she who had sent to Gita and told Gita to come to Canada. She, feeling sorry for Gita back home without a family, at least none that would acknowledge her after she ran away for the third time with Priest. Two children later, and hardly a penny from Priest, Eula had found her a Canadian couple to come and work for. That was how Priest had got the passport out of her, coming to see Gita in Toronto and then saying that he couldn't get back to the States without a passport. Not to worry, he would alter it, he said, get across the Peace Bridge at night when the guards were tired and not looking too closely.

The fact that he was her older brother, old enough to be her uncle, made her rescuing him feel even more felicitous, more righteous. That was her own fantasy, not his. And she had ignored the hiss of threat in his voice when he told her to come, had mistaken it for desperation. Deliberately mistaken. To make herself feel better. But she had begun to remember it as she neared the place he had told her to come, listening to Gita mewling about Priest and what a good life they would now live if only he would settle down. Gita's naïveté startled her. Didn't she know who Carlyle was? Hadn't he ill-treated her enough? Hadn't she seen him swindle people? How could she stay with him? For God's sake, look, she said, pointing to the scar on Gita's face. Gita was quiet in the car for an hour, it was an unquiet quiet. Eula had closed the subject but she sensed Gita's discomfort.

"You don't know nothing," Gita said finally. "My father and them is strict people. I always wanted to leave New Calcutta. Them wanted me to marry a big man, old like my own father. When I see Priest in New Calcutta they did send me to sell ochro and bird peppers in the market. He was there preaching and I like the sound of he voice. He face was pretty pretty and he was young and I know my life was supposed to be with other young people. So I say I going to leave New Calcutta with that boy. I woulda dead if I did stay there."

Eula didn't know that Gita had it in her. She rarely spoke with Carlyle around, she always seemed so deferring, so silent, Eula had treated her like a child though she was older and had two children. "When Pa come to get me and make me go home with the child you don't know the beating I get. So I run away again when Priest come to get me." As if explaining someone Eula didn't know, she said, "Priest is a nice man when he ready. You don't know. We had a good time when we live. Priest take me everywhere, he show me everything. When he have money it don't have nothing he don't give me and the children."

The more Gita talked on their journey down from Canada the more conscious Eula became of her own anger. "What choice is that?" she asked Gita. "Them for him? Feel like the same thing to me." But she knew that she could not persuade Gita. Somehow Gita had calculated the rages of the people around her and chosen one set over the other. Who was she to tell her different?

This understanding, and his threat to tell the authorities that she had lent him her passport that time to cross the border, rankled even more. By the time he emerged from the deportee camp she had remembered the real reason she had got into her car, crossed the border at the Peace Bridge and driven hundreds and hundreds of miles; he had threatened her. By the time she saw him she had remembered everything. Every nervous night of her childhood, sitting in the dark with Mama waiting for trouble. Every piece of this love of his, which was so greedy, so venal he had to inflict pain to feel it. She remembered nights with the same texture as this one as she and Gita sat in the car, a short distance from the INS detention camp between Gainesville and Jacksonville, sat in the car in darkness looking at him running toward them with his double, a shadow, behind him. She had felt like running him down and something had moved her hands on the steering wheel and something had put her foot on the accelerator and she had almost hit him. She had seen his startled face as he and the double jumped aside, but she'd come to a stop beside them and trembled with why she had just tried to kill her mother's child. Shit, now she was fucked too.

"Don't fucking call me again," she told him, dropping them off in Jacksonville. Gita was staying with him. She wasn't going to take them back to New York, she was going to cut across to the 75, find a motel, get some sleep, and head back to Toronto through Detroit. She didn't want any more of them, she wanted to lose them and to get on with her life. He looked threateningly at her and she met his eyes with her own threats.

"I'll send the passport for you, Eula."

"Keep it, send it, I don't care. You not threatening my ass again, okay."

"I was only joking. You could never take a joke, man, Eula." He reached to jostle her shoulder in friendship, sensing that he was losing her. She was the only one of them not really afraid of him and that was why he didn't want to lose her. But all he had was threats. All his skill was violence. So he couldn't say, as he wanted to, thanks, Eula, thanks for coming.

Two months later Priest was set up again, running drugs and stolen sneakers and stolen anything. Adrian was his mule, sometimes running cocaine and hash from Miami to New York. Up and down the fat of America fetching and carrying. Adrian, in a strange place and still bewildered, not knowing why he had met his resemblance, felt as if the wheels of the bus he sometimes took were grooving a sore through the belly of America. He wanted to stand still. He wanted to stay in some small place between those two cities, some small place he'd seen a sign—Midriver or Johnson's Corner. But he didn't. He went back to Priest. The sore grooved in him. He smelled things he didn't want to smell, saw things he didn't want to see, mostly people, poor-faced and dragged-out. He soon lost the old thought in him that America was where you lived well. Maybe they lived better than where he'd come from on the whole but not in the small ways, not in the raw-boned pain and anguish.

He carried the shit, as Priest called it, strapped to his body again, he carried it up his ass, he carried it in his bowels. He crawled through the body of America as small bags crawled through his own body. He didn't see the country, not the country you saw on television, not the one you heard in accents you imitated from the movies, Al Pacino or Joe Pesci, he just saw veins and bloody flesh and shit and whatever it threw up.

He told Priest, when he had a chance to talk and when he could get the words out, that he felt sick with himself. In his little English, he tried to ask what it all meant. Why did they have to live like this, why was it only either this or the life his own father, Dovett, had lived, a life of fighting bosses in the oil refinery in Curaçao. Priest didn't understand. He glimpsed what Adrian said in his broken way but told him,

"Don't worry. Don't worry, man. We going to be living good." If he knew what the boy meant he didn't let it get to him. The doppelgänger was always sad. Maybe, Priest thought, maybe he was missing someone or someplace. He tried to brighten him by giving him blow or his watch. He tried to show Adrian that he would give him anything because truth be told the sadness affected him strangely. If he ever felt pain, if what he felt could be called pain, at this point in his life, he felt it when he looked at the doppelgänger.

He shared the trips with Adrian because he loved it, even though he could be sitting up in New York waiting. But he loved it, loved putting his hand in it, right in the belly of the game. He loved leaning on a bus in Arkansas smoking a cigarette, some threat evident in the colour of his skin, he loved walking into a Denny's in Atlanta for a burger and fries, he loved the fat of it all, the hustlers in New York who came up behind you and opened their coat full of treasures, gold and diamonds, watches and chains, he loved the anonymous gristle of a dark street where he could lean over into someone else's life, he loved the mixed unidentifiable flesh of it squeezed through his fingers, the big how-you-doings of gas-station attendants, car salesmen and store clerks, their smiles saying, Love you, got any money? and their dismissal of your whole claim on humanity if you didn't have any; their hands on your back shoving you out of their stores on Flatbush Avenue, warm and visceral like a predator's; their eyes measuring and balancing how much you were good for against their own treachery.

This was the heart of the world, he thought, palpable and brutal, sucking in blood and pumping it out callously without thought, just instinct, that was its only mission and he was like a vein in it, hungry and just as ruthless. This was love. So he took the trip on the bus or the train gouging whichever artery of America, his hands on the weed or cocaine, and sometimes he would wear glasses and streak his hair grey like an old man's to throw off suspicion. And sometimes he was a young man with a baby, the baby of whichever woman owed him for dope and like a young responsible single father he cooed and changed the diaper packed with coke and everyone on the bus admired him when he talked about his love for the child and how its mother had left strung out on the crack. What a fine man, they'd say, and, wish him good luck. He multiplied and doubled and divided with ease. The sad boy who was his double could not.

A SOFT MAN

~~~~~~~~~

Every day you wake up and there's something trying
to break your heart. Not a day there isn't something
just waiting there lashing your blood right open. Not
a day he hadn't awakened and something wasn't hurting
him. If he tried to tell anyone, Dieter for instance, how
would he explain it? How would he explain something
cracking in his heart like a stiff door opening to let in something you don't want? How would he explain that? And how
would he tell him he didn't know where it came from, this
spoon dipping out his heart like emptying a bowl, how
would anyone feel that, know it enough to feel it when he
himself didn't understand it, just that he got up lonely every
day and every day something was waiting to break his heart
so much he had to clamp it shut quick or pick it up piece by
breaking piece.

He was lying in the kitchen on the floor with his broken
heart. He looked at his hands and they were wet with the
dribble from his sleeping mouth and sea cockroaches were
floating out of him, fat, white sea cockroaches. And what was
his first thought?—Adrian Dovett, your heart is broken.

His first and his last thought every day. He'd crashed in two hours ago, dropped into the kitchen exhausted and wide awake, and had fallen asleep with his heart breaking. Dieter the bastard had made him wait in the square for hours, promising him the stuff. He'd waited and waited, then walked to the hotel above the photo store to see if Dieter was there. Two people looked at him with disgust as he brushed past them. Man, what did he look like? He must have looked bad. He was going to get out of this shit and when he found the bastard Dieter he'd smash his face for making him wait, for fucking him up.

He was cold. It was June and he was cold. A warm night in Amsterdam and he was cold. Cold like when he'd been in that camp in America. Dieter was screwing him. He fidgeted with his shirt buttons, then walked back to the square. Fucking wetback camp. Lucky to be here now. Till he met up with that fucking Dieter! Took his money, said he had a man with good stuff, and here he was waiting and no Dieter. Should have known the shit would take off with his money. Should have followed the bitch. Fine, he was going to have to cut him, make people know he wasn't a man to fuck with, slit his fucking throat.

He wiped his forehead. Jesus, so much sweat; he was hot; hot and then cold. Maybe he'd go sit in the café, maybe do some qat. He couldn't find his way home to the Biljmer anyway. Fucking maze this Amsterdam, fucking maze, couldn't tell one building from the other, one street from the other when he was like this, all cold and sweaty. Couldn't tell who was a brother or somebody from Turkey, somebody from Surinam, all the fucking same. Too crowded. There were more people living in the Biljmer than there should be. Generations, wives, packed up in one apartment.

He couldn't stand it. Had had enough of crowded places. Fucking camps like all over. Not him. He was going to pull himself up. Get out of the stinking tenement, it smelled, smelled like everybody's dreams all chewed up, all mashed together like toes, sweating in cardboard and breath in these small spaces. They'd put these apartments up just for that, right within view of the Schiphol airport, within sound too. White brick crumbling, falling in and stinking with dreams. He hoped that when he got there, when he could stop sweating and got there, he hoped Maya wouldn't be home. She'd told him to fuck off and get out the last time she found him passed out from dope, and he'd avoided her ever since. Said he was a leech just sucking off her. He was only supposed to stay with her a few months but it had been two years now and he was worse off than when he came.

When he came. When he first came to Amsterdam it was all right. Maya had met him at Schiphol airport. He saw her before she saw him. All in pink, bright, bright pink against her dark melted skin. Her lips, pink and her smile when she saw him and smiled at him, beautiful and secretive like when they were children together in that serious house in Curaçao. Children giggling out of tension and the irrepressible childhood even their mother and father could not suppress. When she came to meet him he knew it was going to be all right as soon as he saw her.

He loved her breeziness, her way of making things good so quickly. Maya dismissed trouble. She told him, *forget it*. She was always in a hurry. Always in a hurry to herself, it looked like to him. Which was where he did not know how to go. To himself.

When they were young Adrian had wanted to please their father, but Maya had dismissed him as best she could.

She would search Adrian out across the living room when their father was in the middle of a speech and push her lips up in distaste. He would suffer, but she would listen quickly to her father as if saying to him, Hurry up, I have better things to do. One hundred times their father would say to her, "Stand when I'm talking to you." She always managed to hang one foot in the air or only face him obliquely. She kept moving through his talks and let his sentences trail off in her ears. Her better-things-to-do would be to sit on the back steps curling her hair with a hot curler, or go for a walk, against her father's bidding, through the Punda listening to the noises of hawkers and buyers, squeezing through the crammed markets, listening to life as it never was in her own house. Her better-things-to-do was to stand in the front yard feeling the sun on her closed eyelids.

All in pink, bright, bright pink, he saw her coming to meet him when he got off the plane at Schiphol airport. He couldn't help but also feel in that breeziness a little loneliness for himself. He didn't feel breezy. Light as she seemed to be, there was a part of him that could not be swept up by her. Her breeziness gave out that no one should expect anything of her that they needed, only what she could afford to give.

He was nodding off in the café. It was a small dark café he'd slipped into and sat down. He'd nodded off almost instantly, looking at the smudged menu of Thai stick, sinsemilla, qat.... The guy at the counter came over. "You can't sleep here, eh man, want me to lose my licence or what? Take off now or stay awake. No, no, take off. Just want to use my place to sleep." Fuck him and fuck Dieter too. Cut the bastard when I see him.

The qat made him feel happy anyway. He felt like dancing, he felt like getting a fucking scarf and dancing. Qat made him feel like his chest was bursting one moment with life and he wanted to dance and sing. Couldn't sell qat on the street. Nobody wanted to buy. They wanted hard stuff and Dieter was supposed to fix him today. Probably was in Brussels by now with his money.

He wasn't cold any more, he was happy. He could feel his face peeling back and he was grinning like a fool walking to his sister's. His teeth felt hard and dry as he passed the alleys and the river. Everything else was on the fucking river except the tenement. It was nowhere and he had to walk there, out in nowhere, and the trolley was slow or late or not coming. Look at them all, the fucking tourists. He laughed out loud and a few looked at him. Come to get pussy or get high. Shit. His life was their fucking holiday, any place. He laughed out loud again and couldn't stop for a few minutes. "Want some qat?" he bent over into a woman's face over a railing. She flinched and he laughed louder. He must look like shit, he wasn't going to sell shit behaving like this. Okay, okay. He'd go back to the square again and wait for the bastard.

～～～～

It must have been 2 a.m. The city stank of cigarettes and garbage, the sound of the tram cutting, its iron track squealing, grated on his skin. His skin was like something open and the street looked to him like blood gone vermilion from air. It was like thick blood gone dry already, a seam of it running right through the city, nobody else noticed it but him. It stank because blood was really flesh, and blood left stale was rotting flesh. He pulled his coat nearer to his face and felt it cold on him. He was sweating, just shedding water.

The blocks from Dam Square to the station were lit-
tered with men like him—men from everywhere, duck-
ing into coats even though it was June, a coldness running
through them, exiting and entering the streets off the square
in swift movements. Going nowhere like him, trying to figure out the next bit of money, the next laugh, the next fix.
A debris of men selling anything, anything they could lay
their hands on. Dam Square seemed haunted, though it was
bustling, haunted by these scores of men changing into other
men who looked the same. Haunted shifts of them from
Curaçao, Surinam, Africa. Once in a while an odd woman,
or a woman standing back waiting, coming forward to beg
some skeleton of a man for what was in his hand. Once in a
while a couple of quick-moving women, birdlike and with
their own ghostliness, flitted through selling anything, buying anything.

Adrian was shedding water, or was it blood? He wiped
his face and stood for a moment though his legs felt as if he
was still moving. Here he was like Kamena trying to find a
destination. Dieter. The qat was soft in his head. He wanted
something harder. Cocaine. To hit his head like a sucrier crying at night. Lift him off this square.

A year ago he could see the joy in this square, the gliding
men, the promise of ecstasy. Getting high and laughing all
night long. Tonight he saw no one was laughing and he wondered if he had ever seen it. That high he got when he first
hit Dam Square was downright joy. Tonight it was a burning fizzling low. The real square was alive with anguish, a
cordon of undone and emptied haunts. He wanted to sit
down. He wanted to bawl like a baby. He stooped near the
statue, wrapped his coat around him and hummed.

He didn't want to go back to the, Biljmer too soon.

Maya would be there, coming in or going out. He didn't want to see her, or when he saw her he didn't want to care what she said or how her face looked or that she was going out to make fares, or that she would tell him to find a job, as if he was any man who could get up in the morning and hope to find a job like any man. The city used to smell good, boy, it used to smell good when he first came, now it stank, and look his whole body was weeping, drenched in weeping. He must look like shit in his old tawny plaid coat with the dead fur collar. Maya got it for him two years ago and he'd slept in it and pissed in it and thrown up on it. No use bawling, he had to find Dieter, to whom he'd given his last hideaway money. Money he'd been stealing from Maya.

She didn't know that he'd found her little hiding place, but he had watched her with his eyes barely open one morning when she came home. She took it out of her bosom and she hid it under the head of her green dragon costume. That costume she said she used to dance in as a cabaret girl in Brugge. Once she took it out and wore it for him. Told him how white men loved her in that costume with its red tongue and how she was stunning, so stunning they wanted to touch her. She was a cabaret dancer, not a common whore, and the men gave her money, the old ones said they'd seen Josephine Baker and Maya reminded them of her.

That was where she hid her money now, he'd seen her, and two days ago he'd taken it and given it to Dieter and where the fuck was he. He couldn't go back to the apartment without it. He knew that he could double it, maybe even tell her that he'd borrowed it and give her a share, interest. He'd begged her before. Said give him some, he'd double it, triple it on the corner. She'd screamed at him, "You dirty druggy! I don't want to hear about your drugs

and shit. You're killing people, you're killing yourself."
Then he'd called her a whore. "Whore's feeding you, isn't
she, you prick."

He kept quiet, guilty anyway, this was his big sister and
if his mother heard him calling her whore she would slap
him. Maya never called him by his name any more. He
longed for her to call him by his name like before, when
they were children—"Adi, Adi," she would sing, or call him
"little brother."

In the morning he made her coffee, strong the way she
liked it. It was hard for him to say "Sorry" like he used to,
harder and harder every day, so he made her strong coffee and fried plantains like she liked them, cut thick. Then
he tried again to ask her for the money. His nervousness
wouldn't let him let her alone—ever since he saw her put
the money there after checking that he was asleep, he'd
had an excitement running through him. Juice, a loan, an
investment, look, she didn't have to risk anything, he knew
a friend. Double, triple the money in two days. She spat
the coffee into the sink and looked at him cold. New, but
getting more and more familiar, that new look of hers as if
he were a stranger, a complete stranger, no relative, let
alone brother. So he decided to steal it. By the time he
made it back she wouldn't know that it was gone. He'd
surprise her. Then it would be like when they were home
again. She would be happy with him. They would take a
few days off, go to Brussels, where she said she used to be
a cabaret dancer too, and how they loved black girls dancing in Brussels.

What were he and she trying to do here anyway? The
problem with this city was you were so far away from home,
so far away from his island whose name sounded like the

sound from the lips of a bird. He was fooling himself, he knew. Home was his childhood—not the little house in Willemstad, not the island, but his childhood. Sweet and hot days when the sun hit you just on the left side of your forehead before you woke up and the whole day was like walking with a soft mark across your face. You felt yourself drying and seasoning in the sun, you felt that if you smiled your face would melt. So home didn't matter except for that, and that you couldn't have again anyway. Or else he wouldn't be here in Amsterdam, a world away. And that was a long time ago too, so all that sentimental bullshit was a waste. He had to find that fucking Dieter. And when he did he was going to sell his ass off without taking a single taste. Then he would give the money back to Maya. Tomorrow morning he would make her strong coffee and fried plantains with cinnamon. Then they'd go to Brussels, then, well then.

Dam Square was full and noisy but it felt empty to him. His coat was cold then hot. He wondered if people were watching, if they saw how ill he was. He would walk to the station again, the station and back. He wiped his face with his jacket, feeling the wool slip in his sweat. Yes, somewhere along here he would find Dieter. He was just paranoid from the qat, that's all. Dieter wouldn't fuck with him.

Truth, everybody had fucked with him, why not Dieter? Was he stupid or what? Why, everything happened just to fuck him up. His whole life felt like a mistake. He was blind to every trick. It came from keeping his eyes closed to keep the sun out or to feel the sun stroke his face and wonder at the warm redness on the insides of his eyes. Walking to the other side in Willemstad, his father would say, "Keep your eyes open, you fool. Look where you're going. You'll fall into the water." He was just measuring the inches of the sun, making it fill his eyes. That dreaminess had caused him not to see what was coming at him any time.

―――――

The chill on his bare skin that night in America, the barbed wire of the INS camp keeping him from the world and a life. He'd ended up in that camp with Haitians and Colombians and Panamanians, all like him picked up for being illegal aliens. Not even then did he wake up to the fact that everybody was trying to fuck him up. The cold sweat on his skin glistening and somebody trying to fuck him up the ass in that barbed-wire prison, somebody he'd have to try to turn around and kill, not because he didn't want the warmth of another body but because this ass-fucking was for points and power, not love, and the next morning he had to be still fresh and dangerous for this camp. Wouldn't mind if it had an ounce of tenderness in it, but it couldn't, not here. Even if he noticed that the man touched him almost tenderly, felt him softly, kissed his hands in his own moment of weakness, he had to put him down. You could always mistake these things and then you're gone. The man whispered, "Querido." He thought that he saw iron in his eyes and he had to break his jaw, iron and all, tenderness and all, because he could not be sure, and the other meant that the next morning he would be easy prey, his shoes, his socks, his cigarettes, his pants gone. Then he'd have to sit all day on the benches begging for his pants, bargaining for his cold balls and paying and paying. So he broke his jaw. No *querido*, not here. No, he'd learned *querido* off the coast of Venezuela. In fishing boats carrying men like him, not men yet, but with somewhere to leave and nowhere to go. Fuck that, fuck *querido*.

Everything passed through the waters off the Main, and he was going to pass also, taking anything they wanted him to take, their coke, their crack, their ganja, their sperm if they wanted. Tenderness—well, sometimes they gave it. These were the only men he knew and that was where he learned tenderness. No, he didn't have some kind teacher, just a fisherman who didn't look like a fisherman, who asked him to come with him, carry a package strapped to his groin, the back of his dick, and who touched his dick while taping him up. He felt his fisherman's rough hand go tender and his dick seemed to jump into life. His fisherman was behind him and stopped, taking his ass into his hands instead and rubbing his rough fisherman's clothes into his opening buttock. That was his tenderness. Then he felt something like a knife in his ass and the hoarse voice of his fisherman saying, "Take it, *puto*."

That was it for tenderness. His blood felt like it was coming out of his ears and he should have turned around and looked at the iron in his fisherman's face and broken his jaw but he didn't. He felt broken into and cracked and weak from the shock of something inside him that wasn't there ever before. In the first moments and the rough hand going soft, he didn't look at his eyes for iron or anything, and he vowed the next time he would have to take him.

The fisherman finished taping his dick when it was done and looked at him as if nothing had happened. Nothing like tenderness now. "Get on the boat. When you come within close sight of the Main stop there. Shut the engine off.... Take out the pole. Fish. Someone will meet you. Careful you give it to the right one. The boat will say *El Socorro*."

He waited all day in the middle of the ocean, fishing, dazed, feeling broken. The gulf looked like silver winking.

Sometimes he felt that he was on land and that wave was a mountain or a street. The sun burned down on his head. His baseball cap was still on the sand on that other beach with his fisherman. He passed his hand over his head, he was twenty and had just been fucked and he was sitting in the middle of the ocean feeling broken.

All his blood was in his ears and his fingertips all day long, and bursting from his jaw. The tape on his dick was itchy, or was his dick itchy?

He looked down and wondered if he had passed water in his pants or was it sweat or the thought of his fisherman. He hadn't seen the Main now in quite a while, but he didn't know what quite a while was. He was drifting away and something burst through his nose and it was fear that he was in the wrong place and the fisherman would think that he had sailed off with the kilo taped to his dick. He wanted to start the boat up but he felt dizzy and the quiet was so still, so quiet that he didn't want to make noise. But the sun burned his head and he wanted to go. The boat was an insect with its two fishing poles on either side, an insect with the fisherman's eyes and the fisherman's smell. Why didn't he just turn the engine on and head for the Main, disappear with the dope taped to his leg? What reason did he have for going back? It looked as if he could step out of the boat and walk on the street of the ocean, the sidewalk was glittering. He reached to touch the road, silver and hard, and did not stop until his face was buried in water, and salt burned his eyes.

He swallowed water and couldn't stop coughing. He had swallowed the whole ocean. His nose sprayed blood and water now, and nothing told him to take his head out of the water, nothing told him to breathe, and his hands grabbed the road of water and pushed hard. For a while he thought he could breathe water—it was running in his veins and he wasn't in the boat but deep in the ocean where he had come from in the first place. "Boto, bayena!" his great-grandmother fluted like a trumpet fish when her father came to visit her mother in Culebra Bay. Days it took her father to cross the water, stopping at coves and inlets. His solemn face broke into light when he saw his daughter. One day he would take her home, and Bola too if she would come, but he knew that Bola wouldn't. Bola would not be held. She was the most alone woman he had known. He tried to know her but all he left with each time was a sense of her as the only inhabitant of her life. Culebra seemed empty when he looked into her eyes. Even when they were most together, in her fibre bed in her shack, the children skimming along the beach like blue herons, he could not say that he felt her close. All his lovemaking with her felt like swift tides, caerulean waves of water and senses. He felt overturned. As if she was going one way and he another and he tried to hold her but she slipped out of his hands like the moon. He would have this daughter, serious as he, and he would find a woman to take care of her. He would take her home and come off the water—this endless water with no destination.

Adrian heard an engine close to his ear. The sea water was already in his veins but he heard an engine or some big fish gurgling. "Hey, what the fuck, he trying to kill himself? Oy, *puto*."

The boat jerked and his head reached up for air or whatever was not sea now and he had to breathe air which was as foreign as the water before. Two men, shining like his fisherman, their hair sugary from the sun, calling, "Aye, *puto*, where's the message?"

El Socorro, El Socorro spun in his head. Air made him gasp. The boat was *El Socorro*. He turned from them, opened his fly and untaped the package. They laughed. *Mierda, pendejos*. He turned back, his face changing from water to wood. He was no *puto*. He took out his dick and pissed in the water in front of them, looked at them hard, then threw the package into their boat. He stood there holding all the weapon he had.

They seemed to give up and threw a package into his boat, then turned toward the Main and left. He stayed. Stayed for the rest of the day in the middle of the ocean. Then when the sky could scarcely hold itself open he started the engine. Headed back for his fisherman. *El Socorro, El Socorro. Come*, his brain added, his childhood added, his mother added, the mud church on the outskirts of Willemstad added, *Come and I will make you fishers of men*. He wanted to throw the package away and disappear into the bottom of the sea with it but no, the boat kept heading toward the fisherman, toward the shore. *El Socorro*. And when the ocean swallowed the sun he was there. He bent into the boat, picked up a thick rope knotted on the end, the tether, and his hands brushed and grated against it and he held it and watched the fisherman come toward him. "Come, come, *puto*." What he wanted to feel, which was hatred, he didn't feel, but he held the rope. Nothing like that was going to happen to him again.

So he showed him the rope when he walked toward him, but it wasn't him it was some other *puto*, softer, didn't look at him hard, businesslike, saying his fisherman wasn't coming, counting out money and taking the package from him, saying, "Be here Tuesday, same spot."

He carried the rope with him next Tuesday, tied it to his

waist, hanging from a loop but he again took the package from some other *puto* and taped it to his leg himself this time, and took the boat and went out the meet the two or whoever it was going to be.

He was never sure of what he was delivering, money or dope or just somebody fucking with him. When they gave him bigger packages he thought it had to be guns, but whatever it was he was too scared to find out, too scared to open it and see. He had only enough courage for pissing in the water, carrying his rope and doing what they said. One day he'd get more. He walked the waters off the Main, walked them like streets and dipped his whole head in the whole ocean and swallowed salt looking for the fisherman.

He didn't want to work in the refinery. He wanted to get a boat and run back and forth against the sea. He didn't want to be small, he wanted to handle big life, feel money in his pocket, rubbing against his balls. So when a fisherman called him with his finger one day and asked if he could drive a boat, get some fish out in the ocean, down the Main, his legs sprang water, he wanted to pee, he could taste the big life coming. He had prowled around the bay in Willemstad for months. A piece of fish here, an apple from a cruise ship, an offer to fuck one of the white ladies who came to the market. Offers, but he heard they had AIDS, all of them. That was the rumour flying among the beach boys. He was careful, telling them they would love it when he used his mouth, thinking that would save him, telling them they were beautiful. All day hustling them because he knew they'd have to leave with the ship and by then he'd be fed. Saying he'd take them around, beautiful places, he had a house, showing them someone's house on a hill saying it was being repaired, that's why he couldn't take them there right now, telling them they had taken his heart the moment he'd seen them come off the ship.

He was tired and looking for something steady, looking for something to get him off the island if one of these ladies would take him maybe, but then he'd never have money of his own and his stories wouldn't do, wouldn't last past the moment the ship gave way to water. He was looking for something solid like a boat and a fisherman with a package. Steady money. Hard money. He'd seen them, fishermen who didn't fish, their insect boats, two fishing lines and swift new engines.

He carried the rope for protection and in case he ever met his fisherman again or in case his fisherman had spread rumours. He wanted the money but not for being fucked up the ass, for sitting out in the ocean looking for *El Socorro* and pissing in the water.

In the year on the water, duct tape on his leg, he had never heard his own name. He thought he'd forgotten it. How would he tell anyone now. A name was a liability. And anyway, by the time the world was finished with you, you were not your name. You didn't feel in your skin. How could anyone tell their true name? Why would they tell? They must have thought that he spoke only Spanish or French, or maybe they didn't care.

The men in the detention camp were from everywhere, Paramaribo, French Guiana, the Essequibo, anywhere full of mountains, bush, shanty cities and rivers, anywhere. They had cut cane and hustled vegetables, dug drains and spread pitch, gone to America or Canada to pick peaches or oranges, and if they couldn't run away there or fall in love with a white woman they had gone back. Looking good and talking big until the money was done and they waited for next year, buying the number from the officers so they could go back again. Gone to Quebec, gone to Florida, California. Peaches apples grapes oranges artichokes broccoli. Walked up from Caracas to Belmopan City to Panama City to Mexico to Texas. Walking and running; crossed rivers coming out in wet clothes and moss. They'd sat nights smoking cigarettes cupped in their hands to keep the smell secret.

Up here or down the Main to Brazil or Colombia. He had had to decide. The Main, not an island but a land that is endless, so thick and big at times you might not see ocean water for months and years. The men who fished and the men who played *waroo* said there were cold places there in the interior, colder than any night and colder than water. And that there were rivers and falls and impenetrable forests that only Carifuna people could enter, because they are old like that and know some magic words and they know where there are poisons and they can turn into snakes.

He thought of going down the Main. Hadn't Kamena rolled under the sky and felt the feathery hearts of birds? He could perhaps learn this hermetic magic but all in him was quivering for warm rooms and the touch of people. He'd taken his chances with trembling men and women and children going to America, crossing borders of uniforms and bribes and muddy water and knifings and rapes and hunger. His chances. After measuring the dread of returning to Curaçao against the dread of the water and the sure signs of jail, after ignoring the logic of drowning himself in the Caribbean sea, he'd arrived in that camp in Florida on the backs of coyotes.

So no, not here in this camp in America too. Was there something in his face or what? He wasn't going to be anybody's pussy. He broke the man's jaw and sent him broken against the wire, hauled his face across it ripping it, and he was not sorry and he was sorry all at once. This Cuban, Haitian, islander, fisherman, iron beater, welder, cane cutter, farmer, oil driller, sweeper or prisoner was going to be the dope tomorrow, not him. He skimmed the chill on his chest turning to water when he remembered the fisherman and he saw the fisherman's face and felt the fisherman's hands soften on his balls, and he punched with his bare knuckles when his dick came to life remembering. That's the kind of tenderness a man gives a man, his broken face and his swollen hand breaking it. He didn't ride those coyotes for nothing, which is how he ended up in that camp smashing some *gusano's* jawbone. Sweat forming on his skin and the *gusano's* hard face crumbling soft is what he remembered.

He had become dangerous now, even if the shrinking at his core was something he was going to have to ignore. It would never interrupt him he swore to himself every day when he woke up and felt it gnaw his brain. He smashed his lover's jaw and smoked a cigarette. No one in the yard said a word, the curfew sounded and he strolled to the tents with the others. The *gusano* was still lying on the ground near the fence. He heard the guards telling him to get up and he saw him holding his bloody face coming in. He had to get the fuck out of here now. He didn't want to be the *puto* but he didn't want to be the boss either. He slept and he dreamed of water.

He didn't want to meet the man they called Priest. The camp was so big, so many fuckers trying to keep the chill off their bodies, so many heads in the hoods of sweatshirts, he was sure that he could hide out until he figured his way out. This is not where he had intended to be anyway, he had just gotten swept up in a raid. He didn't know what posse the guy whose face he'd fucked up was in but he didn't want to be no badass. He just wanted to be left alone to figure his way out of here.

He'd heard about someone they called Priest in the camp. Another *puto* running dope and trying to fuck everybody up just to prove that he was a big man. Well, all Adrian wanted to do now was disappear. Why did a man always have to prove he had big balls. Shit, some days you just want to lie down and die and tell them you give up but they won't let you. If you lay down they'd just kick you until you stood up. They'd just tell you you're a man, you can't lie down, you got to get yourself a boner, it don't matter. They wouldn't let you lie down, and it would be some other man just like you doing it, standing over you offering you a cigarette, lifting up your dick for you and saying here this is what you're supposed to do, not lie there like a pussy, if you lie there like a pussy then I'm a pussy too, then what the hell's going to happen, who are we all going to fuck up? So no, he didn't want to meet Priest because he didn't want to meet another fucker who wanted to play this dick-lifting thing.

He slept and he dreamed of water, then he dreamed of the barren cactus-filled island he was from, and then he dreamed of water again, and again. He woke up restless, then fell again into a kind of waking sleep and furious dreams of fear.

He was sitting on the floor in a big cold storage room, there were flowers all over. The room was refridgerated and there were police. Half awake, he was dreaming the raid of the floral company he lugged flowers for. His fingertips were cold and discoloured green. The police were yelling for papers. The floor was wet and freezing and now he saw the rest, the flowers tumbling, all the other illegals, women, men sitting on the cold wet floor in the refrigeration warehouse. He wrenched himself from half sleep to half waking. He was thirsty and his underarms and crotch were wet with sweat.

When he woke up he was standing at the door looking at himself waking up sweating. The man at the door was smiling, something like astonishment on his face, which was the same as how he felt but he knew he wasn't smiling, and he wasn't at the door, he was lying in his sweat, so the man at the door must be different. Did he wake up that morning different, so different that he could stand at the door and look at himself smiling? So when the man at the door said, "Priest, cuz. Son of a bitch," he knew that it wasn't he at the door but some fucking joke, some fucking joke as usual. Whoever put him on the earth was playing him again. The man resembled him and if he hadn't seen Dovett, his father, in his grave after the oil refinery goons broke his head in, if he hadn't seen his father's mashed-up face held together by bad embalming fluid, if he hadn't thrown dirt on that grave and turned his back, pitying his father and saying in his mind that he wasn't going to die for no stupidness like him, if he hadn't regretted saying that, and crossed himself one hundred times to be forgiven for speaking ill of his fucking stupid dead father; if he hadn't, he would swear that his father was standing at the door smiling some kinda wicked smile at him because his arse was freezing and he was wet with sweat in this hellhole.

Of all the fucked-up things to happen he had to meet his spitting image in a deportee camp. He didn't even feel like feeling wonder but he was frightened and that kept his eyes open and dragged him into the feeling of wanting to go back to sleep all at once. But his body was doing the opposite of what his head was doing. Fear stood him up and made him scream. Scream or yell or something, "*Carajo pendejo*! What the fuck . . . ." The man saying, "Cuz, you must be, well I'll be damned, shit."

The man was as startled as he, he realized, but he had something else in his face, something he knew he didn't— jumping up like he was crazy from his wet bunk, frightened to death breaking out in new sweat, "What the fuck, man. . . ." The man was frightened, but he had some other way of controlling it, or at least he'd learned to smooth over every experience into that smile, which he'd cultivated to look a little dangerous too. The man had learned to sum up people and situations quickly, and when he couldn't sum them up he would overwhelm them by some charm, some thing he'd give them that he knew everybody wanted, like happiness. That way he'd cut across whatever was unknowable in them and make whoever he handled think they were ordinary, just wanted happiness and he could get it for them. So his face, this Priest's, was frightened too, but smooth.

All Priest's senses were working, trying to figure out how to angle this new almost double of his and most likely some family, some long-ago child of some man like him, some man in his family, God knows from where, some man repeating himself or perhaps himself, because he had children he didn't even know and why shouldn't some other man in his line have fathered this one and repeated Priest, just like Priest was a repetition of a man, or a woman for that matter, somewhere now dead anyway.

Priest's face was smooth, a rough smooth but smooth, and Adrian knew that he was slipping into it the way you slip into a lie, the way one friend walking along with another, their feet kicking outward in front of them and nothing in the pockets of their jeans, the way a lie is all that keeps them moving. He was buying whatever Priest was selling because he didn't want to be frightened. He wanted to be calm, so he saw Priest's promise of happiness instead of all the rest; the long hard life and the things he'd done that made him wipe his hands with money, the things he'd done that made him open his mouth every ten minutes to crack the tension from his jaw, the things that moved him to nasty anger.

Adrian let all that pass and he saw happiness where Priest let him see it. After he couldn't get anything out of his mouth he let Priest talk. "Shit, you must be family. Where the fuck you from? Home? Who your people? From Abyssinia, Culebra, Port-of-Spain?" Priest ran down the genealogy known to him,

"Venezuela? you one of them 'Pañol ones?"

When Adrian answered what he could understand he said, "Curaçao."

"Curaçao? Curaçao? What the mother's arse is this? Curaçao? Can hardly talk English! What the cunt is this? Curaçao? What you name? What you name, man?"

"Adrian."

"Adrian? What the arse kinda name is that? Curaçao? Jesus fucking Christ! Adrian who? Adrian who?"

He didn't answer when he remembered that he'd given a Cuban name to the camp, Jorge Guerrero. He wondered why just because they resembled each other would he give this man his real name. And Priest, understanding that shock and enthusiasm had taken him over too, made an odd noise on his next word and whispered, "Adrian who?"

"Dovett," Adrian whispered back as if they were children

now. He was twelve and this boy was sixteen and they were trading secrets. They were walking along a road on his island, skipping school and exchanging secrets.

"Dovett, I don't know no Dovett. You look like a sonofabitch Childs. I sure you is my blood."

But it wasn't a road on an island or a road anywhere, it was a camp for *gusanos* and boat people and runaways, a place like all places like this, as far back as any blood between Adrian and Priest would go. It was both the place Kamena wanted to find and the place he was running from all mixed up in one catastrophe of high fences and guards. Refugees and prisoners all in the same singular bodies. Prisoners who were begging their jailers for refuge. There was a hunger holding out there and restless. Adrian didn't know what to feel, fear or happiness or that other feeling growing inside him of defeat when faced with the image of his father, of himself.

Dovett. He hadn't said his own name for a long time. Anyway he had come to think of it as his father's name, not his. It was what his mother called his father. Dovett. By his last name. She said it as if it were a talisman when she threatened him and Maya with beatings. "Dovett will hear about your behaviour." She said it loud and threatening to "Dovett" himself. "Dovett!" she would call, no matter what the circumstance, tenderness or anger. And Dovett would appear, serious and short and dark and thick. Quiet as his great-grandfather Dovett who had been a fisherman following whales in the Gulf of Paria, looking for his chance to run away from his indenture, hoping that the whale would take the boat clear into the broad Atlantic. Till a woman named Bola, who made love like a swift wave, gave that Dovett a nine-year-old girl with a serious face to take with him one day. Cryptic as that woman Bola who spread her children around so that all would never be gathered in the same place to come to the same harm. Quiet as his grandmother, teaching herself to read in lamplight after washing and ironing mountains of clothes, and quiet as his grandmother's son, Dovett's father who took a job in the first oilfield and who burnt up there.

Dovett with all his quietness could not persuade Adrian to take a job in the oilfield with him, not after telling him about his own father's flaming run home one Thursday. That Thursday, Dovett's father had gone the four miles to work. It was the rough and early days of oil. Every week a well blew, every month someone was killed. This Thursday was Dovett's father's turn. The well blew sending fire into his plaid shirt that his mother, the serious-eyed girl, had ironed fresh that morning. Dovett's father had one thought, to go home to his mother so that she could douse his whole body in water. He fled the oil field, running all the way home, a ball of blackening, brightening fire. His whole body aflame he ran all the way to his mother thinking of her, ironing; the one thought in his head of her sprinkling water over him to cool him. She would sprinkle him like a shirt or a linen sheet and he would exhale all the heat burning his skin. When he arrived home he was singed to nothing and fell on the door- step calling his mother to put the flames out.

This story Dovett told his children, Adrian and Maya. He was a small boy himself when it happened. He remem- bered the wail of his own mother and a bright heat at the door, a ball of flame falling and the smell of his father burn- ing. When he told this story his face glowed as if from his father's fire. He himself never forgot and went to work in those oilfields and carried his father like a talisman, a sign that those fields owed him his father's life and they would pay. Dovett worked and agitated in his bitter serious way, and marked himself for beatings by the anti-union goons.

"You're a soft man," Dovett said to him before Adrian left home. "You're a soft man. You're not a Dovett." He said this with finality and pity when Adrian didn't want to follow him into the oilfields and come home like every other man smelling of petrol, smelling of chemicals; seeing his fingertips and palms go stained black until they could not wash out any longer, could not wash the smell out or wash the stain off; burnt here and there, a finger gone like nothing, scars across his face like all the other men. His father said it quietly, making Adrian feel ashamed, his palms soft and sweaty. "You're a soft man." And then he, Dovett himself, went off to battle Shell in the oilfields and to end up with a goon's truncheon to the side of his face and dead.

Adrian came home for the funeral six months after he had left. He threw dirt on Dovett's grave as his mother instructed. He could swear that his father still saw even with his embalmed eyes; he could swear that his father saw his fluttering. He was drowned in the sea of purple- and black-dressed people who came to see his father off. They poured into the church and into the burial ground. They wept, big men, wide women. They were men and women who worked in the oilfield like him, men and women who had called Dovett "Steel." They looked at Adrian with pity—some for his loss but most, he felt, for his weakness.

His sister Maya stood at the grave too but he could see that she was impatient with them all, impatient with her father. Impatient to leave and stop all this crying and for once get on with what she wanted to do. Adrian watched his mother losing all authority, her hands in her lap on a chair at the graveside, her hands almost losing their fleshiness. He watched her leaving all of her mind in the grave with Dovett.

That day, the first day without Dovett, they all broke into pieces and disintegrated. No one could hold on to the other. They all ran off and began to do what they thought they had been prevented from doing while he was alive. Dovett had been the quiet centre of them. He had told stories too well and his children had been too imaginative. Stories he had told for lessons in discipline had inspired both of them to indecision, stories of redemption had taught them only to take what was going in this life and quickly, even voraciously, and stories of courage had taught them to flinch, run like hell. And the seminal story, the story of their burning grandfather, the story of their incandescent ancestry, which Dovett told as if he knew that he too was heading into a goon's truncheon, as if this were their destiny and their duty, it flared and burned their dreaming eyes....

It was the last story Dovett told them each night, and it was the one that Maya was so impatient to leave and Adrian immersed his head in water to stop. He breathed the end of the story with relief the day his father was buried. He had failed in understanding some burning thing he only wished he understood. The expectation that it should make him strong and lead him into the oilfield as well, that expectation confused him, it paralysed him.

The crowd of his father's friends and admirers surrounding him, dressed in mournful purple and black, made him dizzy. He felt their communal rebuke, the weight of their loss of a man who led them and made them hope for better. They made the dirt in his hand seem meagre. If he had any sadness for his father dying they took it back and told him he was unworthy of sadness. Even his hand seemed meagre extending over Dovett's grave. Sadness was too wonderful for him.

Priest got the name out of Adrian—"Dovett"—and his story filled him up as it usually did and he wondered how his mother was. He had not written or seen her since the day after the funeral. He had tried to slip away in the early morning but she had awakened, going to the kitchen to make him cocoa and bread, talking all the time, not wanting to see what was in his face. She talked about when he was a boy and how his father had taught him to walk up his entire body, holding his hands and leaning backward, and how his father taught him to dance with his small feet on Dovett's large ones.

He watched her stir the cocoa tea and remembered dancing with his father because that was what she wanted to remember and for a moment he wanted to remember it too. It was when his father came home at night smelling of oil and tobacco, and he would eat in silence at the table by himself and after he would put on the radio and take Adrian in his arms and dance him. And when Adrian was old enough to walk, Dovett would set his small feet on his and dance to Duke Ellington and Pete de Vlut. He remembered the smell of smoked tobacco leaves and he remembered the smell of crude oil. He felt the rough touch of his father's fingers gripping his small hands and he remembered looking down at his feet on his father's feet, dancing.

After the funeral, his mother had kept him with that memory. He'd spent the day trying to leave her, moving from one room to the other. Going outside she said from behind him, "Don't go out into the sun, it's too hot." As if he were still her child. Once she said, "Lie down and take a little rest," knowing he would leave if she took her eyes off him.

He waited until she was exhausted from trying to keep him and had to rest her eyes. "Your sister will be leaving soon too," she murmured, falling off to sleep, and then he waited almost too long, saddened by her knowledge that he wanted to go, and desperate now, wanting to leave before his sister.

He left walking fast up the road, hoping that his mother's sleep would last long enough. He headed on, breaking into a run, running, knowing that she was looking after him. She was standing at the window her head resting on her hand, her hand resting on the wood, the curtain parted wide. He could feel her frame diagonal in the open window watching him go. He felt her reproach and her sadness, and as if she were ending.

The two of them had left her, he and Maya both, as if only Dovett had held them to her. They'd left her as if they hadn't come from her belly and when they remembered they remembered as if Dovett was her child and they were his. She took care of him and he chastened them.

He was tired of running away from men who were like iron, men who prided themselves on knowing everything even if they didn't. These men like his father made a lot of mistakes with other people's lives. They were so certain. They left him speechless because in the end he couldn't be so sure of anything. Most of all how to make himself like these men.

~~~~~~~~~~

He was still between Dam Square and the train station, deciding to go to Maya's. Home. Her money gone with Dieter. He didn't know what to tell her. Deny taking it for one thing, just deny it. Fuck it. Fuck her anyway. Off in her own self she didn't give a shit about him. She could make it back quicker that he. The one good thing she'd done for him was send him a ticket from New York to Amsterdam after he had begged her for months, months of a slow-burning hatred between him and Priest.

A man, passing, brushed against him and he felt as if he had been touched intimately and he felt fear and he remembered Priest again. The last time he'd seen him. Priest had told him to meet a guy in an underground parking lot over on Fulton. The guy had shot him, just like that. A guy he was used to meeting. Out of the blue, just shot him, and grabbed his bag.

When he made his way back to the store, his wounded hand wrapped in his coat, because he couldn't call the police, Priest didn't believe him. His hand was bloody, he showed Priest and all Priest said was, "You make the man rob you and you en't dead? How come you en't dead, eh?"

Adrian couldn't say anything. He laughed, the pain burning in his hand. He laughed, thinking how he always got caught in his own stupidity, he always got caught in something he just didn't understand about people. And Priest misunderstood his laughter. "You think I get born yesterday, eh?" And he couldn't stop laughing, which probably saved him because Priest couldn't figure it out. Why Adrian was laughing in his face holding his bloody hand out to him. If Priest didn't believe in *obeah*, in magic, in God, he would have shot him himself, right then, but he saw the boy's face, the spitting image of himself, laughing at him and he was revolted by his hand. He noticed that Adrian's eyes were feverish and the sudden don't-care of him made Priest tingle with remembrance.

He didn't shoot because he thought that it might feel like killing himself.

~~~

Adrian's high is cascading in, and the lights on Dam Square seem yellow and small and it is cold. The usual busyness of the streets he can't seem to catch and step into himself. And Dieter isn't coming. No, the bitch, Dieter, isn't coming. Now he's in deep shit with Maya. And he's cold and his high is cascading in, tumbling in on him. Things fall into an ocean, he thinks, like bodies and small pieces of buckles, and bits of shirt cuffs, cloth washed threadbare. Things that eventually belong in the sea and are indescribable on land. Sometimes you find that the smallest grain of sand was a button once. Water is like road if you really think of it.

He has thought of plucking his eyes out. He has covered them with his hands walking whole days like that through Amsterdam. He's sat full days staring at the sun—this last gives him blindness for a while and then he sees a tingling sheet of gold and lemon. He has to go home. Standing on Dam Square, he turns and heads with no certainty, he heads for someone he knows.

~~~

All he could do was lie on the floor in the kitchen. He felt himself convulse as if he were spewing up an ocean and he imagined sea turtles and sea cockroaches coming out of his mouth. His head was dipped in water, in big blue water. Someone was stepping over him and leaving out a doorway. He heard red rustling and smelled feathers. He heard a door slam. And his mouth was open, spitting an endless stream of shells and bitten bone and small white sea insects. He never wants to see the world again.

He woke up to a burning pain in his eyes.

He could hear the trolley, he could hear voices, feet. He smelled crêpes, sweet, metallic sweet and brown. He smelled sugar burning. He smelled the street. He remembered his dream of the ocean spitting from his mouth, he remembered the sun's white light. He saw white heat. He was somewhere outside. There were people running, shouting. He had a burning pain in his eyes and he couldn't see the sun where the burning was coming from.

He remembered doors. He was back in the street. On the square. The back of his head burned. He remembered looking for someone. His fingers were holding something soft, wet. His coat was missing. He was hot. He sat up to see what was in his hands. He couldn't see. There was a burning in his head and people running, shouting. He called out. His words were slurry. He wanted to ask what was going on. His tongue was heavy. He couldn't see. His head was falling. A warm metal liquid was running down his face, he wiped it on his shoulder. He felt his skin. Where was his shirt. The liquid ran into his mouth, he spat. It tasted like blood. His skin was burning, a stinging spreading burning. Like a high starting at the back of his neck. He couldn't see. He called out. Something soft, slippery, was in his hands. He remembered thinking that he never wanted to see the world again. Never. His eyes were in his hands.

IN A WINDOW

———〰〰〰〰〰———

Maya is standing in the window. This is where she is. Framed in a window. This second. Not what comes after and not what came before. She wishes that this moment were all she must live. Right here in the window, framed just so. The left corner, glass and air and the wooded floor shafts angled to the right and the end of the floor mat. This moment framed in a window, every area of space and air composed. She begins in the left corner. Her leg, oiled and smooth, her right leg, planed to her ankle, her right ankle, a fine gold chain cutting the deep brown of her, just one shade of glimmering darker then lighter, her toes unvarnished and perfect, thick, flat, blood purple.

The sun opens the floorboards to light, the light shafts gradually toward her ankle, moves up her body like a brush, feathery. She watches herself in half light and half dark and it is this preoccupation with herself that makes someone stop at the window. Though it is not a seduction but a genuine fascination with the sun creeping up her ankle. And when there was no sun, just the light, the cold dowdy winter light of Amsterdam, the damp light and the grey light, it adds degrees to her concentration. None of this is seduction. And then it is. It is hard play. The window is as calm as it is brittle. Except for the calm in Maya, it is brittle.

The first time that she stepped into the window she thought, "What am I doing here? Why am I on show? Why am I in this window?" And the questions had caught her just so in the window. Paralysed her. What had made her step into the window so casually when inside, at the time, she felt a furious panic. All of her blood sang in her ears. The glass window shaped the lookers outside standing in front of cars, or walking by, glancing at her. She'd felt if only she could turn stiff, stand still as if she were a mannequin then they'd take it for a fashion display and pass on or stand and stare at her inanimation. She had arrived at the window oddly thinking that it was the most ordinary place in the world. A place to look in and look out. A simple transparent place, a place to see and to be seen and therefore a place where complications were clear and strangely plain.

She had not bargained on discomfort. She had thought that once she stepped into the window a preciseness would take over. Yet her first days were self-conscious and she wished that she could turn stiff. Then as a distraction she looked closely at the window itself noticing light and its movement and she remembered the dappling light of early mornings in Curaçao turning quickly, plunging to the heated stark light of midmornings and noons, and then the slow laborious burning flare of afternoons and the brutal dart of night. She witnessed the light on her hands and skin.

So she turned inward to these meditations, picking up where she had left off after her father's speeches, picking up curling her hair with the iron comb on the back steps and

standing in the front yard making the sun warm and heat
her eyelids to a furious pink glow.

She tried making the lookers feel comfortable at first
but that only made her uncomfortable so she made her own
tableaux where she was happy. A chair and a table where
she could have a glass of wine or a beer. A straight-backed
wooden chair and a wooden table. A table she could put her
leg up on when she got tired, and a pack of cards. She liked
cards. And she would dress in her half-slip and her chemise
and some days she would just wear her jeans and merino.

But she decided that she would do whatever she wanted
in her tableau. She didn't look out the window all the time
but thought her own thoughts and if she happened to look
up so be it. Whatever Walter the manager said she didn't
follow, and she didn't have to, because she had clients, sometimes more than the others whom he told to stand so and so
and look out the window and act innocent or act sexy. Pussy
was wasted on women, he'd say, just wasted. He'd make
that thing work for him if he had one. No homo shit, that
wasn't what he was thinking, just plain and simple—pussy
was wasted on women. A man would know how to work
that shit.

He was an idiot. Fucking pimp, she thought, which was
worse than what she was. It was her pussy and he wouldn't
tell her how to sell it. He didn't have one, and that was his
problem. Fucking jealous that's what he was, wished he had
one, wished he could sell it. Oh no, he wasn't queer, he said,
he was a fucking man who wished he had a pussy because it
was a good commodity, he said, and he'd know how to sell
it better than them.

She wouldn't let Walter tell her how to stand, he could
just do it himself if he didn't like the money she was making.

Her tableaux became more and more casual and this is what attracted her customers. Sometimes she would read a book, burying her face in it, and then they would only see her legs and her bare feet disappearing into the shade of the day, sometimes she braided her hair and drank a bottle of wine, sometimes she looked at her fingers, the dark half moons at the quick of her nails. One day she put on a plastic lizard's head with a red tongue slithering out. One day she turned her back. That day Walter was furious and threatened to fire her and let her walk the street instead of sitting in his gilded window any more. But that day her withdrawal caused more sensation than the window had ever known. Soon she did this every few weeks, attracting those customers with a penchant for harassment, those who hated not being noticed and those who wanted to commit murder anonymously.

Sex, Maya discovered, was lethal. In the little rooms at the back she warded off violence even from the meekest-looking men. Their concentration and efforts were agonized slashes of movements used for destroying things. Her or themselves.

Her movement from frontal pose to backward was because, despite her efforts, she was beginning to read the thoughts of everyone passing and those who stopped terrified her. The moment they stopped she could tell that they were not satisfied with themselves and needed a distraction to stop themselves from committing suicide and what could be more distracting than trying to commit murder.

She knew that it was not desire in their eyes but something worse. Desire was already too elusive for them. They could not catch it, so they came and stood in front of her window pretending desire, even longing for it. She could feel their anger disguised in a smile or smirk; their grave joy at the thought of someone to overpower, someone to order around. Take that off, give me this, do it here, they would say, never succumbing to themselves but wishing her to succumb. By the end of it they left feeling coarser, but pretending they had felt something, even as they boasted to themselves and friends that they had overpowered the woman in the window. So when she could stand it no longer she turned her back. In a short while she knew too much about the men who stood in front of her window.

Unknown to Walter, she took one on privately. He asked for nothing. He was as short as she was tall, as white as she was black. He bought her white flowing clothes. He took her to Vlisingen on Sundays, to the beach where he, dressed in black, and she, dressed in white, walked all afternoon. Then he drove her to a small bar in a Flemish town where he was born and they drank Camparis and he treated the whole bar and showed her off and then he gave her four hundred guilders and drove her back to her window in Amsterdam until another Sunday.

Sometimes he took her to musky rich men's clubs of stockbrokers. He wanted her for the show, like the expensive ring on his baby finger and the gold chain buried in the white hair on his chest. He walked her like an exotic, showed her like spun silk from some other country. Maya's job she knew was to drink Camparis and remain aloof, shoo his friends away with disgust and light his cigar. She, on these Sundays, was his way of knowing the world like a sophisticate, a man who crossed boundaries and therefore a man who was dangerous.

The four hundred guilders she hid in her private place, hiding them against her brother. He had been living with her more than a year now in the Biljmer, and she could keep nothing since he stole everything, and whined, and walked in cold sweats, begging her to let him stay each time she threatened to put him out. She was saving in order to leave the violence behind the window, the violence she sensed that she was warding off, or tempting, with the domesticity of her tableaux.

Perhaps this was what women who married men did, she thought. Puttered and puttered at domesticity, fixing curtains and chairs and lamps, decorating the abattoir where they were soon slaughtered; primped and laid out doilies and candles to sup up the odours of violence; kept their own fingers busy with cooking so they themselves wouldn't cut a throat, and perfumed themselves so as not to smell their own fear and rage. Perhaps her mother had done this. Puttered and puttered staving off some violence she sensed in Dovett. Or some violence she sensed in herself.

Years ago now she had left her mother standing in a window waiting for someone to come home. Her mother, smelling of rage and fear and too weak to express them, expressed, finally, helplessness. She had said nothing. It had been understood between them longer than Maya could remember that she would never stay to hold her mother up when Dovett died. She would never remain a day longer than she had to, and that meant the day after Dovett died, when she could finally persuade her mother to give her the money she was saving to leave. There had been too many moments when her mother sided with Dovett against her. She and her mother had an understanding of looks. They had an understanding of decisions made without a word. What they had expected of each other was never loyalty.

Her mother, Maya suspected, had not wanted much of her, had seen her as disappointing her hopes to deliver to

Dovett a first-born boy. Dovett had expected children and her mother had delivered them. Other than that she suspected her mother's wish was to be filled up by Dovett, to be in every room with him, to have him breathe every breath of air for her. Dovett had saved money for Maya to go and become a nurse. He wanted her to return to be a nurse in the hospital in Willemstad. When Maya left that was what she had fully intended, to become a nurse, though not to return home. Nearing Amsterdam, up in the plane, life seemed to start again. And on the drive from Schiphol to the Biljmer, where Rita her schoolgirl friend lived, Dovett's voice, his last hold on her, seemed to let go. To be a nurse would be to have Dovett still express his influence in her life. And he was dead, she reasoned, so he didn't know so much after all. He was stupid dead, killed by people much more stupid than he. So in the end, she reasoned, some things do not matter. He could not have been right about anything.

The minute she saw Rita at the Schiphol airport she felt a mix of nostalgia and gloomy hesitation. Perhaps she wasn't going to be able to get all she wanted with Rita for a friend. There was every sign of Curaçao on Rita, earnest drudgery and dry determination to get by. Rita was full of plans for her though, and didn't know that whatever Dovett had said was slipping away, and whatever Curaçao was left in her Maya intended to get rid of.

In the beginning she tried to be sensible, as Rita said. Rita worked in a hospital for the old and got Maya a job there. Nurse trainee. The first day, Maya threw up at the sight of blood and the smell of incontinence. She couldn't get rid of the smell. It lodged itself in her throat and she gagged continually. There was a clamminess attaching itself to her fingers and her skin. The whole place smelled of incontinence and she bought her first pack of cigarettes to get rid of it. She lasted a week, then told Rita she wasn't going back. Months later she still had the sensation of smelling the humus and death of old people. So much so she would need to spit to clear the scent from her mouth. Sometimes she vomited from holding it in.

And then she wandered down a street near the river, past the train station. Something distracted her from looking at the clutter of boats and she saw a window with a woman, then another and another. Windows hardly distinguishable from any ordinary window. In fact prettier, far more domestic, windows that had tables and chairs and in one window a woman in something loose, blue, a dragon curling to her throat, her breasts flaccid and relaxed. In another, a woman with her hair permed to flat-shine waves, in another still a woman who might as well have been leaning over an ironing board, and stunningly in another a woman pursing her lips inviting Maya in, bringing her half-slip carelessly up over her thighs. Maya stared, not realizing that she was staring, until the woman turned her lips to someone else, her hand resting on her upper thigh as if to smooth an itch or soothe a small ache.

Maya looked to see who had drawn the woman's attention away from her. A man in a mauve shirt and a white belt on his trousers stood near her, smiling at the woman. Then Maya realized what the windows were for. They were not ordinary pleasant women standing or sitting there after making breakfast, sitting in their windows watching the world, but women selling something quite ordinary nevertheless. She was struck by the domesticity of the scenes, their plainness, their obvious clarity, their acceptance of something that happened in the world every day. That simplicity made her decide what she had to do.

It looked easy. All she had to do was sit in a window and then do something quite ordinary when the men came in and she would have more than enough money. Dovett would turn in his grave, she thought, and her mother would finish wasting away.

So there she was in her window, and seeing the Flemish man on Sundays and her guilders multiplying. What life she wanted she wasn't sure, but money was part of it. Money would take her beyond the Biljmer and her brother, whom she refused to help apart from tolerating him in her apartment. What life she wanted she had a glimpse of sometimes. She only wanted to drift down streets or drift out into the country. She wanted a car and a lover and warm weather when she might feel the play of breezes on her body. And a beach. Or cold weather and a sure house and a fireplace and beer or port. That was all. She wanted to be nowhere on time and she wanted incidents of music in cafés and clubs when she drifted into music as if she were music itself. She wanted sourness on her tongue and sweetness too and smells of cooking bread. She wanted kitchens, spotless, without soot or dirt, and well, she just wanted to drift on the cream of life, what else?

Drift. She liked the word, suggesting streams of her appearing and dissipating in air. Like the smoke she blew now constantly. She wanted to stoop down in a quiet place going on with its own business, and blow smoke into ohs and ahs and listen to the sound of glass before it was glass but sand. That is why she liked the window. When she stood there, moments would stay still. Whatever frame she chose remained still and she learned to count seconds as complete eternities. Drifting. Seconds each had their own sound if anyone listened, like drops of water each had a particular tenor, falling in the middle of an afternoon or the beginning of a morning, each different, each singing or tapping. What if she only wanted to listen to moments pass and what if she stood or sat in a window in Amsterdam listening? It was far enough away from burning oilfields and burning bodies, her father's constant anguish, which he spread all over the house in bleak thick silence. Thick and heavy silences dense with his causes. Which was why she had to leave as soon as he was dead, because it wasn't enough that he was dead, he still filled the rooms of the house with his dense needs. He made them all worried and nervous and pessimistic even though what he wanted was what was right, better treatment, better places to live, better pay; but in his body it all felt heavy and distant and dense.

He saved this heaviness for them. She knew because she had seen him once talking to a group of men and he was transformed, the sun glistening off his silver helmet; he was light and smiling and his heavy steps had turned to dancing on his tiptoes when he waved his hands, arguing and convincing. He touched them the way she had only seen him touch Adrian when he was a small boy. The way someone touches a lovely thing. He gave them lightness and loveliness. He gave them courage and said no harm would come to them, nothing more harmful than what they were already bearing. She saw him leaning against a lamppost smoking a cigarette with the men and then he was weightless, weightless against their weight and worry. She saw his fleet-footed leap off the back of the evening transport, waving goodbye to the men in steel helmets, throwing out a last challenge. When he left them he walked heavily home to engulf his family in his doubt and his true feelings of disbelief and dread that the bosses would not yield. He filled not only the house but the island with his heaviness, and she wanted to leave. Her mother was saturated in it, and if she was to become her mother, which she feared, she would thicken like a drum full of lead or cement.

She had been inconsequential to him. Her father. She was not a boy child. She would not follow him anywhere. She could not embody the shape of his own father falling in fire at the doorway. What would become of her? He put aside money for her to become a nurse, but Adrian was to be his flame, the leaf peeling off as Dovett had peeled off from his own father to fly in the face of the oil bosses. Maya was, in his words, to become like her mother, "patient," and in service.

Dovett's ambition for her was that she become a nurse, and able to feed herself. She supposed that was not a bad ambition. In the evenings at the table when he spoke, he spoke to Adrian or to their mother as if Maya were not there, as if the three of them were family, but not she. Only once did he lift his head in her direction. Only once that she could remember. It startled her. She was surprised by the change in the angle of his body, looking straight at her and saying to his wife, "Watch that little girl before she bring shame in here. She getting big." And then to her, "Don't think I don't have eyes. Don't let me catch you down in Otra Banda."

After pulling the paper curlers from her hair, she had gone walking in Otra Banda. Left the dishes in the sink and slipped out the back. Left the clothes to iron after she'd ironed the dress she put on, and gone. She liked walking, feeling the dry breeze on her skin, just before the sun went

down, just when the light is about to turn dark and the
street lamps about to be turned on, just when slinking boys
are unfolding their long frames stretched out on sea walls
and corners. Who could have seen her laughing with them?
Who could have seen her take the hem of her dress in her
hand and brush her dress tail back laughing and dismissing
them? She sat at the evening table, the hot cocoa in front of
her and the bread, and she must have smiled, remembering
her walk, because she felt the heavy dull ring on Dovett's
marriage finger. She felt the flat of it hit her face, wrapped
around his heavy finger. She felt his thick callused palm and
smelled the chemicals on his fingertips. The cocoa fell into
her lap and she jumped up and stood there because she
could not leave the table without asking his permission and
because she was stunned and because she was wondering if
anybody was going to help her.

She wanted weightlessness and limpid sound. And so
in her window in Amsterdam, far away from Dovett in distance and flesh, she listened for the sound of each moment.
She just wanted to be light-headed and ordinary and have
not a care, not a bother. She didn't want to bear the weight
of her father any more, and when she saw how casual these
women in the windows were, how every move they made
was easy and drawling, how bored they looked as if they had
time and were content to be looked at and even handled,
but somehow remained uninvolved, she wanted to step into
the window and live their life.

The world came to these windows with stories. The
women in the windows did not pay attention—only enough
attention to come to no harm, but the many life stories
were nothing to them, nothing but lies and justifications.
And for sure they knew better than to keep these stories or

consider them, even during the telling of them. Their life in the windows, on the other hand, was a dreaming of another life. They would look at their watches and calculate the moments before going back to their life in the window. Sometimes they didn't even listen. They nodded here and there in the appropriate places and even where not appropriate. The stories settled on the edges of their own dreams like buoys to navigate around. If, as happened once in a while, any of these stories took over, that woman would be back where she started. If at any time a woman got tangled up in these stories she ended up sorry. The story-teller didn't notice anyway. So Maya skirted their stories, banished them to the outer places where she was not heading and followed her own dreaming to breeziness and weightlessness.

People always made themselves sound better than they were anyway. More honest, more caring, more of all the things they thought were human—more compassionate, more blameless, more knowledgeable, more naïve, everything all at once; but really at best they were idiots, at worst, evil. They all had more or less the same story but thought that it was unique. She was amazed at the commonness of them all. They all tried to twist their common small life into knots and strangeness just for attention, or gain, or to hide who they really were, she supposed. After all, didn't she have to tell Rita some absurd story—instead of the truth, which was that the job she got her and the job Rita herself did made Maya sick to her stomach? But she didn't want to insult Rita or make her feel small. She didn't want to say, "I don't want to clean old Dutch shit. I can't stand it. I don't want anyone telling me what to do, I don't want to hear their curses without getting paid for it. Most of all I don't want to gag for the rest of my life." Didn't she have to tell Rita that she was living in with a Dutch family, and could only come out one day a week to see Rita? And why, why did she have to make up these lies? Because Rita would write home and tell her mother, who would die, if she hadn't already. Because her mother needed good stories to while away the time until she went to meet Dovett again and tell him everything was well.

All the customers hid their mercilessness and their cruelty, in particular those most merciless and cruel. They hid it somewhere in their words, but she saw it. All the women saw it. It would slip off in a customer's shrug or settle in the middle of their eyes, even those who wanted to make their eyes bland and plain, which was the sure sign, or those who made their eyes innocent, as if anyone at the window could be innocent. In this window where all talk was no talk at all, all joy was induced and all greeting fiscal, who could be innocent? That there was such drama for something so ordinary meant that what was being traded was not sex at all. Too much machinery had to be deployed, too much camouflage, and money had to be negotiated and exchanged. No, this was something else.

She saw Rita less and moved into her window almost permanently. Her compositions occupied her more and more. Her discoveries of regions of the pane and their spectral relationship to the sun, their unrequited openness to the dead moon, these she attended with more curiosity than the job. And the phases and shapes of parts of her body. She liked her body's shine—the way it was when she'd just arrived. She oiled it and put it under a sun lamp in the winter to keep its gloss. Though nothing could beat the shine of an island arrival fresh and full of sand, nothing could beat water and a close sun, nothing could beat the equator's teak breath on the body. She dreamed of just walking in the dry sweat of a Curaçao day along the *laman grandi*, even walking in Otra Banda hearing the rude boys call her *dushi*.

So she oiled and sunned. In the summer she took boats and wore the skimpiest clothes to make sure the sun reached each part of her. She sculpted her calves for running and her thighs for lifting, she pruned the biceps and triceps and she cultivated the deep river running down her back hardening the ridges on either side. She made herself strong and liquid. Her menses made her euphoric. After the initial gravity into which each period sank her, after the day of feeling the world as it was, hopeless and suicidal, after watching her body swell with water, she felt euphoric at the warm feel of her blood gushing uncontrollably as if a breath was let out, as if rightly she could give birth to the world and wouldn't, giddy and spinning, anything possible, and an energy so powerful she felt that she could spring above time, and wondered why she hadn't. Not even the window could contain her when she was bleeding.

Maya followed the phases of her body, not following them at all but being surprised and recognizing them only after they had arrived or left. She became aware by surprise, and each time surprised again and familiar and knew herself as much as any woman did, marvelling at physiognomy, the smell of the body, the sudden appearance of nails, blisters, itches, sweat, hair; the descent of the womb, the clutter and impatience of ideas, and the way a thought jumps around until it is nothing but a fragment of a thing, half of itself trying to remember itself. How her mother managed to devote so much time to Dovett in the presence of her own body confused her.

Walter found out about the Flemish man and asked her

for his share. Sitting in her window she did not hear him at first and then she pretended not to hear him until he waved a knife at her, saying, "That pussy is mine and you don't sell it or show it or even wash it without I tell you."

When she thinks back she cannot decide if her window melted or cracked into shards at that moment. She has a sense of both happening at the same time. She had been sitting with her back to the window and just about to turn around, sensing someone there. Come to think of it she cannot exactly remember seeing Walter's face, but the window melted like ice in the sun even though it was night. It became warm water where it had just been ice, and her leg dissolved into crimson drops.

When she thinks back, Walter looked as if he was about to say something else but she had cut in, "*Fok bo, abusado!*" And perhaps the other language had confused him; perhaps it had been so unlike her that he had fallen to the floor in shock and she had continued to scream, "*Sinbergwensa! Mariku!*" When she thinks back, her arm was running crimson, but the light went out just as she noticed it. And then there were other screams and she asked one of the girls what was the matter and the girl said, "Run!" grabbing her and that was all. She was pulled along, hating to leave not knowing whether her window had melted or cracked into shards, and whether it was Walter whom she had sensed had done it.

When Maya recalls this she is sitting watching television. The Flemish man likes to watch television. He likes to watch the stock market on television and he is dressed in his usual black suit. His white beard is shocking against his suit, and his reading glasses, which he wears for watching the stock market on television, reflect the screen. He says to her as usual, "Don't fidget," as if she were a child. She is waiting for the program to finish so they can go out because the thing she does not want to remember is the last thing she remembers from then. Walter falling and her crimson arm.

She'd gone back to her apartment after the window broke and after Walter fell in the glass, after the girls had all run away, dragging her with them. Her arm was still crimson, and she knew that she had to get away. Her still and beautiful window, broken.

The light came on in the hallway and she saw Adrian lying face down on the kitchen floor again. She had told him to leave so often, but he was weak and kept quiet through her quarrelling, trying to persuade her on his next scheme. She had seen how he had become nervous and driven by some drug or another. She hardly recognized him but then he probably did not recognize her either. She had begun to hide her money, and she had returned to the apartment to collect it. She had to go somewhere else and his body lying there on the floor only made her more certain. She had no intention of keeping him alive, he would have to find some way himself. He reminded her of their father, not leadenness in his case but weight nevertheless, a light nervous weight, a hovering, an unhappy hovering, his face thin and shaky, a film of narcotic sweat glazing it.

She had shaken him and shaken him that morning not yet morning but crimson turning to morning, when she had to leave, and he was in her way. She screamed at him for her money in the middle of tearing everything to bits, but he had only mumbled and thrown up an ocean and in her rage she had left him there to choke on it, stepping over him, feathers dripping from her fingers where she had stripped the green cabaret dragon to pieces, and the red rooster too, even though she was sure she had left her money in the green dragon. The blue monster's head she had torn to pieces too.

Stumbling over him, trailing feathers, she left, her hands stuck in red feathers and green feathers, and oil and a crimson shade that she cannot remove, going to call the Flemish man since that was all that was left for her to do.

Now she is waiting for the Flemish man to stop watching the stock market so she leans back in her chair in resignation. And he doesn't stop until a little girl enters the room. "Ah, there you are. Where have you been? I've been waiting for you all this time, do you know?" The little girl gurgles and runs to him then notices her mother in the room.

They are walking down a street in Brugge now, the little girl is counting cobblestones. She is counting cobblestones because then she can look down and not up at her mother's face. Maya, dressed in pure white, is walking alongside, smiling, holding the little girl's hand. She is thinking circumstances lead you to this, circumstances, and she smiles to herself, mocking herself. She puts all her weight in circumstances, her last night in Amsterdam when Walter's body crashed to the ground, falling away from her, and a crimson oil dripped from her hand; and when she walked over her brother who lay in her path throwing up an ocean. Those were circumstances that no one could predict. Those circumstances had led to now. Or her father falling into his grave or for that matter his father falling in flames at the doorstep.

There was no way to know, really, which thing led to which, if there was a sequence. Had she been heading for this long before she arrived? Was it laid down somehow like a story with an ending, only she was the person wandering through it not knowing the end? Had she returned to that ending or was this her own? She had never wanted to be weighed down by anything, especially not a child or for that matter a Flemish man, and here she was walking down a cobbled street with a Flemish man and a child. Circumstances. There are moments you cannot crack no matter how willing you are. No matter how treacherous or cunning you may be. If your grandfather falls in fire it is a sign.

Feeling a different tension in her mother's hand, the child looks up from her counting, looks up and sees Maya's face self-mocking and detached. Her mother's face is always full of something. Not emotions that she knows anything about but ones she recognizes. She reads her absence, which is quite involuntary. Her mother doesn't mean to leave her, it is just the way she is. The child prefers to hold her father's hand. He is there, but her mother drifts.

Maya doesn't like to look at her child. She sees too much understanding there, plain like water or hot tea. It is as if the child is flooded in whatever she, Maya, is feeling at the moment, and Maya is afraid of feeling nothing or revealing everything. So sometimes the little girl is flooded in crimson and the weight of a man falling, then she is flooded in airy fields and then she is flooded in Willemstad streets, sometimes she is buying the hearts of cactus in a market, and then she is flooded in glass cases and windows. Flooded in coconut oils and perfumes and heat and translucent blue lizards and arid dust. She is smothered in red feathers and green feathers and the sound of birds screaming. She can feel her mother's heart beat even if she doesn't lie on her breast. She must roll under her mother's smiles quickly before their horizons close. She is flooded in a dress-tail swishing, her mother's young laughter and a cup of hot cocoa overturned. She is drenched in things her mother will never tell her. Circumstances, which envelop them both in any room, or when they walk down cobbled streets in Brugge.

BLUE AIRMAIL
LETTER

~~~~~~~~~

Dear Mama.

Hope you are well, and enjoying the best of health. I am
still here in Toronto. I have not written to you for a long
time. Not since the time I went to help Carlyle. It has been
weighing with me. It's taken me some years. Then all of a
sudden yesterday I began this letter.

I wanted to send you a blue airmail letter. Light blue
with thin black lines on the front. I wanted to imagine you
squinting, holding it close to your eyes, holding it close and
far from the light in turn. Trying to catch some of the
lettering by bending it this way and that and then giving up
and getting one of us to read it. Giving up and placing its
precious weight in the hand of a child just home from
school, whom you have waited for, whose big eyes and
halting mumbling speech you have anticipated just to hear
what I have written.

I wanted to think of you as I have seen you so often,
after the small child places the letter back in your hand,
lying on your side on the bed as you would do, with the letter, your fingers thick and small bringing the letter to your

eyes now and then to see perhaps if you could read more out of it, perhaps to feel and imagine your oldest daughters sitting in their bedsitter somewhere in London, their coats still on, writing to you. You would lie on your side for hours like that, holding the blue airmail-letter form, thinking of them.

I wonder what you imagined? Whatever it was, sadness was all I could see, or perhaps it was loneliness for them. Or perhaps it was so separate a pleasure imagining them in Liverpool, Chelsea, or New York, so secret a pleasure that they had gone away, that I took it for sadness. They were sitting somewhere beyond where anything you knew could harm them. I often mistake pleasure for sadness, it is that moment of complete loneliness even if you share it with someone.

Under other circumstances I would not tell you something like this, but when I make love to someone I am sad after. I am sad for how much they cannot know about me, for how single I am. It seems as if in that very moment, which is what people call intimacy, I find myself alone. Someone else can never know you. You live all the moments of your life when you make love and you live it alone. No one can truly be with you. And any thought can grab you and take you with it and it need not be what you are doing at the moment or who is with you. Once I remembered you in that moment. I would not tell you this if you were here or able to read this, but yes, once, just then in the middle of making love, I thought of you and began to cry for you.

I wanted to write to you the way my older sisters had, and imagine you lying there holding my letter as if I were your life, your eyes far away where I am, seeing a gulf

between us, the distance of water and of lives. I wanted
you to lie like that on your side, your head on your hand
and the other holding my letter, and think of me sitting at a
table in my small apartment on Brunswick Avenue here in
Toronto, telling you of the things I've done, the books I've
read, about the winter, the girl from Vietnam across the
hall who lost her child on a boat in the China Sea. She told
me she hid diamonds and jewels in his waistband and
thieves must have stolen him. The last time she saw him
they had been separated into different boats and he was
crying, his arms stretched out for her. She said his fingers
reached and curled and his face leaned to one side.

I wanted to write to say that each moment I wanted to
call you on the telephone, even though we never had a telephone and you never saw one in your lifetime. I wanted
to tell you about Carlyle and how he still seems to be running our lives, even here. How I wish that he would grow
old or die, and how many of everyone's days it seems he
has consumed.

I wanted to think of you quarrelling with some small
child for misplacing my letter, as if it were so necessary for
you to have it and to have some sign of me that was close.
Some small child whose only sense of me would be my letters, their smell of glue and their words that would
describe where she might want to be. This small child
bathed in a fine story about me which you would tell her,
holding the letter as if it were precious and a lesson, a sign
of how life would pay if she only lived right. Some small
child going back to her play after a while, called by the next
candy or game and dropping my letter on the floor in her
hurry where some breeze would take it to a corner under
the bed or next to the wardrobe behind the clothes basket.

Some small child forgetting me, running outside to climb
a tree or beat her cousin in a foot race, to argue this is
mine...no, mine...yes...no...I won't be your friend
any more....I would like to be forgotten by such a child
carrying on with her own play, and never dreaming that she
would ever have to leave you. As I would like you to long
for that letter collecting cuttings of hair and bedsheet dust
and shoe dust behind the wardrobe now. A letter you
would mourn the loss of, and try to recall from memory
how I sounded. Was I happy? was I homesick? and what did
I say about coming home, and was it too cold for me and
did I say that I would write soon and did I sign all my love?

　　I just heard some kind of bird outside. I cannot tell
which but it sounded like a cry of alarm or haste or
distress. I didn't think that birds spoke at night, but somehow it made me start this letter. It might have been the
bird I saw today. For a moment it looked like a swift, the
way it swooped and extended its wings all at once, fast. But
then it stopped at the top of a linden tree and I have never
seen a swift sit down so it must not have been. At any rate I
heard it and thought to write. Why the sound of it would
move me I do not know. I have tried to write before but did
not know where to begin and one thing led to another and it
was years.

　　I remember sitting with you, looking out our window
and plotting to go away, and I said that I would write to you
and send you money and that you would come and visit me
and I would grow up and take care of myself, and all these
things I would do for you. I remember both of us knowing
somehow that this would not happen. Or perhaps you
knew, but I sensed it surely, that was why the air had a
breeze that only you and I could smell or acknowledge

even though the room was full of other people and the
breeze seemed to take what we had said and lift it above
us or out of our reach or our will to make it true.

I wanted to tell you that I have a job in the post office.
I've had it for years now, sorting letters. I love sorting letters because it reminds me of you. I have sorted letters
from all over the world, Amman, Cape Town, Bangkok.
I have gone home at night and looked up those places on
the maps of the world that I keep. I put a small red dot at
every town in the world that I remember sorting that day.

I collect maps of all kinds, old ones and newer ones,
ordnance maps and road maps. That was how I found my
way out of America after leaving Carlyle and Gita on the
road in Florida. In the trunk of the car I had brought all my
maps and when I was so tired that I did not know my way, I
would pull off to the side of the road and search my maps.
Any one would do, even a map of France or a map of
Guyana. Their steadiness steadied me, it did not matter
that they were not where I was. Their definite lines
brought order to my head.

When I first came to Toronto to live with Sese, she had
already bought my coat. She bought a brown coat and
brown boots. They seemed desolate. They made me look
like an old lady and at first I didn't want to disobey Sese, as
you had asked me not to. So I put on the coat and the boots
and I felt like a child who wanted to scream but I sulked
instead. When I got my first money I gave Sese only half. I
bought a coat, a red one with a hood and a flared skirt, and
I would leave the house in Sese's brown coat and streets
away I would change into my beautiful red coat. After a
while I didn't care if she knew and we had a row.

In the two years that I lived with her she called me a

whore, first when I became pregnant and then when I
decided to leave her place. She said that I wanted to be a
whore, to spend money and not to save and send home to
Terre Bouillante for my little girl. That was the end for her
and me. I could not live with her any more, telling me
what to do at every turn. I got to know the city by myself
and I found another job and quit the one Sese had found
me. She said I was ungrateful and had embarrassed her in
front of her boss. True, I left without notice but I couldn't
stand it any more. I thought that I had come here to be
independent, and Sese seemed changed from when I knew
her. Now she went to the church all the time. I have nothing against the church, but she would want me to go
with her and read the Bible every morning before going
to work.

I didn't want to write and worry you so I suppose I
didn't write at all and disappeared instead. I know that Sese
wrote and told you that I was a whore, and I cannot tell you
any different if she meant that I thought I should enjoy life
and not work until my face was as hard as hers. I won't
deny that I drank in bars and met many women who
worked the streets. They at least were living and their faces
were soft, too soft perhaps, so soft they came apart in
men's hands. At least they could feel every moment they
lived. I would dance with them all night long sometimes
trying to figure out how they lived in life with so much
abandon. Of course by the end of the night things would
fall apart for them and all the partying would end and I
would go home to my maps and they would head for the
street quickly as if they had only stolen their life for a
moment in dancing.

I was not tough enough for that. I didn't want anyone

bothering me or holding me up. I could not help but hesi-
tate on a thought when it came along, and to live their life
you have to hurry and be quick-witted, you have to trust
your senses and I never trusted mine. So I drank every
night at the bars but I ended up at the post office at eight
every morning. I moved and I didn't give Sese my address
or phone number.

Once I saw her on the other side of a street and I could
swear she saw me but walked on. I saw her and faded
into the glass of a building until she passed. I don't know
why I did that, Mama. After all, she is my sister, but it was
as if I had left her completely and left this family. And that
one glimpse of her on the other side of the street confirmed my decision. I haven't seen her since and dread
ever doing so.

Mama, it's just that I wanted to be in life but Sese was
punishing herself as if just because she gave away her own
child she had to suffer. I know we don't say these things out
loud, and I hurt Sese when we had that last row, telling her
how she threw away the child to white people here and
she had no right talking to me and trying to run my life.
At least my child was with people at home and I was not
ashamed of that, but it was as if she wanted me to be
ashamed too.

It was the wrong thing to do, I know now, but I can't
make it up, it just won't come out of my mouth even
though I know that Sese, well, I saw her just shrivel up
when I said those words but I couldn't take them back.
She looked so bad and the more I said the more she dried
out. We can't take back what we do. I never saw Sese again
until that day on the street and by that time I could not
reach for her.

I can't help thinking of that breeze that passed over
you and me that day, with you lying in the bed sick and
promising to get better as if you had control of it, and me
believing you because you had control of everything that I
knew of. All our lives from our eating to our sleeping you
made with your hands and your tongue. But that moment
we knew that neither you nor I could ignore that breeze
that said I was going somewhere no longer ruled by you.
The feel of it not cold, not warm, with a fresh smell to it,
a waft, as if rain would fall but not soon, but rain at the
change of seasons, not the rain in its season or the sun in
its season but the middle of the two, the exchange between
them and the way they promise each other nothing. I've
never felt that breeze since.

No, that is not true, I've felt it in a different way when
fall comes here when it isn't the end of the summer yet.
One day, suddenly. I am walking at the back of a building, it
is afternoon and I feel it, something like it, at my back, as if
someone is walking behind me and I turn around and there
is no one but that breeze moving as it moves to end things,
but seeming not deliberate just saying, "There. It is over."

My forehead feels like thin paper, the kind you use to
trace a figure or a map. I can hear it rustle under my fingers, if I let go all of it will pour into my hands, all of my
thoughts and the thick oxidizing matter of me. The creases
of lines on my fingers are dusty like crushed paper.

History opens and closes, Mama. I was reading a book
the other day about the nineteenth century and it seemed
like reading about now. I think we forget who we were.
Nothing is changing, it is just that we are forgetting.
All the centuries past may be one long sleep. We are
either put to sleep or we choose to sleep. Nothing is

changing, we are just forgetting. I am forgetting you, but
it is work, forgetting.

No, I am exaggerating. I do not forget you at all. It's just
that I am too lazy to go through all the emotions it involves.
I will never forget you. How could I when only an airmail
letter lying on the floor reminds me of you, when only a
bird I cannot make out says something one night far away
from you and I remember?

Once I felt you sit on my bed. I did not imagine it, I
know. A weight just like yours sat on my bed as I was about
to fall asleep. I woke up and called "Mama?" and felt peaceful. I know that it was you, just your weight as if you sat
and rose there on my bed, just the feel of you sitting when
you are tired. I knew that it was you. All of a sudden my
room was warm and familiar and it was as if I had not left
you. Many years after I prayed that you would come again,
but I remembered that feeling as if you had given me something, as if you were near.

I heard from Priest—that is what he still calls himself,
your oldest son, Carlyle. I know you had me late but I wish
that you had never conceived him at all. I suppose you
wished that too. I don't know how he found me after so
long. I left him and Gita at a bus station in America six
years ago. I have been hiding from many people, he most
of all. Even over the telephone—he, somewhere in the
States—even here on this small secret avenue his face
comes to me, it overwhelms me. It is as if I am not hearing
him but seeing his face.

I drove out of America so fast when I left them, Carlyle
and Gita, and a boy who was Carlyle's double, Mama. I
don't know where he came from. He was Carlyle's spitting
image. I imagined the wheels of the car blurring as I put

distance between us. All of the highways felt like him, vibrating with a hardness, a steeliness. I didn't notice until Erie that my jaw was clamped shut on my tongue.

I can't lie to you, though that is a lie, but he and I are the same and that is why I drove so fast leaving him in the middle of nowhere. He pushed Gita's head out of the door of the moving car to make me stop and I almost didn't. I knew that I could have kept driving. I could have smashed the car with all of us in it. I eventually stopped not because I was afraid of him or because I felt any pity for Gita—I stopped because I could feel him become afraid, just for a moment, afraid. In that moment I was as cunning and violent as he and he understood it and that was all I needed.

After I'd left them, all the way driving back up to Toronto I was so tired yet so full of a violent energy, I drifted off in daydreams that seemed electrical and strafing. I remembered what you said about Marie Ursule with her iron ring, limping through forests. I saw her caught in vines and tangle, hurrying back before daylight. I thought that I heard the thudding of her ring on wood and stone until I opened my eyes and it was the rim of my tire on a curb. The car swerved across a median and spun but I was in a delirious control and pulled it back to my direction north. I was awake but not really awake. My face was hot and my tongue was dry, but I couldn't stop driving to eat or sleep.

I am writing you this letter because I have no ordinary things to tell you. No things we share now and are used to. I am writing only to imagine you reading it with children around your bed. I recognize this fantasy because of course there are no children and no bed. I am writing to no one. You are dead.

Everything should have been said a long time ago. My
decisions happened as any day happens, with no spectacle
or anyone knowing. I was just living. Yes, living and forgetting like any century. All the small details you do not
remember, the pebbles of air and the pebbles of pebbles,
you forget them. I am only writing to commit an act, to
write a letter. I have nothing to ask you except to still be
lying on your bed with small children circling you and
to squint your eyes at the print and then give it to one of
them to read for you. I have no small things to exchange.
I wish that I did. But it never occurred to me to save
them or at the time I didn't think that telling you was the
proper thing.

My older sisters must have lied to you when they wrote
those things they said, so ordinary and everydayish, that
I read out to you: "London is wonderful," "I love fish and
chips," "The head nurses are kind here," "They treat us as
their own," "I am missing home."

I can't lie to you. I wish that I could remember the
everyday things or had cherished them enough to remember them. One year I lived in the living rooms of friends,
one year I drank from morning till night, one year I went
to England and stayed with someone in Ilkley. One day
there we took a walk along a shore but that wasn't in Ilkley,
it was the other town where they take the ships to Belgium,
not Dover, the other town. I saw the ferry to Belgium, it
was large and cars drove onto it. One day we took the ferry
and we went to the bar and drank Campari. My friend said
that this was good for the crossing but I was sick to my
stomach and wanted to get off right there in the middle of
the English Channel.

One year I tried to go to university but I didn't finish

because I felt that everyone was staring at me. I was study-
ing modern drama. I tried to fit in. I could have gone on
living a life that way. Anyway I didn't last. Off and on I
went to the university but I could not get over my shyness.
I discovered though that it wasn't shyness at all. I was afraid
of what would come out of my mouth. I was afraid that it
would seem unintelligent and some days I simply wanted
to curse, to spit at the whole room of people and the
teacher. I felt burning, the front of my chest and my head
was consumed in anger and I wanted to curse. I don't know
why. Sometimes it wasn't even what they were saying,
more that they seemed all sly, gesturing toward me with
their eyes and smiles and the things they knew. Last year
I studied French at a high school.

I wear black boots. I wear black all the time, and no one
knows it but I carry iron knuckles for when I walk at night
and yes, Mama, I drink a lot and see too much. I go dancing. I dance to anything. I dance alone in the middle of
the floor with the light revolving and I dance until I am
exhausted, then I go home and sleep deeply, forgetting.

I am living in a city at the end of the world, Mama. It is
rubble. It is where everyone has been swept up, all of it,
all of us are debris, things that a land cleaning itself spits
up. It is the end of the world here. The office buildings and
factory buildings and houses and shops and garages all
wreathed in oil and dust and piled up on top of themselves.
It is as if some pustule erupted from the ground and it is
this city. It is bloated and dry at the same time, crumbling
with newness, rubbled in glitter.

I dropped everyone as I did Sese. I had to stop thinking
about Gita and what harm she would come to with Carlyle.
I didn't want to be emotional all the time, to miss things

and want things and long for you and be disappointed.
I didn't want anyone to become old or sick and die right
when I loved them, so I had to make space and find other
people who didn't want me at their bedsides or when they
hurt themselves, others who would not ask and not expect.
I didn't want to be the kind of person for whom life is a
burden. I didn't want people to care for.

Don't think that I'm sad. I'm just trying to explain it
to you so you will know why I did not write sooner. I'm
forgetting you even as I write this letter. The more I write
the more I forget. Perhaps that is why I never wrote until
now, perhaps I need to forget you now, though that fright-
ens me.

How is your knee? Is it still scarred from the fall, and
your back, does it still hurt? Mine does. I feel as if there are
knives in my shoulders. My head burns with small things
that repeat and repeat: a stone I saw covered in moss, a rag
in a wet place under a tap, slime was gathering on it and I
was scared—that was when you sent us to those people in
Paxton Bay. I was afraid to go outside to their shower room
and they pushed me and at the corner of the room was the
rag filled with slime and I felt that it was in my throat or
crawling toward me.

My mind now stays on those things and I am afraid of
corners and wet rooms. Their rooms were large and dark
and there was the smell of pee and wood. They had a piano
with pictures of their whole family on the top. There was a
lace cloth on the piano and all the pictures stood on the
lace cloth.

Our life always scared me. You had so many of us, there
was always so much confusion. I got lost at the end. Everything was uncontrollable. Our house was so small with so

many people and things changing there every day. Yet Terre
Bouillante was so quiet outside, so hushed, it was at the
same time as if life was not going on. I am not blaming you,
perhaps I now only remember the uncontrollable days.
Surely there were days that went slowly, as if we had the
time and were happy, but I only remember the full rooms
and the discomfort.

Mama, I am afraid of wet stones and wet leaves and wet
cloth and wet hair and all the small things that human
beings give off or drop or leave and never notice, but I do
notice, and each day it can be a different small thing that
scares me—dead flies and wet soap, a strand of hair or a bit
of paper, mildew, decay, the way things decay like bodies.

The streets here are full of decay. People hunched up in
their filthy coats and shirts and blouses, their moulting
shoes and pants. Mama, everyone here is decaying. When I
first came they were all new, at least they all seemed brand
new all the time. Now they are all decaying on the streets
and the streets themselves seem old and crumbling, the
concrete is chipped and old garbage decays in the gutters.

I am so sick, Mama, I am so sick with seeing. It is as if a
film, the film that we usually see through that would make
being human acceptable, this film has lifted from me and I
find us filthy and decrepit, walking decay. I am so sick,
Mama, so sick from seeing. I wish that I could get my eyesight back where this is only human, what we leave, what
we are. I hate this sight of everything.

Perhaps I took it that somehow we were not like birds
or lizards or rats and we didn't have leavings or droppings
and could not be suddenly devastated by the climate or the
growth of trees. Perhaps I took it that accidents of great
proportion could not happen, that one day in the middle of

the street everyone would be wrecked. Wreckage, Mama, that is all we look like, pure wreckage. The street is full of human wreckage, breakage and ruin.

I saw a woman yesterday whom I really could not bear to look at, her skin was flaking off and her hands could not touch her face. It was as if she had forgotten it. Forgotten her face, forgotten her hands. I imagined where she lived and I saw a small musty room that smelled of her skin and perhaps cooking and I had to turn away. Her coat had once been khaki-coloured but now shone with a grim juice of living.

My mind is not calm. It is always running, running, running. I cannot come home now. I will see the drains and canals. I will see the creases of things and in the rainy season I will suffer from wet places. I've seen many such people. Sometimes I do not leave my apartment in case I see them. Why doesn't it seem to occur to anyone else that this is happening? I notice others not noticing and going about as I did before, taking coffees and breakfasts and not noticing the floor, not thinking of the oil layered on the walls, or the cook wiping his hand against his nose before breaking the eggs and stepping on flour on the floor until it is rolled into a grey dough under his shoes.

I have moved to different neighbourhoods to avoid the father of the child. He hunted me down, saying that he wanted his child. I moved to Korea Town right after I sent her home to you. I lived in a room above a store. There was a cinema opposite called Eve. They ran a film called *Emmanuelle* perpetually. Perpetual desire, it said. The child's father found me and I moved again. To a street with warehouses where I thought he would not look but one morning I saw him go to the Portuguese bakery next door and ask for me. I stayed inside all day until he left. I have moved all over this city because of this man. I wasn't afraid of him; I simply did not want to do something bad to him. I have lived in Greek places in the east end, Italian places in the west, I've lived above a store selling saris and above a store selling halal meats.

One day I stopped moving. I became tired of him. I surprised him coming up my steps on Brunswick and I told him, "Go away now." I showed him a small gun that Carlyle had given me once, which I kept as a joke. I was tired of moving and he had gotten the wrong impression altogether. He left. All the challenge and danger in his body gave out.

Dear Mama, I wanted to tell you that your dream had come true, that I was living well, a manager in a store or a supervisor in an office full of computers, and would send barrels of clothing for my child and you, that I would come home one day dressed in lace and high heels and greet you as the person you wanted me to be. I wanted to tell you that I have slipped easily and happily into life, that I am resilient and quick to laugh. No, no, I don't think that you wanted me to be false or pretentious. I know you wanted me to be my best self, but I don't know what that is now.

I remember a calypso. "Take me, take me, I am feeling lonely, take me back to Los Iros. . . ." Why do I remember that? I have never longed for Los Iros but I longed for longing for it. As I long for you. I wish I could long like the man singing of the woman longing. I wish there was a place like Los Iros that I could long for. I could see them now in that small village in the twilight with the sea turning milky in the evening, and a small wood house with a lamp perhaps, and the smell of cooking, smoky and secret, and a small

bed, she fanning a fire at a coal pot and he sitting in a
shadow watching her, and the village all around them curious, wondering why she has come back again. I can see the
night dark and just the lamplight from the houses and her
skin so amber in the lamp, sweat shining her and her face
peaceful and settled over the coal pot, and she planning the
early early morning when she'll walk on the beach before
anyone else. She with her reasons, her sickness of the city
and her body thick and secret with knowledge.

I can see her. I love her. I want to look at her all night in
the lamplight. I want to take her back there to Los Iros and
we can live in lamplight in the small curious village and I
will watch her for her secrets and sit in the shadow breathing her in. I want to watch her and I want to be her. I want
to long as she longs and get my wish as she gets hers. I
know that she knows too much, which is why she wants to
go back, she is sick as I am though she is full of knowledge.

But she can voice a longing and I can't in all honesty.
I can only envy her and the man who takes her to Los Iros
and the lamplight and the village and the milky ocean they
walk toward when the bus drops them off. I can only envy
their walk and envy the paper in her amber hand fanning
the coal pot, I envy the warmth between her legs from the
fire and from the knowledge. I love the centre of her, the
way she can long, and her sadness which is ripe.

After the child; when I sent her home to you I felt all
new again. That is why I did not write after a while. If I had
written to you I would have been reminded of her. I didn't
have money to send and money was all that would be valuable. I hated the child. She was an intrusion. She was so
certain. She looked as if she knew everything from the day
she dropped out of me like a moon, and she knew that I

was incapable. I could not wait to hand her to Sese to give to you. I knew that I would never see her again. I did not want to look at her face. I knew that there would be reproach there. But I looked and there on her face was something like pity.

How could a baby have pity, Mama? Or perhaps I flatter myself that it was pity. It wasn't. It was like someone who did not care. Perhaps over the years I've reconstructed that look of hers to say pity, but I am not as honest as I would have you think, it was harder than pity and more distracted. It was as if she was going her own way and found me trifling. Perhaps it was my own look, which she mirrored for me. I wonder if she asks for me. I don't suppose so.

Yes, Carlyle called me. "Eulalie," he said, "I am out in the street, I am in Brooklyn. I am eating garbage...." I could hear it raining wherever he was. I could hear it raining over the telephone and I listened to the rain and how it made his voice more sinister. So I tried listening just to the rain. I did not want to hear him. I wanted to put the phone down, my hand felt numb. "Your brother is eating out of the garbage," he said, "I am eating out of the garbage." Then he said, "Eulalie, I couldn't get a hard-on with Gita."

Why was he telling me this? I hated him. What intimacy did he think that we shared? I could not bear it. All the way over there and he is standing in the rain in Brooklyn, telling me this.

"I'll send you some money when I get a job," I told him, "next week perhaps." I wanted him to go away but I kept holding the phone because I wanted him to take back what he had said. Why was he giving me this story to keep for him? He is the kind of person who empties himself on other people and leaves them to handle the consequences. He thinks that he can relieve himself on anyone, on me, so I waited for him to take it back. "You hear what I'm saying, Eulalie, I couldn't get my cock up the last time with Gita."

"Priest," I said, "Priest"—just like any stranger would call him—"I'll try to send you some money. Where shall I send it?" I was thinking of Gita.

He wasn't stopping. "I am eating out of garbage cans, do you hear me? Your big brother is eating out of garbage cans."

I put the phone down and let him weep the rest to the floor. I'm not a puritan. It was the idea that the story was his, and his perverse telling of it in the middle of saying that he was starving in Brooklyn. And telling me. Why? We never spoke of these things, he and I. I don't want to know his life. He made my skin crawl. I didn't touch the telephone for a day and since then I don't answer any more.

Priest sucked on my breasts when the house was crowded and we slept in the same bed. I felt his spit on my chest. I had no breasts but he sucked where they were supposed to be and bit my nipples. I wanted to tell you. In the morning he looked at me and pointed his finger. The next night I took a pin and stuck it in him hard when he was doing it. He couldn't cry out so he hit me in my face but I kept pressing and I screamed and you called me to your room. I told you he had hit me. I think I left the pin in his side. I put it in like a nail.

Even now I feel his mouth on my breasts. I feel revulsion. I have to hold my breasts and rub his spit off. In all the years he never mentions it nor I. Instead he calls me starving from New York to tell me his secrets.

How can I mail this letter to you? I didn't want to burden you. I didn't want to send you any stories I couldn't

bear myself. I just wanted to write to you. To hold a pen
against a blue airmail-letter form and write, "Dear Mama,
Hope you are well and enjoying the best of health." Those
words came to me out of the blue and I wanted to write
them to you, hoping to only send you words as light and
blue as that. Only words might reach you now. Paper has
no strength where you are.

Dear Mama. I only have tenderness for you. I can never
recover from you. I was walking along some street and I
noticed that no one there looked like you. They were going
about their own doings and I too, I was going to the store
on the corner for something, and suddenly I noticed that
no one had your shape and I had not seen your shape or felt
the weight of your thoughts for so long. I stood there not
remembering what I was going for.

I used to feel your thoughts. Did you know that? I used
to feel your thoughts the moment I got to the head of our
street. I felt them whether they were heavy or light. When
they were light I smelled your thoughts. They were whiffs
and they lifted and strafed and scattered. I would run home
quickly to see your face. All the flowers wilted when your
thoughts were heavy, the hibiscus fences lost their leaves,
the ixora bled. I knew the minute I set foot on the street
that you were worried or some hard thing had happened.
That was how I came to hate Carlyle. He caused it most
of the time, he caused the fences to bend and the house
to break.

I would like one single line of ancestry, Mama. One line
from you to me and farther back, but a line that I can trace.
I don't know why I thought that or ask you. One line like
the one in your palm with all the places where something
happened and is remembered. I would like one line full of

people who have no reason to forget anything, or forgetting would not help them or matter because the line would
be constant, unchangeable. A line that I can reach for in
my brain when I feel off kilter. Something to pull me back.
I want a village and a seashore and a rock out in the ocean
and the certainty that when the moon is in full the sea will
rise and for that whole time I will be watching what all of
my ancestry have watched for, for all ages.

.   I would like a village where I might remain and not a
village I would leave. A village with tin shacks and flame
trees. A village like the one you used to tell us about,
where great Mama Bola once lived. A village that I long
for, with a light in a wooden house.

I want a morning when I wake up and decide all I must
decide and all I must decide is what will I eat today and
what rush of sweat will catch me at one o'clock hurrying
home to lie down until the heat has died.

I want the comfort of pity for others. No, it isn't that I
want others to suffer just so I can pity them, but I would
like to know what it is to be so happy as to pity. I pity nothing. Not myself. Not even the child that I sent to you. I did
her a favour, I sent her to the past, to be with you.

I see the man I made her with now and then. He doesn't
bother me any more. I avoid him. I cannot imagine how I
even lay with him, let alone had a child. I was not drunk
or lonely or in love or anything. I simply had sex with him
the way one does anything, the way one walks or talks or
answers back to a question. I am lying, but not entirely.
I did feel as if it were that, but I was also trying desperately
to feel something for this man because everyone said that
I should.

He was from Ghana, Mama, and he was good to me.

Good to me, well, all of my friends said so, meaning that he loved me, I suppose, and thought me some kind of catch. He took me to meet his mother and all I wanted to do was run out of the room. His mother was a round woman like you, short and round, and she was shining with expectation and he too, but all I saw was a room full to the brim with all that they could buy and stuff into a small room. And a mother. Full of expectations. The room was full. I cannot tell you how I felt choked. I could not breathe and he smiled so lovingly at his mother and then at me and I felt hopeless and wanted to run.

Instead I got pregnant. Why is it that I always butt up on the ordinary—and fail it time and again. I wish that I could have left well alone and sat with him and his mother and planned to go to their country and meet his other relatives and be a woman twenty years from then with four or five children and a husband and a mother-in-law who reminded me of you when I first saw her.

But some vice in me told me to leave him. Some vice that thinks happiness is a stupid endeavour if it depends on a smiling man and his smiling mother and worst of all me. I didn't even tell him the truth about the child. I just said that I was sick of him and that he bored me. In some ways he did. He was not intelligent. He only wanted to be happy and for him that meant me. Can you imagine? I felt greater than he and at the same time smaller and inadequate. And like a liar—because what had I said to make him think he could count on me, or that I was capable of doing all these things, let alone holding his happiness in my hand?

I don't like people giving me anything. How terrifying to have to handle their souls, to touch their moist soft insides with your hand. What a presumption to give to you

like that——who do they think they are, coming to you so
open and throwing their whole being on you so you must
take care of it.

I always prided myself, Mama, on being self-contained.
I could hold all of me in my own hands. My one failing in
this was to get pregnant. For a moment I lost my hold.
Looking at his mother who looked like you, her face so
full, so glowing, I let go. It was not even for him but for
her. After I met her in that room for a moment I lost my
shape. We ate and I went home with him and I pretended
that it would be all right even though I saw his face over me
and felt his bones brush me like flailing sticks, even though
I heard him say how long he had wanted to do this, when I
would not let him, and he pushed himself in me harder and
harder and assumed that he was being tender and I could
not wait to get out of his small room or go to sleep, seeing
my mistake. I turned my head toward the wall, I felt as if I
were in a coffin.

These are not things to tell you I know, and now I am
not so much writing to you as saying what happened.
Because if I were to write to you it would not be to tell you
these things but to scar a blue envelope with my love for
you and imagine you smoothing your thick warm fingers
over my words. And if I had written you enough words
perhaps you would have saved them at the bottom of the
bureau drawer, or lost them only to find them in the
clothes basket or at the back of a shelf. When I think of
writing you the room turns blue. Perhaps if I had not seen
the resemblance between you and his mother. . . . But I cannot blame memory.

I left long before he woke up. And when I got sick with
the child I suppose I decided that this was my fate. I could

have thrown it away but I was paralysed, and fascinated with how my body had betrayed me. It was as if I were living inside it, sharing it with the child like a corner, a bus shelter or a room. My body was an animal wanting food voraciously, suddenly heavy and falling down where it was, anywhere. I wanted to throw the child out of me, to cleave it off like meat. Well, the child was just another inhabitant after a while, and as soon as she came out I got rid of her. But I am thankful for one thing. It gave me the sense that I was separate from anything physical that might happen again. I would never be in my body as if it were me.

I hear you named her Bola. I hope you have never spoken to her of me. I don't want her longing for me, longing to know who I am and what I look like. I don't want her hearing how much she looks like me, has my nose, my mouth or my way of turning around. Don't saddle her with a memory that's not hers.

Forgive me. I know I cannot give instructions. That's not what I'm doing. I'm just trying to say, why make her long for anything? Anyway, this is not why I wrote to you. But I wanted her to sit in your lap as strongly as I wanted to get rid of her and live my life. I wanted her to sit in your lap and listen to the song of sucrier and think of Kamena wandering through the balata and teak and tangled undergrowth trying to find his way to Terre Bouillante. I wanted her to misplace my letters to you in her hurry to run outside.

I wanted her to be such a child, and I of course could not be such a woman fondling a letter waiting for a child to come home to read it. You and I planned that I would not be such a woman. You were that woman already.

I confess I didn't write while you were still there, and

it's so like me to write when there is no one there. I suppose the girl is with my older sisters now that you are
gone, she must be. I have years of letters from them. I
haven't opened them. I don't want to know what's inside.
I can tell by their handwriting. So furious. Sometimes I can
tell their urgency by how frequently they come. The one
time that I opened one it was so vicious that I tore it up.
I keep them but I don't open them. If the girl is in their
hands she is in their hands. Why blame me?

Sese said I was your favourite but of course I was the
youngest. She said you were blind to how wicked I was.
She stole the papers you gave me with Mama Bola's drawing. When I confronted her she lied and said I was crazy
and that I was always a liar. It is always about who was loved
the most or the least or not at all. One day I came home
and found her lying on her bed, holding Mama Bola's drawing. She didn't know I had come in, she was looking at it,
pulling her fingers along the outline, then along the creases
of paper, she played with the sand in the creases of the
paper. Then she looked up at me as if she knew that I'd
been there watching her and said, "Why did Mama give this
to you? Why do you always get everything?"

I was afraid she would tear it up so I remained quiet.
I suddenly saw that she had always been in the middle,
between the older ones going to England, and Carlyle so
dramatic, and Job and me. We were that way for a long
time, me standing in the doorway and she holding Mama
Bola's paper, looking at me with resentment.

Then she got up and left it on the bed. She walked into
me at the doorway, I could swear that she hit me in the
stomach and I felt all her hatred but also her sadness. What
would she have done with the paper, I wondered? I wanted

to give it to her if that would make her happy, but she'd wanted you to give it to her. It was nothing. Only an old yellowing paper, moths had eaten at the creases and it was stained in water or food and it seemed that once it had been crumpled up to be thrown out. Mama Bola had put sand in it from her time and she had stained it with roucou or her hand must have been stained in roucou when she touched every part of it. Sese just wanted it because you had given it to me. I must admit that I didn't know what I'd done with it until she found it in my things and took it, but at that moment with Sese it was precious and something between us.

There on the bed when she left was another bit of paper. I looked at it quickly and it was piece of a newspaper. A picture of her baby in the *Toronto Star*. Child of the Week, it said. It was a baby boy, Kevin they called him, baby Kevin. She had written the date in her handwriting, August 9th, 1970. "Baby Kevin is cheerful and inquisitive...," it said.

"I know where he is," she said, startling me. She had come back into the room. "I've seen him in the subway at Yonge. He was leaning against the wall. He was wearing a windbreaker. It had a number on it. He was with a white girl. His little sister maybe, he was holding her hand. I saw him. I know it was him."

She was lit up. All bony and bright. I noticed her hands, how small they were compared to mine. One gripping and rubbing the other. She wanted to talk, but I didn't. I had a vision of her haunting the subways, looking for any boy who looked like her baby Kevin. Going up to them, perhaps asking them their names, frightening them. I now knew why she came home later and later. I don't think that she wanted to find him so much as follow him, watch him

in his life. When I saw her that day, after I had not seen her
for years, she must have still been following baby Kevin.
What is he now? A boy, a man in a suit pacing the subway
platform, feeling the strange look of a small woman, sensing her behind him? Is he now a hockey player in Sarnia or
Peterborough? Does she spot him at Union Station with
bags and his sticks, in the middle of white friends, feeling
uncomfortable under her stare? Or did he see her at the
beginning of a summer when he was trying to decide what
to do with his life, did he see her, recognize who she must
be and take off in confusion to Alberta to sit in a tower,
watching the vastness for her, and for fires?

I never really knew her. I only remembered her in the
polish-shined corners of our house, lurking. She never
spoke. She cleaned every corner of that house as if she were
rubbing out her thoughts. She shined everything spotless.

I remember her only as half a face leaning on the jamb
of your bedroom door, listening to you tell of your papa.
You saying he searched the beach for his mother's footsteps, stepping into them so that he would be safe. That he
felt nauseous and dizzy, taking his own path, thinking the
ocean would suddenly lash out, slip the sand from under
him and drag him in. He stepped in his mother's footsteps
so that he would be safe.

We all loved it when you said that his grandmother
Marie Ursule loved us and sent us to the future because she
could not hold us, and in turn we could not hope to hold
our own lives together and that was her art and ours. We
loved that, not understanding it at all. We with no ambition except ruthlessness, delivering clots of blood, standing in windows and running off just for the speed of it. She
had sent all of us to make mornings, you said. How could

she know what kind of mornings? Perhaps it didn't matter, that was her art and ours.

Sese had a smallness and a secretiveness just like the corners of the house. Did you know that even her name was a secret to me until I grew older? It never seemed odd to me that we called her Sese, *soeur* said twice in patois. I only saw her real name on her pay cheque from the hospital where she worked here in Toronto. Margaret Childs. Margaret Childs who cleaned house like the big sister and was forgotten in all the letters from her bigger sisters in England because when it came her time there was no more money to go and she was considered too old by the time there was. Sese's face, I remember, as luminous as the doorjamb she had shined, a fear of her own beaming through. Of what, I am growing to know. Of simply falling. You said that is how your papa ran away to Terre Bouillante and why he built that almost airless house of ours, so strong, so impenetrable.

What a hunger! Was it childishness or something more? What would she have used it for? It's only a drawing of a rock and an ocean and a far shore with sticks for someone swimming in the ocean. I looked at it for some time, wanting to see what Sese saw. It was drawn with a stick burnt to charcoal and drawn many times over I could tell and then she must have tried to make it stay by putting the roucou over it. I can almost see her licking her lips and looking out to make sure she drew the place right. There are birds in the air and the ocean is big and the far shore only a trace. There is no one in the drawing but the rock, the ocean, the far shore and man-o'-war birds in the air. She had so many children, so many lovers, so much life, I wondered why this is all she drew.

I folded the paper up and searched the room for the other things you gave me, the dried bush in the gazette paper and the shell ground to powder in the tin can. I've kept them now all this time and will send them with this letter.

The child can have them. Whoever is there can have them. I have no use for them.

I know you loved that paper and that was why you gave it to me. You loved it as you loved letters from abroad. It is the past. I hate the past and for that matter the present. Did you spend hours too, looking at the far shore? Did your father give it to you I wonder, or did you find it as you found old letters behind doors and old chests? And what made Sese want it? Like wanting something ungettable— a boundary.

I heard a mot-mot this morning. I woke up and I heard a mot-mot. It was not my imagination, I know. I heard it. Just as I woke up. There must be a mot-mot here. A kind of mot-mot or something. Believe me, I dream of nothing, so it was not a dream. I lay in bed for some time awake, listening to it, and I thought how beautiful. I remembered it all day, even when I noticed that the floor was dirty and needed to be cleaned, I remembered it. Then I remembered it when I looked out the window but I couldn't see it, I couldn't even see a tree. The morning was cold, last night it was colder. I began to write to you again. Immediately I heard the sound of the mot-mot—I could see its head red and green and yellow and blue. It sang for a long time, until I got up, and then I forgot it again till now.

Dear Mama, I stand on the corner of a street and I am falling away. People go by me, so ferocious. They are lurching forward with such ferocity, such greedy determination for life I do not understand. I think that I am with them.

When I was twenty or so it was all I could do to hold my-self to the platform of a subway, not to leap. I walked close to the walls, tracing the names of them all, tracing the let-terings with my fingers to distract myself from noticing the rails waiting. Y-O-N-G-E. C-A-S-T-L-E F-R-A-N-K. B-R-O-A-D-V-I-E-W. At any moment I might have leapt, yet I was drawn to the subway to watch when I noticed this involuntary greed of bodies. I would go every day to think of how I could leap, how I could leave all these people with no purpose, just lurching into living.

If I had written enough words to you, perhaps I would save myself. If I had sent them to you instead of only writ-ing them in my head or tracing them on the walls of subways in this city, perhaps I would hold myself together. As it is now with all the words lost and the things unwritten. All the paper bluing on your breath now could not save me.

I never had the courage to come home. I never had the courage to have you comfort me. The farthest back I've been is Jamaica and there I saw people clinging to the rim of that island, gripping tight to the dry heat and the broken buildings and I knew that that was as close as I could come. All that desperation frightened me. The suicide of whole villages, the water creeping to their feet and the knives of rain and the harness of the sun.

I saw a little girl one day step into a small dirty canal to let a car pass in Annoto Bay, and in that moment she brought a handkerchief to her face to wipe away sweat and I saw her sorrow as big as a grown woman's. I could not help crying as I passed in the transport. I could not help feeling that I was leaving something weak at the side of the road and that I should go back and take her or else kill her.

I saw a woman waiting for a bus next to a field near Port Maria. Her dress was alive until I realized that she was standing there with butterflies. She alone, holding her hat on her head with butterflies, butter-coloured butterflies with round wings swirling around her.

This is the kind of stupid thing that happens soon after you see a little girl who should be taken out of her misery. And I cannot make head nor tail of it, Mama. Why would I see them both the same day and walking the same ground? I've seen that little girl before. I've seen her in many places I've gone. I've seen her resting against a wall like that with her handkerchief and her age, her misery and her loss and the impossibility of her life, as if it had suddenly occurred to her as she waited for the transport to pass, bringing her handkerchief to her face as if to wipe the heat, the water, away. Did I look like that as a little girl, in Terre Bouillante? She is going to collect water or she is going to pick up some money from her father or she is going to deliver a message to someone, a dress measurement or a price for so many green figs.

At any rate, at that moment the world passes over her face when the transport passes by and she is overwhelmed and she knows it is useless because her true face arrives and she must dry it, pass her hand over it and collect herself. And if someone recognizes her from a transport then they take that glimpse of her away, not because she lets them but because she has unintentionally thought of everything at that moment, and so whoever sees this is let in on a confidence. I felt as if I had seen something shameful for a moment then sad.

And the woman with the butter-coloured butterflies, the round wings fluttering and swirling around her, the dress was brown and now I remember there were white flowers on it and I don't remember her face. It said nothing. If anything a small impatience with the butterflies, but she looked as if it was a usual thing to stand waiting with butterflies swirling around you.

It is all happenstance, Mama, whether we are miserable or not. We are a tragedy, Mama. A whole broken-up tragedy, standing in the middle of the world cracking. I think of Carlyle, and that boy he was with from God knows where, and me, rushing down those highways in America in a temper. Cities rushed by us, and roads. We never saw them. I felt as if we had been scattered out with a violent randomness. As the girl with her sorrow. As the woman with her butterflies.

Dear Mama, is it warm there, are you sleeping in the afternoon with the curtain blowing against your cheek, are there children around you, playing, waiting for you to wake up, impatiently opening your eyes with their fingers? Are you dressed in blue? I always waited for you to wake. So my life would continue. I was not always mindful. Sometimes I would plot against you or forget you completely but as soon as your eyes were closed for too long I worried. Dear Mama, hope, hope you are well.

BOLA

~~~~~~~~~~

If you saw us in our home, a mother and daughter sitting on the back steps, never leaving our little house at the bottom of our street in Terre Bouillante, you would immediately see how much we enjoyed our life.

My sister said we had to move from 30 McIntyre Street. She said she could hear people walking outside as if they were walking in the house. She said so one morning after our mother died. She said the street was coming into our house, she could hear people outside walking and we had to move away.

Our mother grew sick and was taken away to the big hospital on the wharf. Then she died and came home in a coffin. They cleared out the living room to hold our mother's coffin and put the coffin near the windows where the sun shone and the breeze came and the curtains blew. But they had taken the curtains down when they heard our mother died so she couldn't feel the light breeze through the windows when she lay in her coffin when she came home. Our mother lay in her coffin beside the windows with her eyes closed, lying on her back.

"Well, that's the end of that then," my sister said after my mother lay there with her eyes closed. My sister said this after a day or two, when our mother would not move or listen to us cry. "Well, that's the end of that," she said.

Our mother had gone and died just like that. My sister said our mother was tired, that was why. My sister said I had not behaved and our mother had become tired of it. Our mother lay in her coffin under the windows on her back with her eyes closed no matter how much I beseeched her to wake up. We promised never to do certain things again but that didn't wake her. I promised to clean and not complain. We promised everything, I even promised to stop crying because I thought this was making it unpleasant for my mother and not any kind of scene for her to return to. But with all our promises our mother just lay there under the windows.

The house seemed empty except for our mother's coffin. All the curtains had been removed and all the mirrors had been covered in black cloth and there seemed nowhere to sit so once or twice we leaned on our mother's coffin and then it felt just like leaning on our mother as she lay in bed or sat at the table or stood at the sink, washing wares. And in a short few days we became used to our mother lying under the window and we became used to leaning on her coffin and complaining.

We heard they were taking her to the Paradise cemetery soon, but we thought nothing of it. We could go on, we all agreed, living with our mother in our house with the curtains taken away and the mirrors covered. We did not mind our mother lying in her coffin under the windows and we could live that way fine, if we had to, so long as our mother was there. After my sister said, "Well, that is the end of that," we realized our mother had abandoned us, was gone and left lying under the window like that, not moving. The day our mother had to leave for the Paradise cemetery we became afraid of our mother.

My sister came and told us to get dressed and line up to kiss our mother goodbye. My sister said this and stood there and we stood too, waiting for my sister to make a plan. My sister just said, "Well, that's the end of that," and stood there.

We lined up to kiss our mother and we were afraid. Our mother did not look at us. She looked up at the ceiling and lay in her coffin under the windows. She looked up at the window with her eyes closed. When we kissed our mother she did not sigh or hum, and she didn't say a single word. We began to scream. Not a word, not a sigh, not a hum. We screamed and screamed and screamed and wept.

Our mother's coffin floated in our tears. Our tears fell like rain filling up the whole living room and wetting our clothes, our faces were bloated from the soak of tears and our shoes slipped when we tried to walk to our mother's coffin under the window. There were water marks on the windows and the mirrors under their black cloth were melting and slipping out but our mother lay there quite quiet. She simply lay there floating away in her coffin as if she were only waiting for our tears to float her out the house and sail her down to the Paradise cemetery.

I was sweeping the back steps just as our mother was dying and a ladybug flew at me. I thought at first she was a fly and tried to brush her away but she lighted on my hand and I knew that it was our mother. Then, that night, while they were removing the curtains and covering the mirrors the same ladybird appeared on the bread at the table, then she got attracted by the light. I had never seen a ladybird at night and neither had anyone else and that's when I knew for sure it was our mother. She was red with black dots and I knew it was a good sign. Our mother had not died but had gone into another shape.

The big people kept quiet and stared at me because the ladybug had landed on my piece of bread and it was all I could do not to say "Mama." Ladybugs never came at night before and no one at the table wanted to say too quickly that it was our mother, but all of us knew when she landed on my bread. I left the bread sitting there and she climbed around it and then flew to the light. Then I thought she would burn up so I begged them to turn the light off so that our mother could see her way out and not burn in the light. They turned the light off and we sat in the dark for several minutes. I could hear my sisters crying because we all knew that it was our mother. When they turned the light on again our mother was still sitting on the bulb and we began to weep again until they turned it off. We heard the voice of our mother even when she didn't speak, even when she hummed, even when she was silent.

That afternoon, when I was sweeping the back steps and the dust blew thin and brown and the light grabbed each grain, I knew that the ladybug was our mother. That afternoon it was gold and black and flew up in the dust.

I was thinking of the guava tree and thinking that while our mother was away I could climb it and pick the guavas green and dip them in salt and eat them and our mother would not know because she always warned me not to climb the tree and to let the guavas ripen first, and then sometimes she said girls climbing the tree would blight it and the guavas would wither. She didn't know that I climbed the tree all the time behind her back and nothing happened.

But I was thinking I would do it at my leisure before she came back and then I could confess to climbing the tree when the guavas withered.

Just then the ladybug, which was gold and black in the afternoon, came flying through the dust. The dust flew even faster, it was as if our mother had disturbed the sun and the sun was pouring out dust. I stopped and waited for my mother to settle. But I looked up and I could see the sun pouring more and more dust out, spilling over as if my mother had disturbed the sun's dust with her wings. I had to squint to see and then it settled and then she flew off.

In the night when our mother came back and lighted on my bread we were having evening tea. I was about to soak my bread in hot cocoa, a thing my mother hated me to do. And then my mother lighted on it and I began to cry in anticipation of her licking. After a while sitting in the dark waiting for my mother to leave or find a more suitable spot, a spot where perhaps she could live till tomorrow, I fell asleep at the table. The big people tried to turn the lights on but I would not have it. They tried to make me go to our bed but I would not budge. Finally they left me there at the table with the cold cocoa tea and the lady bug somewhere in the room.

I had read that lady bugs do not live very long. Why would our mother take this ephemeral form? If I were to die, for example, I would become a big piece of stone. Stones I know have eyes and they move even though we may not think so, they are very cunning. So I would be a stone, a black stone with grey dust, and I would sit and watch all the time.

They made us form another line in the street when they were ready to take our mother to the Paradise cemetery. I

felt ashamed standing in the middle of the road with the
whole street watching us. I wondered why our mother had
decided to make this display. She hated that ordinarily. Our
mother would have been happy to lie in her coffin under the
window and have us read to her and tell her our troubles
and now and then take a sip of guava juice and now and then
yawn, but no, people who did not love her like we did were
sending her to the Paradise cemetery.

So we lined up in a parade, feeling stranded, behind
our mother's coffin. Our feet felt like stubs of dead wood
and they burned in our shoes and we walked weeping and
stranded all along one street then another then turning onto
the main road and then to the Paradise cemetery, where our
mother was now going to live.

I kept the dead ladybird in the pocket of my funeral
dress. I had found her that morning lying on the window sill
beside my mother's coffin. It was brown now with red dots
and there were many others there with it, so many, crowds
of ladybugs on the window sill, so I had to be careful to find
the right one, which was our mother. I called my sisters to
help me find our mother and as we looked and looked the
big people screamed at us to stop and get dressed. Just ladybugs, they screamed, a swarm of ladybugs passing through.
But they could not convince me that our mother was not
among them. So I didn't listen but searched and searched
for the prettiest dead ladybug on the window sill or the floor.
When I found her and we agreed that it was dear Mama, we
carried her in turns. My sweet sisters allowed me to carry
her in my pocket since I was the one whose bread she had
lighted on the night before and I was the one sweeping the
back yard when she first appeared.

So in the procession to the cemetery I held her in my

pocket and checked all the time through my tears if she was still there. I knew she should have chosen a more durable shape but it was her decision to be a ladybug and to fly with a swarm of ladybugs and to fall asleep on the window sill next to her coffin. After all our mother must know what she is doing. I wished she had not placed us in this embarrassing situation by dying.

"Well, that's the end of that," my sister said through her tears as we walked behind our mother with everyone watching. I had never been ashamed to walk with my mother before and now here I was walking behind her coffin and ashamed and wishing she had not done this, or that she had done it so privately that I would not notice. And here I was carrying her in my pocket with only the shell of her left.

We passed by girls from my school who smiled at me as if they were happy for my mother's death, or jeering. And I smiled back as if we were having a celebration and then I was ashamed again at feeling a tinge of happiness at the small celebrity our mother had brought us. Our aunts peered at us from the only vehicle in the procession and looked stern at my laughter and happiness. I wanted to spit at them. Where had they come from, sitting in the car while we walked with all our tears and our mother sailing along the road? Who were they to direct us as to what we should feel or how we should walk?

I ignored them all the way to the cemetery and put a slowness in my step so that I would not arrive. I delayed the procession with loud weeping and fainting half of which I surely felt but half became performance for my friends at the side of the road and the big people. All of this I would explain later to our mother so she would understand, I did not mean to laugh at her. All my feelings were happening at the same time and I became confused, not knowing what to laugh at and what to cry for.

After the funeral my sister moved us from 30 McIntyre Street to another street in another town, August Town. Well, we moved but I never believed that that was the end of that. I visited our mother in the Paradise cemetery for many days and then many years. We had conversations. Well, at first it seemed that I talked to myself but I knew our mother was listening. Lying there in her coffin she could not be deaf to me, and not for one moment did I believe my mother was rotting and turning into a skeleton; not when I knew how she loved talking and listening.

After some years my belief and devotion paid off because my mother came out and sat beside me on her grave. Her dress was the same as when they laid her in the coffin, a blue satin with blue lace over the bodice and small fake pearls around her neck. She complained they had not given her any shoes, just stockings, and that her feet had been cold. But my mother was beautiful and laughing as ever.

Luckily, that day I had brought her some of her favourite sweets, paradise plums, the red and yellow stripes with white sugar dusted on them. I asked her why, why had she left us. She would not answer but began to yawn as if she were weary and this led me to believe my sister had been right. I had tired our mother so much by not obeying and doing my work that she had lain down in a coffin to get some rest. I stopped asking why, why did she leave us, because I understood, and because I feared she would remember and leave again. And some days when I arrived and she was lying in her coffin, I would cry and beseech her to come out but she would not. I would wait for night to come so I could hold the silver cross from my mother's coffin.

Jesus was impaled on it, and I held his feet next to my head with both hands and I prayed nine prayers. The next day I could not wait to go see our mother, and there she would be in her blue-lace satin dress and fixing her hat.

All my plan was to get our mother to come back home. Of course home was not where she remembered and I circled and circled the subject, not wanting to tell her we had moved. Finally I could not tell her. We discussed the people laying wreaths, or the priests who came at night and talked to the dead tugging their cassocks and screaming, or the lovers who came to the Paradise cemetery to make another kind of love in privacy.

And so we whiled away time. Whiled away time. If you came to the Paradise cemetery on these days you would find us sitting close together, my mother in her lovely blue satin lace and I in my school uniform, our heads together or me holding my mother. I liked it when we were alone. I liked the pleasure on her face when I unwrapped the brown paper full of paradise plums. I liked the rows and rows of headstones and the empty cemetery with its quiet and hush. There is no place like a cemetery for quiet. Everyone there is finished with saying whatever they have to say, every thought is concluded.

Since my mother spoke in her mind and only rarely would she speak out loud, the cemetery was filled with my voice. When I realized this I tried to speak in a whisper but even my whisper burst the quiet and I could hear the echo of myself against the cemetery and hear it clang on the gates with the iron curls so sometimes I would have to speak in my mind also.

Our mother loved to speak in her mind. She too had said all she needed to before she climbed into her coffin and I began to understand little by little why she had lain there under the window with the breeze blowing through the curtain, just looking at the sun. I dressed in my uniform to meet my mother. I decided to wear it forever so that she would recognize me or until she became so used to me that it would not matter, but just for convenience's sake and to help my mother remember I wore it for ever.

We continued in this way for many years, my mother and I. My sisters carried on, they changed clothes, they brushed their teeth, they had flings with boys, they chatted as if our mother was gone and they would look at me strangely when I said I had seen our mother. They stopped in the middle of conversations as if I had interrupted them from more important things, they looked at me and sucked their teeth and told me to shut up.

My sister said, "They going to lock you up if you don't shut up." At other times she tried to be more consoling, saying, "Just don't tell nobody else. Is just we secret." But when I took this for her friendship and knowledge and told her some message our mother had sent her, like don't forget to water the plants and don't mash down the aloes and save the orange peel for fever, she shouted at me, "Shut up." I would then hide under the bed. I felt that her voice was so powerful that it blew me under the bed, all I would see was her mouth large as the sky at night and I would feel a wind blasting and the air between us would shake.

At other times I would hide behind the hibiscus hedge at the new house and there I would squeeze flowers until the red of them cut all my fingers. I would put the blood on my face and wear it all day as an armour against her windy voice. But my sister would often surprise me at the hibiscus hedge or trap me under the bed and haul me to the bathroom

and tear off my uniform. She said I stank and didn't I see
that my pink blouse was purple with dirt and my overall was
in tatters? I would run to find the silver cross from our
mother's coffin. My heart would beat so fast in my ears it
sounded like someone walking.

After these excesses by my sister, I would have to sneak
away in the night to the Paradise cemetery to see if our
mother was still there. I would stay all night with our
mother and the morning would find us looking at the sun
coming over the Paradise hill. My sisters were unfaithful
but I sat beside our mother and vowed never to leave her. I
complained to our mother but she did not seem to hear and
I dropped the subject, since I had noticed that there were
subjects which she did not want to go over.

My mother wanted a new life even as I wanted an old
one. This bothered and upset me but my frowning and pout-
ing had no effect on her. And of course I wanted to know
what could be more perfect than our life now. I wondered
what new life she wanted even as I held her in my arms in
the cemetery. I would tearfully beg her to come back to our
old selves but these times she seemed more distant and
asked me where did I get the paradise plums from and why
hadn't I brought more. I always had an extra supply for
these moments and she would fall on them ravenously and
that would be the end of her trying to go to her other life.

It was beautiful to watch us, I'm sure, sitting side by
side. Two figures sitting bent over in thought, our mother's
blue dress with lace and I in my new crisp uniform the way
my mother liked it, ironed to a shine, the gravestones white
and grey, with their flowers dying, and their candles waxed
to their heads, the emptiness of the cemetery perhaps in the
afternoon just as the sun breaks an afternoon cloud, how a

pink light would suffuse us turning orange on the brass of
the Paradise cemetery wrought-iron letters; how settled
the cemetery is then, how like life going on away from the
town streets.

Every day in the Paradise cemetery is like Sunday. I loved
sitting on my mother's own grave with her. I brought her
food. She said bring flowers, lilac and white ones, orchids
and fern. So I did. When I went home every day I could not
take the image of me and our mother out of my mind. Just a
woman and a girl laughing and talking at a gravestone, the
beautiful afternoons when the sun would purple and rise to
the west of the cemetery and our slender figures would part
clouds and hold the sun just there, and the droplets of
clouds in the seams of the strafed clouds and our laughter
and my mother's thoughts filling the cemetery and my voice
answering hers.

I wished that my sisters would come but they didn't,
they sent flowers instead and I think one day after some
time they forgot all about our mother.

"What the hell wrong with she?" I heard my sisters saying. "She always wearing the old clothes, is crazy she crazy
or what?"

I hated them now. How could they forget our mother? So
all this time they had only pretended to love our mother?
No, I did not want to believe that. Perhaps if our mother
came back they would remember and love her again. We
had been so happy, all of us together. Didn't they remember
how our mother used to dance with us and how, to stop
us from sucking our thumbs, she'd give us pieces of cloth
dipped in sugar and how when we had worms she'd stay up
all night bent over, pulling worms out of us? Didn't they
remember our mother scalding her hand with hot milk to

make sure that our tongues would not burn on the nipple, didn't they understand the sacrifice of our mother balling hot rice with her fingers and blowing it to cool before putting it into our mouths? Didn't they remember our mother waiting at the window for us to come home, didn't they remember her curled up on her bed when she was sad?

If nothing else they should remember when she was sad, when our father, wherever he was, would not write or come or think of her and she was sad and we gathered about her and combed her hair and cut her toenails and made her tea.

All of this we did for our mother because when our mother was happy she gave us cherry wine and dates, and put lipstick on our mouths and allowed us to wear her dresses and her high-heeled shoes and laughed at the way we stumbled around. Our mother cooked and cooked and danced the Castilian and oiled our feet. Was our mother someone to be forgotten and abandoned just so, just because she had died? I could not believe it. Perhaps their grief was so great that they could not show it, perhaps they were afraid it would blow them away far into the sea and then there would be no hope of seeing our mother again. Yes, perhaps they were so distraught they could not bear to even look unhappy or think about our mother. But if they knew, if they would only come with me to the Paradise cemetery and sit on the gravestone with our mother and hold the sun to the west and part the clouds, they would not look at me so strangely and rip my uniform off my body. So I decided to persuade our mother to come home.

A letter came for our mother today. It is a blue airmail letter, the kind our mother used to get from people abroad. The kind my sisters used to read to her. My sisters read the letter and then hid it from me. I know this because when I asked them to see it—because our mother would always ask each one to read the letters from abroad and it was my turn—my sisters hid the letter from me. I searched and searched one day while they were out but I could not find the letter.

I heard a mot-mot this morning. As I woke up I heard a mot-mot. And I could, by hearing it sing, I could tell that it was saying something. I listened for quite a while, lying in my bed on the floor. I could hear it under the door coming in with the breeze and then I had to get up quickly and run to the Paradise cemetery to tell my mother.

I have persuaded our mother to come home with me. I told her that I went to school today and the teacher put me out. Our mother would always come to the school with us when anything was wrong. I persuaded her that if she were home with us the teacher would not put me out of the school. The teacher was so rude to me, I told my mother. She said I was too old, she said my uniform was filthy and I should not come back there. She would never say this if my mother were at home and if my mother would come to the school with me.

Our mother looked cross because it was lunchtime when I arrived and I usually visited our mother after school. She came out as usual in her blue dress and she looked vexed and I felt bad because my uniform was ripped at the hem and our mother was tired of sewing up hems, so I promised her that this time I would do it myself and told her that I was very sorry but the teacher had put me out of the school.

Our mother sat on her gravestone a long time, watching me in my poor state. The sun was so hot I began to sweat because it was lunchtime. My head was itchy and a headache started to come down the centre of my forehead. Our mother just sat there not answering me. So I stood up after a while and began to walk away. When I reached the gates I looked back and there she was still sitting in the sun in her blue dress with the lace and I thought, "This is the last time I will see my mother." And then her head turned toward me and she looked angry, so I began walking quickly. What was she saying? Should I go back to the school or should I go home?

And that is when I decided to go to where we used to live in Terre Bouillante, at 30 McIntyre Street, before my sister said, "Well, that is the end of that." I could not go back to August Town after they put me out of the school. My sisters would laugh at me and tear up my clothes—my sisters were always telling me I was too old and they should run me out of the school. Just because *they* did not wear their uniforms, just because *they* did not go to see our mother, just because *they* were talking things I could not understand . . . I could not go back to them so I decided to go home.

I walked along so sad all the people were looking at me. They must have seen how sad I was. I could not stop crying because the teacher had put me out, and now where was my education going to be, and then my mother did not care and only sat on her gravestone looking at me because I had been put out of the school and my uniform hem was ripped. I would become nothing now, just as our mother had said. I know the people must have felt sorry for me along the way—I was crying loud and some of them started to run away from me because they could not bear my grief. Some put their hands to their faces and sobbed for me. I heard them say, "Poor thing, poor thing."

The tears were blinding me but somehow I found myself

in the old streets where we used to live, before the people came and took our mother to the Paradise cemetery while we walked behind. I cried so much that my books were frayed and wet from my hands. My whole body cried and my book bag was torn and frayed too and when I passed in front of the gasoline station I saw my face in the glass case and it was old. It looked older than who I was and I could not recognize it properly except that I had my red ribbon in my front braid and that is how I knew it was me. But the rest of me was older.

I stopped there after staring at myself in the glass case and that is when I saw our mother following me, just as I was telling myself that it was the glass case distorting the age of my face. There she was coming along the road in her blue dress with the lace and no shoes. She stopped to look at a run in her stocking, then she walked on toward me but she seemed to stay the same distance. I saw her in the glass case and when I looked around she dodged behind a car but when I looked into the glass case again there she was. I forgot about my face and walked on. And so our mother little by little was coming home with me.

When I arrived at our old house on McIntyre Street it was still there and I sat on the steps and I cried. It was still there, the gate to the gallery and the brown wooden door. When I turned to show our mother, she had disappeared again. And then I thought perhaps she was loitering at a neighbour's. Yes, surely she had to say hello again to all the people she had not seen since her funeral, so of course she must have been next door with the neighbour.

So I waited on the steps for our mother to come home just like before. I went into the house to wait and I removed all the sheets from the chairs and the mirrors. There was dust everywhere and I was dusting when my mother said from the door, "Don't dust, it will only grow again." But when I turned to the door she was gone again, perhaps she was in her room, the front room where she used to lie. She was so tired I left her alone to rest and did not go to her room. Yes, my mother and I would be very happy here now. I felt happy, I felt content, I did not even have to turn a light on when the evening was coming as I used to beg my mother to do. I was so happy that I was not afraid.

I sat there and planned to go to my sisters and tell them that our mother had returned just as I had said. I was always telling them that our mother could not find us in a new house but they would not believe me. I never went back though. I could not bear to leave our mother. Each day I remembered that I meant to go to them and try one last time to persuade them, but I would get caught up in our mother's laugh or her calling and then the day would be gone.

Some people came to visit us today. They were two women and they resembled my sisters, only they were much much older. Yet one of them reminded me of my sister, because she said, when the other one asked me to leave with her and I said no, she said, "Well, that is the end of that." Just like my sister.

I told them I had to comb my mother's hair and I had to cut her toenails and then I had to do my homework and get ready for school in the morning. They talked and talked. One of them said, "She's mad, I wash my hands of her," the same one who had said that's the end of that. The other one said, "We should write to her mother in Canada and get her to come for her."

I remembered that I had planned just today to go to tell

my sisters that our mother had returned, but again I had forgotten. That was why the one who said "Well, that is that" was reminding me of my sister then. But where would I find the time now, with everything to do, how could I go? I did not know why these two came but they didn't disturb me and I let them sit in the gallery and I gave them water to drink. They talked for a long time and I hemmed my uniform as my mother had taught me and I listened. They were saying that their mother should never have taken some child and that she should have told the child everything because now the child had gone mad.

"Damn irresponsible, she was always damn irresponsible." The other one looked at her harshly and said, "You never got along with Eula, you were jealous of her because she was the youngest. Mama was too old when she had her, that's why. But you could never understand that."

"She is up there living life, God knows where, and we have to take care of her trouble. You don't call that irresponsible? How long now? How long? Sixteen years. Look at this crazy girl. Who the hell is responsible for that?"

They looked at me as if they were asking my opinion, but what was I to say? These strangers who looked and talked like my sisters but weren't, just sitting in our gallery talking to each other. I didn't know them, why would I intervene? I didn't want to get into their fight. Suppose they woke up our mother from her nap? I tried to tell them that they could stay but that they should speak quietly. They could not sit there and be waking our mother. Our mother would have no peace at all.

"She's filthy."

"But she looks happy now."

"What people going to think? They'll think we abandoned

her. They don't know how much trouble this has been for us and her mother off living big as usual."

These two seemed to visit all the time when I first came to live in our old house with our mother and then it would be months before I saw them again. They were nice enough but I never understood why they had to use our gallery to sit and talk.

One day I was fed up with their talking and I said to them, "But, look here, why don't you leave this girl alone and this mother maybe she had her reasons like my own mother whom I had to walk all the way from the cemetery to get to come live with me, and still that was after what seemed like many years of persuasion." And I said to them, "Why don't you go and find this woman and take her some butterscotch perhaps or read her her favourite book, and then maybe she will come."

That day I insisted that they go and when they did not move off our gallery I took a stick from our guava tree and I ran them away. You can't spend so much time in deciding and deciding. You have to make up your mind and all will come true. I ran after them all the way to the gas station and I only stopped because I saw our mother in the glass case again fixing her stocking. I stopped and saw them too in the glass case next to our mother. They looked at me as they always do, as if I were speaking from a deep well and as if they could not hear me, and then they turned away, caressing our mother and I dropped the stick and began to walk home because I knew that our mother would follow me. Months later I found them again in our gallery sipping their tea, which I had made them. I didn't mind them so much but they always spoke too loud and I was afraid that it would wake our mother, so sometimes when they came I hid behind the curtain at the window just as our mother used to do and I pretended to be away. And they called out my name, Bola, Bola, as if they knew me. I did not remember telling them my name but perhaps I did. Even though our mother called for me to say what was that noise and who were those women, I did not move. I stood still, still still as a ghost. They looked as if they saw me. They looked as if they saw through the curtain, but I stood so still.

We spend our days sitting on the back step and talking, our mother and I. That is also why sometimes we miss the women at the front. Though I have not seen them for some time now, ever since I turned to a ghost and they watched me through the curtain as if I was there and not there. My mother and I sit on the back steps. We take in the sun and we talk. We sit and we smell mango trees come into bloom and we listen to the bash of calabashes falling and breaking and we smell guavas and we smell the grey sluice in the drains. We hear sugar birds and we stone them with slingshots. Our mother sits on the top step as usual, in her blue dress with the lace and I sit on the bottom step as usual in my uniform. Though I have not been back to the school since my mother came home. My mother doesn't quarrel with me about going. Ever since that day when they sent me away. What can I do if they don't want me to go there? I was a scholar, our mother said. I was her scholar, she said when I recited my lessons for her. So to comfort her I sit on the bottom step and I recite my lessons which I have learned by heart.

Our birth is but a sleep and a forgetting:
The Soul that rises with us, our life's star,
Hath had elsewhere its setting,
And cometh from afar:

Not in entire forgetfulness,
And not in utter nakedness,
But trailing clouds of glory do we come
From God, who is our home:
. . .
Thou, whose exterior semblance doth belie
Thy Soul's immensity;
. . .
Full soon thy Soul shall have her earthly freight,
And custom lie upon thee with a weight,
Heavy as frost, and deep almost as life!

My mother loved these lines and I would recite them for her when she seemed far away. They seemed to lift her even though they were heavy words and words I did not understand and only knew from memory but not from any life.

The neighbours do not come over since our mother came back. They are giving her time to rest, I think, and our mother was never too sociable anyway. But when we sit on the steps to talk and me to recite sometimes I can see them trying to get a peek at our mother. I suppose they also cannot believe that she has returned. Once or twice they've asked me who I'm speaking to as if in disbelief or just to make sure. They smile and I know they're just asking to get a smile out of me and we can share this happiness. My life is perfect here with my mother.

. . . and deep almost as life!
O joy! that in our embers
Is something that doth live,
That nature yet remembers
What was so fugitive!

I memorized these lines for the teacher, Mrs. Palmer, and I was the best memorizer and when our mother took me up in these lines she loved them so much that she made me say them even after we were past that lesson.

One morning in our earlier life I woke up and saw our mother's face as a face I would never see again and as she prepared me for school I decided to stay with her. I hid outside the house behind a post until ten o'clock and then I called to her. She was startled and then angry and raised her hand to me and said, "What about your education? Who will mind you?" And I said to her, which does a person need more—a mother or an education?

Our house was peaceful again. Our mother had visitors of her own now and then. A boy came to visit and our mother called him "Father." He kept hiding and hiding and looking at my mother and when she called he would not answer. After a while my mother paid him no mind and he left.

I woke up to his little voice one night and I listened to him telling our mother that after his brother Juvenal was taken by the hurricane he mistrusted the wind and the sea even more.

My mother said, "Father, Father, don't go over it again. Let it rest."

But he continued, saying the hurricane had ripped up the shacks along the beach and sent some of them sailing out to sea. Banks of sand piled up to the windows and doorways of the shacks that were left, covering all inside with the fine gritty dust. Trees, half their bodies flayed by the winds stood one-sided, as if they were mad, as if, he said, they were raising their only arm for help.

Our mother said, "Father, you know how you get when you remember. Please forget."

The boy wept and I fell asleep to his small weeping. The next day I thought that I had had a dream only, and that the boy was not real. I asked our mother about him, and she brushed me away saying, "You were sleeping."

Then again in my sleep I heard the boy come back every night until his story was finished. His mother did not lose her curiosity about the sea. "I begged her," he said, "I begged her for us to move."

Instead his mother told him, "Go your way, my boy. Go your own way."

She made a wreath of twigs and dead flowers and limp herbs to her hurricane-gone son, sailing it out on the water and singing the name of her own mother, Marie Ursule. She made a wreath every day until the hurricane was not so bad a memory. Using what she found, her wreaths becoming more beautiful as the shrubs and plants caught themselves and as flowers struggled to appear. She still spent hours in the sea, her dress ballooning like a sail.

When I dreamed this boy's life I would wake up as if I had not slept. When he stood standing on the sand, waiting for his mother, he hated the way little waves would edge toward his toes, bubbles of sea froth would creep toward him and the waves would pull the sand from under his feet making him unsteady and dizzy. I would have loved that, I told him. I like to spin and spin around until I am dizzy. He feared the bash of huge waves, their violence, he said, and noise, but he would stand there waiting, steeling himself, closing his eyes out of fright, waiting for his mother. He kept me awake so much I have forgotten the rest of what he said and if I ask our mother the next morning she says, "Don't worry yourself in old people's business."

If you walked down our street the year our mother came

back, you would find our house on the corner at the bottom
of the street. Our house was painted cream and brown and
it sat at the bottom of the street and so there was land
around it and a small ravine on one side and a neighbour
whose house was yellow on the other and across the street
was neighbour Tanty and then there was the playground,
which our mother never let me go to. The children there
were not nice, she said. And if you came down our street to
our house, especially in the afternoons when our mother
and I sat on the back steps, you would see our house, peaceful and quiet except for my recitations, which I recited low
and continuous because my mother loved them, or if you
listened closely you could hear our mother telling me in her
soft low voice to hem my skirt or shine the windows or
sending me to the shop for messages or telling me to cut the
grass. If you came to the bottom of the street to our house
in Terre Bouillante, you would see us living an ordinary life
with no funerals and strange people coming into the house
to cover the mirrors.

I had thrown all the mirrors into the back yard when we
first arrived even though our mother told me to leave them
alone. After those people had come, when our mother came
back from the hospital in her coffin, something had happened to the mirrors. So that when our mother and I
arrived this last time and my mother told me to leave the
covers I was disturbed by the mirrors underneath. They
had turned into jumbies and I knew every time I passed by
them, I knew that they were not mirrors any more. I had
glimpsed someone there. She was there and I could only see
her eyes, which were closed and only opened for a minute
to watch me and then I dropped the cover. In that simple
moment I saw that she was not me, not a girl with her

mother coming happily home, but she was . . . I cannot say
what she was. . . .

So one day when our mother was asleep I took the mirrors down and threw them in the back yard. The wardrobe
mirror and the bureau mirror. I wrenched them down from
the wood and I threw them away. I turned them over and I
put sticks and dirt on them.

When our mother woke up she said, "What was that
racket yuh making when I trying to sleep?"

So I gave her her favourite flour dumplings and she ate
them, saying, "I know you do something, don't think I'll
forget just for dumplings."

But I knew that she would forget. She was exhausted
and she always forgot when she was tired. I left the jumbies
down in the back yard and soon I forgot them and then
they died.

A letter and box came for our mother today but my
mother would not give me permission to read it to her. She
said, "Here, take the box." When I begged her to let me
read the letter to her as my sisters had done before, when
we would all gather around her and tug and pull while she
tried to read the letter holding it up to the light, she said,
"You will lose it and then I will not be able to find it any
more. You children always losing my things."

The box was a brown box with a twine tied around it.
There was a paper inside with an ocean and a rock and a far
shore and a figure standing on the rock. And there was a tin
can with a bush tied around with twine. The paper smelled
old and there was sand in it and I licked the sand. I had never
tasted sand before. It was salty. It was fine and brown and
black and shiny if you looked a certain way.

Our mother always promised to take us by the sea but

she never had the chance. It was expensive, she said, and it was a long journey and with so many children it would have to be when we got money. So I licked the sand because maybe this was my mother's way of taking me to the sea. I licked the sand and I smelled the sea in it. It was salty and I saw our mother walking on the beach where, she said, her father, the boy, was born. I didn't eat all the sand, I saved some for our mother and my sisters who never went to the sea either. I tied the bush around my neck and my mother said that it was pretty and that it would keep away bad things.

Our mother lay on her bed with the letter in her fingers and I asked her again if I might read it to her but she just looked at me and then after a minute held it up to the light. It was night and there was only the light of the moon through the window now and it came between the branches of the guava tree and when the breeze blew it shifted the light and my mother began to read. The words my mother read were in gibberish and I had to put the g's and l's back in to understand.

"Deagelar Magalama, Hogolope yogolo argarla wegelell agalan egelenjoygoloyigiling thegle begelest ogolof hegeleath."

It was very hard to understand and soon our mother tired again. Her eyes were not good so she stopped and I asked her again if she wanted me to read for her but she said no and asked me to recite my lesson. She was sad now and I suppose that is why as soon as she was asleep I threw the blue letter behind the wardrobe so that it would not make her unhappy to read it.

Many letters have lain there over the years. My sisters and I sometimes deliberately put them there so that our mother would not be distracted. We saw that sometimes they made her unhappy as well, sometimes they gave her hopes, but we did not like this other life our mother had of blue airmail letters that could break up our house or fly away with it all at once. So I hid the letter.

I kept the box with the drawing and the sand because I liked the picture, and the twine made a good ribbon for my front braid and when next our mother remembered and asked me for the letter I told her I did not know what had happened to it.

The next day after I put the letter carelessly behind the wardrobe I waited for the postman and I told him never to bring another letter here. I waited for him behind the hibiscus fence, to stay out of the way, in the shade, and when he broke the fence line and saw me he jumped back as if I had frightened him and then I told him, "No more letters, no one here can read them."

We lived for what seemed like years this way, our mother and I. I am content as I have never been. One of my mother's visitors, a lady, came limping to our house as if one foot was sore. I gave her a place to sit on a stool in a cool corner of the house, and a glass of water for the heat. She had a heavy ring around her ankle and a rope around her throat. I loosened the rope, I fanned her as I had fanned our mother when the sun was too hot. She sat and began humming a nice tune. I asked her what tune was that and would she teach me. She looked right through me. She kept humming as if I had not asked, the sort of tune our mother used to sing to me when I was falling asleep. *Pain c'est viande beque, vin c'est sang beque, nous va mange pain beque, nous va boit sang beque.* . . . My mother joined her and I lay down and fell asleep to their sweet voices.

Our mother doesn't mind sometimes if I do not hem my skirt or bring in the clothes from the line when it is raining.

But if I miss and the rain comes pouring down and the clothes are wet and I am anxious my mother says, "Clothes don't melt, Bola. Pick them up another day." If the rain pours in through the windows she doesn't mind. When I run to close them she says, "Let the rain fall. It's not bothering anybody." We set aside one room for spiders when our mother said, "Spiders are good. We'll give them one room to themselves." When I swept the floors our mother said, "What you sweeping, sweeping for? The house going anywhere?"

Sometimes we left the doors wide open at night and sometimes all day we kept them shut even though it was hot. "Air," our mother said, "doesn't always want to be let in and out, in and out. Sometimes it wants to settle." So I am content because nothing has to be done exactly the way it used to be since our mother returned from the Paradise cemetery.

Sometimes the drawing of the far shore disturbs me. There was something familiar about it. Perhaps from our mother's stories about the sea. The far shore seemed so far away and sometimes looking at it I would feel the house move and our mother rolling in her sleep. The paper was reddish in some parts and I could make out a finger here and there and I put my finger in those places. I have never been to the sea, I have only seen our small street and our small town and August Town. Now I only know this small house where I live with our mother, and I only long for this.

The picture was for some other longing, which came and went when I looked at it. So I put it behind the wardrobe as well, but our mother asked me for it with such longing herself that I took it out and put it in the middle of the floor for her. I put it in the middle of the floor and I put fine dirt around it for sand and I polished around the sand as brilliant as the ocean might be and I left it there for our mother to swim to any time she wanted.

One day when there was a storm outside a boy rushed in from the rain holding on to a piece of galvanized zinc. His face was covered in bushes. I had left the door open to let the storm through. I liked the mist left by the speed of the rain. I like the smell of rain on hot dry ground. The boy suddenly blew in in a hurry reaching his hand for our mother. His eyes were open wide and I saw all that he wished for, all the things he might have been and it was all I could do not to let our mother go, it was all I could do to hold on to her else she would have been swept away by him. I myself could have gone. I myself could have rushed to my own might-have-beens.

When I see butterflies on the zinnias I want to go out and catch them, but my mother says, "They do anything to you? Just leave them alone." So I follow them or stand still near the fence to watch them. My sisters and I used to tie thread to their bellies and fly them like kites. Then we would blow all the dust off their wings and they would stop flying.

I miss my sisters but I can't leave our mother alone. I tried. Once I started off to visit my sisters but when I reached the gas station at the top of our street I became so anxious that all the people there could see it and kept asking me, "What do you? You don't see yourself or what? What do you?" So I had to turn back. And when I turned back they said, "Go, go on now."

It was so kind of them to notice how distressed I was that I thought they needed an explanation, so I smiled and thanked them and said it was my mother, I felt so nervous about leaving her by herself. They said, "Go, go on now, quick!" And I returned home because I thought I hadn't told our mother how long I'd be, and I hadn't told her why I was going, and suppose she thought that I too would not return and then she'd leave and go back to the Paradise cemetery. So I was relieved when the people at the gas station said, "Go on home!"

Soon after, the two women came to visit. I saw them coming down the street walking briskly and arguing. One of them held her jaw so tight it looked like a blade and I hesitated to open the door or go outside. The other was sweating down the sides of her face and dabbing with a handkerchief.

I stood behind the curtain for a while until the one with the blade face found me and pointed that she was coming into the gallery. My mother and I never left the door locked anyway so she walked in and began screaming. I could not understand her and said, "Lady, what are you saying? Lady, your face is as sharp as a blade." The other one burst in after her and tried to calm her down. I went to get her some water but seeing our mother lying on her bed with the letter once again I stopped. So she had found it behind the wardrobe. Oh, well. She was holding it up to the sunlight, just like old times, and I sat at the foot of her bed and listened to her read.

When I remembered the two women sitting in the gallery I listened to hear if they were still agitated. Perhaps, when they were calmer, I could give them a letter to my sisters and ask them kindly to deliver it seeing as how I could not leave our mother by herself. They stayed there talking and talking and when it seemed that they had talked themselves out I approached them and made my request.

"Misses," I said. "Would you kindly do the favour if it

isn't too much to ask, because as you see I have my mother here and she is recovering and I cannot leave her so if you would be so kind as to take this letter to my sisters who I am sure would like to know that our mother is here."

I used my best school English to impress them and then I curtsied the way our mother had shown us, to show respect to our elders. I put the heel of my right foot into the instep of my left foot and I clasped my hands and I curtsied to persuade them to take my letter. They seemed impressed and taken aback and one of them reached out to me, frightening me, and said, "Do you remember us?"

"Of course, miss," I said, why wouldn't I remember them? God knows I didn't ask them to come but I let them sit in the gallery any time they wanted.

"Will you come with us?" the one with the handkerchief said.

"Of course not, miss, that is why I am asking you to do me this great favour of taking my letter. I can't leave our mother alone." And I ran behind the door and shut it behind me. I put my ear close and heard paper tearing and the other one said, "There's nothing written here." Naturally she couldn't read it. I had written it for my sisters and that was precisely why she could not read my handwriting. I could only hope that they would deliver it and pray that my sisters would come.

"She's not in the world," the other said. I was a little vexed now that they seemed to have forgotten my request and moved on to their usual topic. At least I am always in the world. My sisters are forgetful but I remember everyone. Our mother said that I had a good memory and she would give me little things to remember for her. I am full of memories for her—where her slippers are and where she

hid her money under a stone in the back yard and how many
cups of flour for the bread and what date it is. I recall everything. When our mother gave me these things to remember
I would sit on the back step and hold my legs and repeat
them to a tune so I would not forget, and I would rock to
the tune and keep everything in my head. I never forget.

I am so busy. So caught up with living. Our mother is
coming out of her shell more and more. Once she even
went to visit the neighbour over the fence. She tiptoed over
and begged for a cup of water just to start a conversation,
and she showed the neighbour her stockings and said
they were spoilt because she had walked in them without
shoes. When she came back to the top step she told me,
"Have nothing to do with that woman. Don't take a thing
from her, it's poison." And she smiled at the neighbour and
waved. From then on I watched that neighbour. "Watch her
well," our mother told me. "Watch her well." If any mangoes or guavas from her trees fell on our side of the fence
I threw them back over and if she tried to give me anything
I turned my back.

We try to live peacefully and quietly. I make small things
for our mother and I bring her paradise plums and sugar.
And I shine the part of the floor that I made into an ocean
for her. We live peacefully and quietly and you would not
know that we are living there except sometimes for my
recitations and our mother's instructions. It is a quiet house
as my mother loved it, quiet and calm. The back yard is
quiet and the windows are quiet and now and then the trees
move and the rain falls and my mother and I sit on the back
steps and watch.

Sometimes I can't sleep because I'm afraid I'll wake up
and it will be like that morning when our mother went to

the Paradise cemetery, but then I fall asleep and wake up and there she is sitting on the bed in her blue dress with the lace and it is a morning with sweet light coming through the window and the guava tree is either leafy or bare and I am lying on the floor at the foot of our mother's bed and my fear leaves.

It is my birthday. Our mother told me to bathe and clean myself off and get ready for my birthday cake. I am so happy. I have cleaned myself off and here I am in the gallery, waiting for my mother to bring out my birthday cake. I can't but smile to myself at how well our mother has planned this party. I can smell the baking, the sweet flour and the vanilla essence. Every now and again our mother calls to me to make haste and put on my clothes for the party.

I am waiting for my best dress to dry. I am sitting here in the gallery, letting the sun dry my body, and when the neighbours look over I tell them that our mother is making me a party. The sun is so warm. It spreads all over the gallery and if I close my eyes for long and let it in, deep into my eyelids, when I open my eyes everything is dazzling. The street is dazzling and the trees are dazzling and my skin is dazzling. I close my eyes and smell our mother's baking and I open my arms and let the sun warm my whole body.

AT THE FULL
AND CHANGE
OF THE MOON

~~~~~~~~

All day Bola watched the Venezuelan Main appear and disappear under the rainy-season sky. The peninsula flat at its tip and rising gradually toward the east. She counted the showers of rain falling far off in the ocean between herself and the Main. There, rain fell in separate misty circles and at times she counted five, six falls far out there. There, rain turning milky with smoke covered its own imaginings of islands. Rain played its own circle games, fingering ripples of sea water, turning them solid and pouring water into water valleys, lifting itself over water hills. There, rain, steaming and misting and smoking soft grey, made the sea brow and turn dead glistening white.

She saw the man-o'-war frigates head out to sea and back again. A flock so thick as to cloud a sky: if they come in to land it is more rain, if they go out to sea the skies will lift. But that day they could not decide. She'd never seen the frigates alight where birds alighted; on Gran Rock. High in the guano-stained crevices was where they lighted. Her eyes followed the frigates all day out to the Main. Appearing and disappearing. It was as if they were carrying and taking messages, those birds that do not fly but float high and never flap. White-bellied, red-throated, black-bellied.

The sky lifted and fell, the clouds grey blue. Even rain could not disfigure the blue. At every turn it was a different sky, strafed in blue and then in red, in goat shape and eye shape and then the shape of houses and boats and legs and arms. When it rained the sea kicked up sand and the water was bile green and brown as far as the eyes, until the great depths turned turquoise again. Today the Main was visible, rising out of receding mist. Then sun, burning a hole through the steam and passing rain. Her dress ballooned out around her like a raft.

The frigates wafted and dipped using only the air under their wings. She swam out to her rock to get a moment's peace from the children. But there they were, following her, though not into the sea. Strung out in a line, like little blue herons scraping the beach with their toes. They were waiting for her to come out of the water. Bony-legged, they dipped their feet into the steaming froth of the surf, each with their own concern, food, sticks, pebbles, complaints about each other.

She had made them it seemed one after the other. Their fathers were different, one smelled sweet, one loved gold things, one loved to fish, later one was blind—she loved these men for what they loved or what they didn't have. And then again it was more selfish than that. She had a great appetite for anything.

She had left Marie Ursule—who was a woman with little

else to give but this ocean—she had left her early one morning long ago, riding on the back of her father, Kamena. When they arrived at Culebra and she saw the ocean, she loved Marie Ursule and Kamena even more for giving her the solitary wide ocean and later, when she understood, for sparing her the humid estate and the dreary barracks. So when she saw Culebra turn into a village, and the loneliness of life with Kamena ended, she craved everything. Like some endangered tree she bloomed, devoured, fell into all her senses.

She loved them, these children strung out across the beach. Their bird-like heads strained to see her. They wandered after their own thoughts then remembered her and waved at her. Straying along the sand, waiting for her but doing their own business. One who loved dolls with her mouth in an O, one finding a stick to hit another, one lurking back because he hated the sea and hated to see the sun go down in the horizon. Two tried to unfasten limpets from a coral rock. Faces like the moon. Deep and open. Robust like any dawn here. She liked to watch them like this, like blue gaulins puffing up, their stick legs so fragile and strong. She liked to see one of them break into a run or rear back and pitch a stone. They brought her sea cockroaches and green medicine bottles washed up by the sea as gifts.

Culebra Bay winged out from one point to another. She could see the flame trees on its small hills and the tin shacks. The small riverbed where she used to walk on warm stones in the dry season, in the rainy time it pitched to the ocean. Perhaps she could see the swept dirt and the rocking chair of her old age, the grandson who went off to war and whom she waited for, to tell him that his mother, Augusta, had died.

Culebra was not large enough to be anybody's harbour but hers. She hovered over its stray wood and shells and boats washing in and out. Some things that go out come back again and other things never return. What is taken by the sea is taken, she knew. Her children might get to see a thousand glistening harbours, as some of their fathers had seen, some might spend nights brooding and days brooding and afternoons watching even in places with no harbours and no sea, but she would stay here in Culebra, blowing her shell and watching the Main appear and disappear.

She could see the nuns' broken house from here, the entranceway where she and Kamena first walked in, their bodies forming a cross with a tree growing out of it. It was not hard to remember his voice, though he spoke little and only long when there was some direction he had to give. Before it slipped his memory, like the fortunate way to Terre Bouillante, he had recounted their life like a psalm.

"At the full and change of the moon. Everything get measured here by the moon. And when it was a good moon, as it was big and round and the rim of it was white with clouds, they say that it was not a good day for the leaving. A good day was at the end of the moon's rounds when the evening come dark, so dark as they could pass the medicine without discovery. Your mother made the preparations to take everyone to the heavens and to rid them of the wicked world of slavery they had entered and to give them their deliverance from the hands of Mon Chagrin estate. Full-moon nights, your mother slip away to find the medicine. That last night when you was already put to sleep the singer sing a last song and the people of the convoi make many speeches, every one, and one by one after everyone was together they bless the poison your mother had gather to send them all home.

"Not two years good before, the boiling house had been set on fire and the whole of the whites was going to be dead, but for the betrayal of a few frightened and treacherous. The whole thing end up in punishment and the work was started all over again. The chopped heads of the copper keeper and the plantine grove keeper, as them was the leaders, King and Dauphin, was raised on sticks at the beginning of the estate where there was a bell. You was still in your mother's belly but you was there as we was all called to look upon them and beware. And the heads was made to wither on sticks at the bell pole so that we would know that there was no departure.

"When your mother done served her time and her foot released from the ring, she was left to discover some root so as to take life itself away. Marie Ursule, she could smell the wind which made the cocoa crop fail in disease and she know the ants what make the sugar red from rot. The year the crop failed your mother did seen the insect which come in the wind and shrivelled the leaves and blow out the following October. She did seen the swarms blow in on the winds of August not knowing where they would light and sensing that they had come to help her purpose.

"And in her goings about she discover medicines that cure all sickness. And life was a sickness itself. And your mother and me and the remaining of us last out and wait. By innocence or trick or patience we went about our direction and bide our time, until the day I leave to find my maroonage and which I did find when I roll under the sky. Until Marie Ursule send for me and dropped you and me into her dream when she was getting ready to leave."

Bola has her own hymn, "Life will continue," she tells the children, "no matter what it seems, and even after that someone will remember you. And even after that it could be just the whiff or thought of things you loved."

It is her own hopelessness and her skill. Her faith doesn't believe in endings. Marie Ursule moved to light the fire; it is her gibbous back going to its doings that Bola recalls, which is why she loves whales.

The line of children stretched out unending on the beach. One girl child, a cloth around her shoulders, billowing like a grey sail, ran headlong past the rest. The others catching up to her grabbed her by the cloth and they tumbled down in the sand. The one who loved gold things waved at Bola, jumped into the water and tried to swim out alone.

Whenever she would take a lover they would skip around him in excitement saying, "Is he mine, Mama? Is he mine?"

"Yours is the one who smell sweet sweet and give me the palsy... yours is the one who' skin was gold, yours is the one who wouldn't leave me alone... just like you. No one is anyone's. How much time I must tell you?"

The jumble of them would go quiet for a brief moment then they would turn to each other, taunting, "Well, he not yours neither!" Then Bola would shoo them out of the shack to fly along the beach, flying to some other argument over a shell or a limpet or the number of times the surf came in before it touched their feet. "Go your way, go your way." As she held the coarse fingers of the next father.

Bola dipped her head into the water and came up. She had to come out now, light a fire, make some food. It was becoming breezy. A spray of sand along the beach obscured the children for a moment. She could hear their voices in surprise, the laughter and astonishment.

She swam back to shore to hear their complaints and have them hover at her dress tail for the rest of the day. Her dress lost its sail, it clung to her hips as she came out of the water and the crowd of them clutched her wet body.

"Mama, Rafael Simon . . . ."

"Boto bayena mama . . . ."

"Why do you leave me?"

"Quiet!" she sang out above the sea noise. "Or I'll go back in the sea."

ACKNOWLEDGMENTS

I would like to thank Louise Dennys for her patience and her painstaking editing. I would also like to thank Diane Martin, Ted Chamberlin, and Jennifer Kawaja for their helpful readings at various stages of the writing of this book. Thanks also to Denise Bukowski for her tireless work; Kwame Dawes for his inspiring insight; Filo and Anandan, my only visitors at Burnt River, Ontario, where this book was written; Ted for his survival tips on bear tracks, fox tracks, porcupine tracks, etc....Dionne and Jennifer for their generous home when Toronto was necessary. Leleti for her much tried faith in me.

This book was written with assistance from the Canada Council for the Arts.

Historical information in this book was drawn from E.L. Joseph's *History of Trinidad*; Eric Williams's *Documents on British West Indian History, 1807–1833*; John La Guerre's *Calcutta to Caroni*; Bridget Brereton's *A History of Modern Trinidad, 1783–1962*; V.S. Naipaul's *The Loss of Eldorado: A History*. In this last, I found the story of Thisbe who in 1802 was hanged, mutilated and burnt, her head spiked on a pole, for the mass deaths by poisoning on an estate. At her hanging she was reported to have said, "This is but a drink of water to what I have already suffered." She became my character Marie Ursule. Thomas Jefferys's (Geographer to King George III) wickedly elegant observations of the island of Tobago have been borrowed here and given to the character Kamena. The French nuns Mère Marguerite de St Joseph and Souer de Clémy, were apprehended in Père Labat's *The Memoirs of Père Labat*; Labat was a seventeenth-century priest, his memoir an account of his travels in the Caribbean. Some of the names of enslaved people were taken from the accounts of a planned slave uprising in Trinidad in 1806 and the respective punishments they received after its failure. These accounts and details of First World War soldiers from the West India Regiment were taken from *The Book of Trinidad*.

Lines in a letter home from a First World War soldier in the West India Regiment were taken from Bridget Brereton's book named above.

The lines of poetry quoted in Chapter III are from Charles Kingsley's "Sands of Dee".

The line of calypso quoted in Chapter VIII is from Growling Tiger's "Los Iros".

The lines of Poetry quoted in Chapter IX are from William Wordsworth's "Intimations of Immortality from Recollections of Early Childhood".

I have played with names of places; I have invented some.